THE CULTIST

Also by Mark Boss

HIRED GUNS
THE CULTIST
ONE BULLET

The Dead Girl Series
DEAD GIRL
DEAD GIRL 2: FADER BOY

The SARZverse Series
SUPERHEROES ALIENS ROBOTS ZOMBIES (Book 1)
ROBOT REVOLUTION (Book 2)
ALIEN INVASION (Book 3)

The Cultist

Mark Boss

Cover by Tony Felty Jr.

ISBN-13: 978-1470015695
ISBN-10: 1470015692

http://markboss.net

Dedication

There are two constant sources of love and support in my life, God and my Mom. Thank you both.

Acknowledgements

For the last eight years, the Cheshire Writing Group has provided critique, insight, and encouragement. Thanks to its past members and current members who helped me, including Tony B., Ruth C., Rich K., Carole L., Tony S., Marty S., Milinda S, and Lynn W.

The Panama City Writers Association offers a sounding board and a supportive atmosphere for writers, especially Wayne G., Ed P., Marj S., and Barbara W.

It's odd, but sometimes writers like to work by ourselves, together. Thanks to the Chapter One Writers Group, including Rob D., Mike L., and Eve and Chris W.

Sanity (and lunch) provided by the Syndicate of Brady C., Lou C., Jayson K., Mike L., and Tony S.

Thanks to Tony Felty, Jr. for the cool cover of the cliff dwellings.

Thanks also to Nick M., Lee B. and Bessie G.

I am forgotten like the unremembered dead....
-- Psalm 31:13

Chapter 1
New Mexico, USA
Day 1

As his father drove them deep into the wilderness, Tyler Burroughs realized he was going to die.

The caravan of cars crept through the night, a glowing chain of headlights and taillights. Tyler read the street signs as they left Silver City and rolled down a two-lane road into the vast Gila National Forest.

The boy sat on his hands in the back seat. His thrift store navy blue sport coat was too tight, and the sleeves ended well above his wrists. Up front, his mother scanned radio stations for a weather report.

"If it clouds over, we won't be able to spot the ship," she said.

Mr. Burroughs leaned over the wheel and looked up. "Don't worry, honey. It's fine."

Tyler squirmed in his seat; he needed to pee.

The boy looked down at his Spiderman sneakers and smiled. He was supposed to wear his dress shoes, but in the dark his parents hadn't noticed.

Tyler wondered why his mother worried about clouds--they all knew Silas had gone ahead to locate the exact landing site. Earlier in the day Silas had shown Tyler and the other kids a hand-held global positioning unit accurate to within three meters. Tyler's friend Calvin asked what a meter was.

Tyler stared out the side window at the star-filled sky and shivered. "Dad, will it hurt?"

"No, son, it won't hurt at all. Silas told us that. You have to trust him. Just think, when you're in heaven you'll be looking down at the stars instead of up." Mr. Burroughs slapped the steering wheel. "Think of the view."

They turned off the paved road and followed the other vehicles west along a rough trail. The taillights of the car in front of them bounced as it labored over the ruts. Tyler pressed his cheek to the cool window, but a drop jarred him loose and left him rubbing his jaw. "Is it much farther?"

"I think we're close, son. Why?" his father asked.

Tyler shrugged. "I'm cold. Do they have video games in heaven?"

Mrs. Burroughs shook her head. "No, because video games are distractions. And anything that distracts us from God is evil."

"They're pulling off," Mr. Burroughs said. "We're here."

While his parents got out of the car, Tyler reached under the seat where he'd hidden his father's small notebook computer. He needed the computer to play *Lair of the Hydra*. He'd played the game twice using his father's account while his parents were at meetings.

As he got out, the boy tucked the bottom edge of the computer inside his belt to keep it from sliding free, and buttoned his coat over it. Outside the car a stiff wind blew across the desert and threw sand into his eyes. Tyler blinked and stared up at the others.

The men wore collared shirts. The women wore dresses and heeled shoes that sank in the sand. Silas came out of the darkness, his tie flapping in the wind, and asked, "Is everyone ready?"

They assured him they were.

Silas led them into the wilderness. The trail was wide at first and the adults carried flashlights, but the path soon became narrow and rocky. Tyler took his mother's hand.

They crossed a dry streambed and Mrs. Proctor tripped and broke her shoe. Tyler's bladder ached, but he was afraid to go into the dark bushes beside the trail.

His father's free hand rested on Tyler's shoulder while he swung the flashlight back and forth in front of them. They followed the other families up the steep trail. Parents carried the smaller children.

Between the dark and the incline, the column fragmented and slowed. Silas moved past, calling, "Just a little farther, folks."

Finally they reached the top of the mountain and the ground leveled off. The trail left the trees and scrub bushes behind and they stood under an open sky with the wind in their faces.

Silas lined up each family and had them join hands, with the mother and father on the outside of each group. Tyler's family was second in line. Ahead of him, Ruth Ann stood with Calvin and their parents. She looked over her shoulder at him.

Tyler stood in his tight sport coat with his mother squeezing his left hand and his father crushing his right. He fidgeted, twisting back and forth between them.

"Stand still," his mother hissed. His father tugged Tyler's arm straight.

Silas collected their flashlights and put them in a neat pile. Without the flashlights, it was so dark that the only way Tyler could guess where the horizon began was by looking at where the stars ended.

At the front of the line, Silas spoke to Mr. and Mrs. Seward, and leaned to pat Ruth Ann on the shoulder. Hands clasped, the Sewards marched forward into the darkness and disappeared.

Tyler gaped.

There was no noise or smoke or anything--they just disappeared. Like a magic trick.

Tyler almost forgot his need to pee.

His dad squeezed Tyler's hand. "See, the Sewards just went to heaven. We're next."

Silas approached. He still held a flashlight and in the yellow beam his bearded face was calm. "Okay, folks, are you ready?"

"Yes, sir," Mrs. Burroughs said.

"Okay, the ship is here. Walk forward until you see the lights, then take one more step. I'll see you on board." Silas walked down the line to the Proctors.

"Dad, I need to pee." Tyler pulled against his father's hand.

"Son, you can pee in heaven," Mr. Burroughs said.

"No, he can't," Mrs. Burroughs said. "You can't pee in heaven. It would foul the soil."

His dad shrugged. "Tyler, just hold it until we get on the ship. Let's go." Mr. Burroughs tugged the family forward.

Tyler's mom pulled back. "He can't go to heaven full of pee. It's unclean. You can't run around heaven urinating everywhere."

Tyler stumbled as his father pulled one arm and his mother held the other. "I gotta go," the boy said.

His father hauled them forward several steps and peered into the darkness. "I see them. I see the lights."

Tyler stopped struggling to look. He swung his head from side to side, but he didn't see any lights. Then he looked down. He saw red lights flashing way, way down.

His mother let go of his hand and stepped forward. “It’s the spaceship, Tyler. It’s here.”

Tyler reached for her. “Wait.”

“No, it’s time, son, it’s time.” Mr. Burroughs lurched forward, but Tyler tugged his hand free. His father went over the cliff. Mrs. Burroughs spun and grabbed for Tyler but missed. Her back foot stepped down on open air and she plummeted from view.

“Mom!”

Tyler looked over the edge, but saw nothing except the flashing lights. On and off, on and off. He turned and the beam of a flashlight blinded him.

“Tyler?” Silas called.

Tyler heard the compact man crunch up the trail toward him, his flashlight bobbing. Tyler ducked out of the beam of light and ran parallel to the cliff edge. The computer slid from under his coat, but he caught it and kept running.

“Tyler, come back. Your parents are going to heaven without you,” Silas yelled.

The boy heard Silas say something else but the wind snatched the words away. Other voices rose up. Other fathers, other mothers. Tyler looked back and saw a second flashlight. Then a third.

He ran faster.

* * *

Chapter 2
Tokyo, Japan
Day 1

Takara locked the store and waved goodnight to Yoshi, Atsushi and Madoka. She shuffled into the stream of humanity slogging along Chuo-dori. By now she was immune to Akihabara's riot of neon signs and enormous television screens.

She went down the stairs to the Metro, let the machine snatch her pass card from her fingers, then retrieved it as she passed through the gate and boarded the Yamanote circle line train. The metro car was crowded and warm. Takara swayed a few inches above a sea of dark heads dressed in dark clothes. Her eyelids fluttered.

I need another can of coffee.

At Ueno Station a woman and her son boarded and stood next to her. The boy looked to be nine or ten, still dressed in his school uniform, hands and eyes glued to a Nintendo game system. The mother looked tired, but happy.

Takara leaned over to see what game he was playing and the boy looked up.

"I found a magic spear," the boy said. "I'm a level nine ninja."

"Not bad." Takara smiled and looked away. He's about the age Akira was when the earthquake hit.

At Sugamo Station she switched to the Mita line. The crowd thinned and she dropped into an empty seat and slumped against the window.

Soon the train braked and she watched the names on the wall outside flash by until they were slow enough to read. A half dozen people on the car stood and shuffled to the doors and she joined them.

She pushed her hair out of her eyes, and stomped up the stairs to the sidewalk. Under a street lamp she checked the time on her cell phone.

11:51. Better hurry.

Takara stretched out her long legs and let the breeze wake her. Her bag swung from her shoulder as she walked.

The street was quiet. Towering apartment buildings threw long shadows, turning side streets into inky canyons. She marched past a construction site with its metal scaffolds and plastic sheeting snapping in the wind. Takara stared up at the half-finished building. It looked the same as dozens of other sites throughout the city. Signs, dusty vehicles, garbage bins, orange cones. Residents of Tokyo joked that the national bird must be the crane.

After the cacophony of Akihabara all day, Takara appreciated the silence of her neighborhood late at night. She stopped at a well-lit vending machine. As Takara fed it coins she noticed her hand trembled. A stubby can of Boss coffee dropped into the hopper. She popped the top and drank.

Settle down. If you don't focus, you're going to get hurt.

Two more minutes of brisk walking brought her to the bicycle shop. The front sign wasn't lit, but she saw the light over the counter. She pulled open the door and headed to the repair room in back.

The repair room was neat and well lit, with work tables along two walls and tools and spare tires hanging above them. Shoda sat against the wall, attempting to touch his toes.

"Hey, Tak." The stocky young man popped up and smiled. "How's the online world? You kill any dragons lately?"

Takara rolled her eyes. "You sound like Aunt Shiori." She'd known Shoda since a pick-up game of soccer in junior high, but Takara wondered if they had anything in common other than Midnight Judo.

Takara went into the bathroom and changed into a faded jiu-jitsu uniform she'd bought online. She came out and slid down the wall to stretch her long legs. Skinny Kyle slipped in and sat beside her. Kyle's real name was Kiyoshi, but he insisted everyone call him Kyle.

He's even more pale than normal. I wonder if he ever leaves his room anymore.

"Hey, Tak, how's things at Game Mania?" Kyle asked.

"Busy. We sold a zillion copies of *Ghetto Kings* this week."

Kyle rolled his narrow shoulders. "You better get an account on there to make up for *Lair*."

Tak took her mouthpiece out its plastic baggie and stuck it above her ear. "What do you mean? I sell tons of stuff on *Lair*."

"Haven't you heard?" Kyle asked. "*Lair of the Hydra* is dying."

"What?"

"I sent you an email," Kyle said.

"Our Internet connection was down all day."

"*Lair of the Hydra* is dying," Kyle said again.

"*Lair* can't end. It's my top seller. You know how many virtual swords I've sold for real money on that site?" She grabbed Kyle's arm. "If this is a joke, I will break--"

"It's true. The company is charged with ripping investors off. The American SEC is investigating. If they shut down there won't be anyone to maintain the game." Kyle pointed at the television on the work table. "They talked about it on *X-play* last night."

"Damn it. I have to get home." Tak grabbed her gym bag. "If I didn't know, there must be other players who don't either. I've got dozens of items stashed in that world I need to sell before people realize they're worthless."

Kyle shrugged. "I wouldn't hurry. The announcement was two days ago, so most of the players have probably already quit."

Takara shook her head. "I can't believe this." As she stared at the far wall, a small, chinless kid came in and rolled on the floor with a heavy punching bag.

Shoda stood up. "As soon as Jiro gets here, we'll start." Shoda led the class because his father owned the bicycle shop. And he'd taken three years of formal judo in high school.

"Who's the new guy?" Tak asked.

"That's my cousin, Fumio. He's from Kyoto. He's going to school here now," Shoda said.

Fumio looked up at Tak and grinned, and then grabbed the bag with both hands and slammed a head butt into the thick leather. His face recoiled off the bag and he sat holding his nose.

Shoda laughed so loudly Tak didn't hear the front door open.

A bright red backpack sailed into the room and hit the wall between Tak and Kyle. "What's up?" Jiro blew in, spiky haired and smiling. He wore a sleeveless black Tap Out shirt.

While the others stretched, Jiro bounded around the room shadow boxing. When he bounced past Fumio, Jiro barked, "Welcome to Midnight Judo!"

The new kid stared at Jiro's lean, tattooed arms and swallowed hard. His eyes grew big.

Kyle leaned over to whisper to Takara. "This is bad. Jiro's acting bipolar again."

She nodded. "I hope he doesn't spar Shoda tonight. Shoda won't want to back down in front of his cousin." Takara's heart rate bumped up, and the can of coffee in her bladder felt like an ocean.

"Okay, let's get to work," Shoda said as he clapped his hands.

With Jiro and Fumio supporting the heavy bag, Shoda stood on a chair and clipped the bag to a chain attached to an exposed beam in the ceiling. Takara and Kyle unrolled a thick wrestling mat. The edges curled up and she stamped them down with her bare feet. Kyle scooted across the blue mat like a crab and stared at a dark spot on one end. He touched the stain with his fingertip and held it to his nose. "Did your dad get a cat?"

"Yeah, to keep us company during the day. It's still learning to use the litter box." Shoda split the other four into pairs, and they took turns holding and hitting the bag while he cleaned the mat with a rag.

As she drove her elbows into the heavy bag, Takara tried to remember the technique she'd brought to share. The club met once a week and each member was supposed to teach a technique from their arsenal, but often it was something they'd seen on television. None of them could afford a real dojo with instructors, and they all worked odd hours, so they invented "Midnight Judo."

Earlier in the week Takara watched a YouTube video of a jiu-jitsu rear-naked choke. She tried to get the move straight in her head while she pounded the bag.

"Keep your left up. You're dropping your left. Tak, move your head, you're going to get clobbered," Shoda called.

Finally the kitchen timer chimed and Tak's three minutes were over. She stood panting while Jiro unleashed a whirlwind of kicks to the taped-up old training bag.

The timer rang again and Jiro finished with a sloppy spinning back kick that nearly caught Kyle instead of the bag.

Eyes wide, Kyle whispered to Takara while they leaned against the wall to put on their pads. "I don't want to spar tonight."

"Okay, new rule," Shoda said. "To keep it random, we each roll a dice. Closest numbers spar each other. Simple." He handed out five 20-sided polyhedral dice. Takara received a big, semi-translucent green die. She dropped it on the mat.

"Eighteen."

The other four squatted to roll like they were gambling in an alley. Kyle rolled a nine, Fumio rolled an 11. Shoda shook his die and dropped it. "Two."

Jiro bounced his die off the wall and looked up at Tak. "Twenty."

Takara put in her mouthpiece.

Shoda cranked the kitchen timer. "I'm referee. Three minutes. No biting, no eye gouges, no stuff with the groin, no hair pulling. When they tap, you stop."

Everyone but Fumio had heard it before.

Takara bit down on her mouthpiece. She wore kempo gloves and a white chest protector with a big blue dot in the middle, but no head gear. Jiro used boxing gloves that made grappling impossible, and tattered red shin guards.

Shoda herded Fumio and Kyle back and yelled, "Begin!"

Jiro opened with a stream of sidekicks, driving Takara straight back until she bumped into the heavy bag and spun away. Jiro took a moment to whip a roundhouse into the bag and laughed. Tak jabbed at his open mouth but the lean man ducked.

"Tak, don't retreat straight back. Circle, circle," Shoda called.

Takara evaded a front kick and tried a low kick of her own at Jiro's knee, but he stop kicked it. She knew she couldn't match Jiro in strength; even skinny Kyle was as strong as she was. But she had height, and therefore reach. And a new chokehold he didn't know.

Tak waited for Jiro to punch and then dove for a takedown.

Instead she caught a knee to the jaw. Spots exploded in front of her eyes and Jiro rained blows on her shoulders and arms.

"Time!" Shoda jumped in. Takara realized she was down on one knee. Shoda knelt next to her. "Tak, you okay?"

Takara nodded by reflex, but her vision blurred. She took a deep breath, stood and got her hands up.

"Continue," Shoda said.

For the next two minutes, Tak tried to take Jiro to the ground where she could use her rudimentary jiu-jitsu, but Jiro sprawled and danced away. At the end of the match, Tak's forearms ached from blocking kicks and she tasted blood in her mouth.

"Stop. Nice work, Jiro. Tak, you have to start from closer in to get those takedowns. Think of Randy Couture for example. When he goes for a double leg..." Shoda explained and Takara tried to listen, but her head hurt and finally she just sat down against the wall to watch Kyle and Fumio.

When Shoda called "Begin", Fumio screeched, ran straight at Kyle, and leaped into the air with a flying knee. Kyle twisted aside. Fumio drove his knee into the wall and landed in the cat's litter box.

Cat dung and litter flew everywhere.

Shoda stared at the hole in the sheetrock, looked at his cousin and shook his head.

"I'll get a broom." Takara limped to the front of the shop.

By the time she found a broom and came back, Fumio sat against the wall, sniffling, and Shoda stood red faced and panting.

Kyle spread his hands. "Maybe we should move on to techniques?"

Shoda taught a two-fisted strike he said came from Thailand. Jiro showed them a heel kick that no one else could get above their own waists. Kyle demonstrated a palm strike Tak recognized from one of the *Tekken* games. And Tak managed to bring off her chokehold so well she made Shoda tap out in seconds. Everyone praised the move, even Jiro.

Half an hour later they shuffled outside and Shoda locked up the shop. Takara picked white clay kitty litter out of her hair and waved goodnight.

She hurried toward the apartment she shared with her aunt. Kyle's metro stop was just past her building, so he walked with her.

"What's the rush?" he asked as he struggled to keep up.

"I've got to log in to my *Lair of the Hydra* account," Tak said. "I didn't know the game was ending, so there's probably other people who don't know yet, either. I have to sell all my items before they realize they're useless."

Kyle shook his head. "Same old Tak. Always looking for an angle."

She pushed her damp hair back. "People want special items to get ahead in their games, and I supply them. It doesn't matter that they pay me real money for virtual things, it's just supply and demand."

They reached her building and she turned off. “See you next week.”

Kyle nodded and disappeared into the night.

She limped through the well-lit lobby and down the hall to her door. When she went inside, the small apartment was dark and still. It was a middle unit on the ground floor, so it only had windows along the front and back walls.

The lamp her aunt always turned on when she left was lit, and the door to Shiori’s room was open. Takara remembered her aunt was performing inventory on a grocery store this week and wouldn’t return until morning when the store opened. The thought of shuffling through a store at 3:00am with a bar code reader checking how many cans of dog food there were made Takara grateful for her job at Game Mania.

Takara slipped off her shoes and tapped them into place until they lay even. In the bathroom she washed her face, gently brushed her teeth and examined the cut inside her lower lip. It had stopped bleeding, but her jaw was sore. She took her mouthpiece out of its plastic bag, rinsed it and set it on the sink.

She needed a shower, but instead she went to her desk and woke the computer.

* * *

Chapter 3
New Mexico, USA
Day 1

Tyler ran.

At first he ran along the edge of the cliff. He couldn't see it, but he could feel it--feel the way the air changed and the wind gusted into the big gap in the earth.

The boy turned away from the cliff, afraid to stay near it any longer. He ran through the dark until he stumbled to a jerky walk and bent over, shaking. Five, ten gulps of air and he pushed himself into a trot.

When Tyler looked up, the stars shone bright above him, but he didn't know how to read them like Christopher Columbus did. His shin hit a rock and he flopped on the ground. The notebook computer slid out from under his coat and he grabbed it and held it like a football. His chin and palms stung from the fall.

Did it hurt when they hit the rocks? Did Mom and Dad scream?

Tyler heard a yell and looked over his shoulder. The yellow beam of a flashlight swung back and forth. He scrambled to his feet. His Spiderman sneakers were good to run in, but his stupid sport coat was too tight. He almost threw the coat away, but he wore a bright white shirt underneath and he knew they'd spot him. Ninjas never wore white shirts, and the navy sport coat was almost black, so he kept it on and fastened all the buttons.

Tyler panted. He gulped a mouthful of air on every other step. Pain stabbed him between the ribs and Tyler pushed his knuckles into the spot while he ran.

He thought about stopping to hide in the rocks, but didn't. It wasn't the snakes. Tyler wasn't afraid of snakes. It was the Gila monsters. He'd seen them on Animal Planet before his dad got rid of the television.

During the show about Gilas there were no people in the picture, just rocks and dirt, so Tyler wasn't sure how to scale them in his mind. Were they the size of mice? Or were they the size of hippos? Either way, the scientists clearly labeled them "monsters" so they had to be dangerous. And they were poisonous. Big, possibly giant, lizards with scaly skins and nasty mouths full of rotting chunks of the last child they ate still wedged between their teeth.

Tyler imagined himself crouched between a pair of cold rocks while Silas and the rest ran past swinging their flashlights. And then suddenly a chilling hiss, and the scrabble of long claws across rocks and the flickery feel of a cold forked tongue on his bare neck just before the monster struck.

He bit his lip to keep from screaming.

Without a watch, he had no way to know how long he ran. The flashlights were so far behind now they seemed to wink as the people who carried them passed behind rocks and trees. He couldn't hear their voices anymore.

A rock tumbled to his right and he whipped his head around so fast his vision blurred.

"Gila monsters. Crap." Tyler broke into a ragged dogtrot. The wind sucked the warmth through his sport coat and he shivered.

Then he saw the cave.

The cave should have surprised him, but it didn't. After playing *Lair of the Hydra* it seemed normal to find a cave. The entrance was low, about at his waist, so he might have missed it. An adult would not have seen it, but Tyler spotted the black hole in the rocks and knew it was a cave--a cave too small for a bear or a hippo-sized Gila monster.

Tyler dropped to his hands and knees. The loose sand stung the scrapes on his palms. He crawled a few yards into the cave, curled in a ball and turned the collar of his coat up around his neck.

Then he watched for flashlights.

* * *

Chapter 4
New Mexico, USA
Day 1

Silas searched the desert for an hour and then led the others back to the cliff. He knew they were worried about missing the spaceship.

He wondered about the flashing lights he'd placed at the base of the cliff. He had no idea how long they would function before the batteries gave out.

It took a moment for families to reunite in the dark. Silas got the line set up, then went to the edge of check the lights. They still worked, so Silas went back to his followers. "The ship is still waiting with the others on board. Walk forward until you see the lights, then take one more step. I'll see you in a few minutes."

He walked down the light, collected the flashlights, and put them in a pile.

The compact man leaned against the piercing wind while the remaining families marched hand in hand over the cliff. Silas estimated the ground was 100 feet below. Maybe 110. It was difficult to be exact, even though he'd scouted the location months ago in the daylight.

The cold cut through his worn wool suit coat and his throat was dry. He made the long walk back to the cars and opened them one by one. None were locked. The Sewards had a metal thermos stuck in the console between the front seats. He unscrewed the cap and sniffed. Hot chocolate, steaming and sweet.

Silas smiled. He knew how to pick good people. Thermos in hand, he retraced his path to the cliff. It was late and he was tired, but a friendly, steady wind caught his back and legs, carrying him along over the broken ground.

Other than the cold, it was a beautiful night.

He went to the edge and looked over. The lights still flashed. On and off. On and off. Hot silver flickers. Like a doorway to a spaceship. Silas chuckled.

Tonight was the culmination of four years of work and he savored it as he sipped the hot chocolate. It took time to find the right people--the right combination of desperate and needy and hopeful and directionless. And to make up a story tailored to fulfill their dreams.

Silas didn't see his art as brain washing, but something much more subtle and fragile. Fragile in the way that sometimes someone just woke up one morning and left the group. And then he had to work doubly hard to keep the rest believing. There was an art to it, an art of influence. Constant, subtle reinforcement of ideas and structures and suggestions.

Once that foundation was built, all it took in the end was the simple act of pointing them toward the edge. They marched off the cliff not out of obedience, but out of trust. Silas smiled. His power was greater than that of a general or a president. It was the power of a parent over his children. Like Jim Jones.

Silas thought about his life as a boy in the Peoples Temple Agricultural Project in British Guyana. It was 1978 and he was ten years old and his parents were fervent communists. People called the commune Jonestown, and Jim Jones encouraged the kids to call him 'Dad.'

He shook his head. Jones used poison and bullets. Silas used his voice.

And yet in one day Jones killed 900 people, including 280 children. But not one purple-eyed young boy named Silas.

Which brought his thoughts back to the escaped boy, Tyler. Tyler didn't trust his parents. Tyler didn't trust Silas. There was a flaw in the boy. Some deviant trait. But his parents trusted. Into the wind and right off the cliff.

He figured the odds of the bodies being discovered was small, but eventually hikers or the Border Patrol or Park rangers would find them. Or someone in Silver City would notice the group hadn't come in to buy groceries in a while. It might be days or weeks.

He wanted to find the boy, but Silas knew he couldn't track him in the dark. Better to wait until daylight. Chances were the wilderness would take care of Tyler for him, but... Silas kicked a stone over the edge and listened to it bounce off jutting rocks in the cliff face on its way down.

He might need to help Tyler do the same.

Silas took one more look at the stars and then walked away. He hiked back to the vehicles, put the thermos in his car, and started the engine.

* * *

Chapter 5
New Mexico, USA
Day 1

Night in the desert was not like night at the house. When Tyler took the trash bag to the dumpster behind the trailer park, it was dark, but not black. There were lights from the other trailers, shining through the windows. There weren't many cars because their dirt road was far from the highway, so sometimes his mom let him play flashlight tag with the other kids. Tyler usually won. He was good at hiding.

Night in the desert was like sitting in a closet with the door shut and a bag over your head.

He crouched in the cave entrance, his knees to his chest. Tyler saw stars, a lot of stars, but then the clouds came and smothered them. The trees swayed. Wind moaned down the arroyos. Bushes became bears. Tyler's pupils swelled, rods and cones straining to detect threats.

Tyler wished he had a weapon. Something to hold. He knew there must be sticks around, but getting one meant leaving the cave.

The wind shifted into his face and he scooted further inside. The cold air swept down the tunnel behind him and up a chimney with a low bellow.

Tyler's head snapped around, but his eyes were useless.

Bears sleep in caves. But could they get through the hole?

He listened intently, the silence painful. He sniffed the air. It was cold, dusty, and stale. But it didn't smell like a wet dog or a cat's litter box.

No bear. There is no bear.

He faced outward again.

The wind tumbled through the bushes below the cave. Something coursed with it. Smudges of light-colored fur slipped through the brush.

Coyotes.

Tyler peered at the bushes. If he had a spear, he could keep the coyotes away. It wouldn't stop a bear, but a coyote was just a dog. But if he went out to get a stick to make a spear, the coyotes would surround him. One would bite the back of his knee, he would fall, and then they would snap off his fingers and dig their bloody noses into his throat, pushing deep inside him while he screamed.

Tyler's bladder reminded him he still needed to pee. He bent forward, stomach in cramps.

I can't leave the cave. I have to wait until morning.

He tried to think of something else. He counted to 100, but lost track in the 70s when a tree branch broke on the hill above him. He thought of Legos and what he might build with them. How might he build a bridge big enough to cross the floor of his room? Would there be cars on it? Workers? Policeman? Monsters?

His stomach clenched. He stood to stretch and it hurt. He couldn't go deeper into the cave to pee. There was no bear, but there might be a deep hole and he'd never see it until he fell.

Tyler thought about tumbling down a dark, wet hole. Landing hard, legs twisted, stuck in the earth like a blind worm. A mouthful of sand. Cold dirt in his ears. Pebbles down the collar of his shirt. Then something cold and sticky touching his cheek. A Gila monster, testing the prey with its tongue. A quick flick of the questing tongue, and then the crunch of sharp teeth on his throat.

Tyler bolted out of the cave.

He ran ten steps, stopped at the nearest tree and pissed all over the trunk.

Cold wind stung his bare skin and he rocked on his feet, hurrying to finish before something came out of the night to snatch him.

As he scurried back to the cave, he stopped and grabbed a handful of loose stones. Inside the entrance, he sat at his post and sorted the rocks by touch. He kept five good, smooth ones. If coyotes came, he would throw them at their faces.

The run warmed him up and he leaned against the cold rock wall and shut his eyes for a moment. Tyler reasoned he couldn't see anyway. He might as well just listen, and sniff the air.

He tucked his hands under his arms, grinding the rocks together in his fists. His head bobbed, snapped up, and bobbed again.

I have to stay awake.

Tyler had never stayed awake an entire night before, but he knew it was possible. People did it. People trapped on cruise ships turned upside down in the ocean. Or people captured by terrorists. Or ninjas. Ninjas worked at night and slept all day.

I am a ninja.

But soon his chin dropped to his chest again and he sat up. He stretched and his hand touched something hard and flat.

"The computer!"

Tyler flipped the small notebook open and found the power button by feel. The screen winked on, almost blindingly bright. He turned so the light wouldn't shine out of the cave entrance.

The desktop came up, but there were few icons. His mother had removed most of them after Silas told her the Internet was dangerous, especially for children.

Although he'd looked for them before and knew they weren't there, Tyler searched for Internet Explorer and Firefox. He thought about emailing the police, but there was no email, no instant messenger, no options.

He opened Adobe Reader, but there was nothing there to read, not even a story. Tyler checked the trash can in the corner of the screen, but it was empty, too.

All he could find was the little spear-and-shield icon for Lair of the Hydra. He'd only played the game twice. Once when it was his parents' turn to drive into Silver City for groceries, and a second time when they were at a church meeting.

Tyler shrugged and clicked the icon. At least it would pass the time until morning.

* * *

Chapter 6
Tokyo, Japan
Day 1

At home in her apartment, Takara flipped the rocker switch on the surge suppressor and activated her computer. She opened the folder containing her game accounts. At the bottom was the sword-and-spear icon for *Lair of the Hydra*.

She still had objects stored in the game world. Although the value of those objects was probably now zero, she was curious what was left. It was difficult to keep track with all her different game accounts. If she could find players who didn't know *Lair* was ending, she could sell her items at irresistible prices.

At worst it would take her an hour to wander around and find all of her stuff. Maybe say goodbye to some friends. After three years, she knew a lot of players in *Lair*.

She brought up her character's screen and eyed her stumpy avatar, Takeus of Thebes. The big-eyed fellow spun slowly, his leather pack on his back, bell-shaped cuirass and bronze helmet and greaves equipped. His weapon slots held a +4 Sling of Eye Piercing, a Silver Shield of Athena, a Spear of the Myrmidons, and a +2 Spartan Short Sword. The slots below showed the contents of his pack--one iron key, one spool of thread, two wax candles, three bottles of Greek Fire, five torches, eight healing potions, a blue portal orb, 13 gem stones...and a lot of memories.

* * *

Lair of the Hydra

Takeus of Thebes stepped out of the portal into a dark, muddy street. Even at night he expected a press of merchants and wagons and mules and shoppers and chariots. Instead Takeus faced an empty road, flanked by unlit buildings.

This isn't Thebes. Stupid portals must be malfunctioning. Where am I?

Uncertain of his location, the short warrior turned right at random and moved south through the town. At night the cheerful white stone structures faded to gray, and doors and windows turned into empty black mouths.

A temple loomed over the buildings on his left, so Takeus veered toward it to orient himself. Suddenly he remembered the town, and the wooden hut he'd rented there. Now certain of himself, he located the city square and marched to the Temple of Apollo--a boxy building with stout Doric columns and a huge fresco of the sun god chasing three half-naked dryads.

No vigil fire shone forth between the columns and no white-robed acolytes came forth to perform healing services and accept donations. Takeus rolled his eyes at the fresco as he circled a mound of white cloth and walked into the temple. He lit a torch, ready to loot any loose treasure. Tak raised the torch and realized the mounds scattered across the floor were dead priests.

The short Theban drew his sword and backed out of the temple. Murder was common in the rough towns on the Phrygian border, but killing an acolyte meant either death by a local mob or a precision lightning bolt from almighty Zeus. The slaughter of a dozen acolytes was unthinkable.

Takeus searched for a gathering, assuming there would be a farewell among warriors who'd fought beside and sometimes against each other. But the green sward at the center of town stood empty, except for a broken shield with a bull painted on it.

"The blacksmith."

Takeus knew the blacksmith in every town, because he'd bought and sold weapons across the entire Mediterranean. Orienting himself by the temple, he quickly found the shop. The red glow of the forge pushed back the black night and Takeus smiled as he strode under the awning. "Greetings, son of Hephaestus!"

The blacksmith lay sprawled over his worktable, a spear through his broad back. Takeus yanked the spear free and threw it aside. The soot-coated man slid to the ground and rolled over onto his back. Takeus knelt next to him. The big man whispered, "Beware the cave."

"Blacksmith?"

Takeus shook the dead man. "Blacksmith?"

"Hades." Takeus raised his torch to examine the room. The shop was empty except for a few unfinished blades and a smashed water barrel.

A shadow passed the open doorway, and Takeus spun, sword held ready for a low stab. A thick-shouldered boar trotted down the street, gore dripping from his tusks. Takeus stood very still, and the creature did not spot him. He counted to 20, then slipped into the street. His torch flickered and died.

A gray plume of smoke rose in the air a few streets over and the Theban watched as the fire leaped from roof to roof. Mindful of the boar, he decided not to light another torch. Takeus moved away from the spreading blaze, keeping to the darkest streets.

Shrill cries sounded from a tangle of market stalls ahead. Takeus crept to a corner and peeked around.

A lone Hyperborean warrior stood in a maelstrom of spotted coats and snapping jaws as a pack of hyenas attacked him. The tall, fair-haired swordsman stabbed one hyena, but another filled the gap, and two tore at the backs of his legs to hamstring him.

Takeus sprang forward and drove his spear into a giant female hyena. Its head whipped around and seized the wooden shaft of his spear in her vise-like jaws. Abandoning the spear, Takeus yanked out his sword to hack at the back of its neck. Another hyena grabbed the bottom of his shield and tugged, dragging him to his knees. A third grabbed his sword arm just above the elbow.

Then the tall Hyperborean waded in, his blade slinging blood as he cut his way to Takeus. Takeus rose and back to back, they dispatched the rest of the pack.

Shaking his dripping blade, Takeus booted one of the dead creatures with his studded sandal. "Stupid hyenas. I hate these things."

"In hyena packs, the moms are the biggest ones and they tell everyone what to do."

Takeus stared up at the barbarian warrior. "What?"

"I saw it on Animal Planet."

Takeus sheathed his sword, then planted his foot on the dead alpha female and pulled his spear out. "So she was the boss?"

"Yeah. I think so." The barbarian tilted his head. "Are you a real person?"

"Of course. Why?"

"I thought you were a game person, like the people that sell weapons and the lady at the inn."

"Oh, those are NPCs. Non-player-characters. Yeah, the scripting here is pretty good. They can fool you for a sentence or two," Takeus said.

He's got to be a kid. Sounds American, too.

Takara put out her hand. "I'm Takeus of Thebes."

"Oh. I'm Tyler. Of, uh, Silver City."

"I've never heard of Silver City. What land is it in?" Tak asked.

"New Mexico. In America."

"Oh, I get it. That's where you're from in meat space. So, are you new to *LOTH*?"

"Loth?"

"*Lair of the Hydra*. This place? Are you new here?"

"Yeah, I've only played twice." The big, ropy-armed barbarian fidgeted with his scabbard.

Tak nodded. "I've been playing this game a while and I've never seen you before."

"My dad used to play here. This is my mom's computer, but she doesn't turn it on anymore because Silas said the Internet is evil."

"Who's Silas?"

"The man at my church that tells us what to do. I wish the game people would come back. When I played before, there were lots of people. Now they're gone."

"Yeah, it's too bad. All the people who prepaid their accounts for the next year must be pissed."

"Where did they all go?" Tyler asked.

"Other places. They don't come here anymore because this game is ending."

"I thought monsters ate them. They ate the men at that church."

"You saw that? Yeah, that was ugly. It's not supposed to work like that. Zeus is supposed to protect them," Tak said.

"Maybe they ate him, too." The tall warrior pointed. "There are snakes coming."

Tak turned and gasped. A writhing wave of snakes, small and large, oozed down the dark street toward them. "Come on!" Tak ran to the nearest tall house and dashed inside. Once the barbarian joined her, she barred the door. "Let's get upstairs. Most of these places have a flat roof with a wall."

She charged half way up the steps and stopped. "Are there any ground floor windows?"

"I don't see any," Tyler said.

"Then we might be okay. Come on." They ran up to the roof. Stepping to the edge, Tak watched the snakes boil past. Somehow the mass of individual reptiles formed a body that moved like a single huge snake. "Damn. The spawning programs must be out of whack. Without people constantly killing them, the monsters multiply too fast. They'll overrun this town soon."

"Maybe we should go to a big city where there's lot of people," Tyler said.

"Yeah, let's try Athens. Wait for the snake storm to pass first, though. I don't want them following us through a portal." Takara put a foot on the edge of the roof and leaned to watch. Fire spread through the town and monsters careened through the flickering shadows, attacking each other and sometimes just slamming themselves into walls. "This is freaking weird."

"I wish it was day time. I don't like it when it's dark," Tyler said.

Takara turned around. "Are you all right?"

"Yes. No. I'm scared."

"I don't blame you. This is pretty scary.

"I wish I was big, like this." The warrior flexed his thick arms. "Then I wouldn't be scared. I wouldn't be scared of being home by myself. I wouldn't be scared of the dark. I wouldn't be scared of Silas."

Takara leaned on her spear. "Everyone has things they're afraid of. I don't like closed spaces. Like elevators or really small rooms. I always have to prop the door open so I can feel air moving."

"How come?"

Tak shrugged. "When I was younger I was in an earthquake and I got trapped in the rubble of our apartment building. My mother and father and my brother all died." She picked up a broken roof tile and threw it over the edge.

"Sorry. What was his name?"

"Akira."

"That's a cool name." Tyler picked up a tile and threw it at the building across the street. "Where is Thebes?"

Tak pointed with her spear. "That way. You can use the mini-map feature to find it."

"I mean in real life." The barbarian stepped back toward the stairs. "Is it in New Mexico?"

"No. Tyler, I live in Japan. Tokyo."

"Oh. So you're not from my church?"

"I'm not in anyone's church. I don't go to church. I'm Shinto and Buddhist. Sort of."

"Okay." The big warrior nodded. "I guess it's okay to tell you. I need help. I'm lost."

"It's no big deal. This world is huge. People get lost here all the time. I can show you how to use your map function and set way points."

"No, not lost here. Lost there." The barbarian waved his thick arms. "In real life."

"What?" Tak tilted her head. Behind Tyler, flames surged up the stairwell to the roof. "Damn, this house is on fire. We have to get out of here."

"Wait, I'm really lost. We went into the desert to meet the spaceship and--"

"Tyler, there's no time. Use your portal. Meet me in Athens." Tak activated her orb and stepped into the blue light.

* * *

Chapter 7
Lair of the Hydra
Day 1

Takeus of Thebes stepped out of a portal orb and stood on a hill above Athens and watched the city burn.

I better find Tyler before he gets himself killed.

The short hoplite trotted down the hill, spear and shield held ready.

Creatures of nightmare and silliness raged through the city's streets. Screeching, snake-haired women. Prancing fauns. Rape-minded centaurs. Most were bipedal, humanoid monsters occupying a single hexagon, but giant, multi-hex monsters rampaged along the wider avenues or squeezed into alleyways in search of prey.

Nonplayer characters died at their posts. The candle maker and her husband fell to dire wolves, still calling, "Copper a candle!" The lame bowyer died firing arrows at an arrow-proof lion. Horses trampled a street urchin into red paste. The blind beggar at the corner near the temple was lucky. A cockatrice turned him to stone just before a horde of rats could strip the meager flesh from his ribs.

Fires raced across rooftops and engulfed the sacred grove. Flaming dryads burst from their bark-clad homes and fled screaming. A cyclops methodically kicked over columns with his huge feet.

Across an open space used for discus hurling, Tak spotted a tall barbarian exit a portal. "Tyler, over here."

The Hyperborean ran with her down the street and back up the hill to safety. Takara leaned against a tree. "I wasn't sure you made it. What were you saying before about being lost?"

Down the hill, a figure fled the doomed city. As the player drew closer, Tak saw that it was an eight-foot giant with gnarled limbs and a studded wooden club.

"Hey, over here," Tyler called.

The player veered toward them. Tyler put out his hand. "Hi, I'm Tyler of Silver City. What's your name?"

The giant smashed Tyler over the head. He fell to one knee.

"Hey, what's with the player versus player?" Tak yelled. "There's plenty of monsters to fight."

The giant booted Tyler aside and turned on the stubby hoplite. "So what? This is a PvP server. It's legal. I want his stuff."

Takara moved well outside the giant's reach. "His stuff isn't worth anything. It's a regular iron sword and bronze helmet. This place is ending. What's the point?"

The giant hefted his club. "The point is I like kicking ass. And your asses are the only ones around."

Takara took a step back. "Go fight some monsters." She pointed at Tyler. "He's just a kid. He barely knows how to play."

Tyler got up, but his spear was in two pieces. "You didn't have to break it."

The giant backhanded the Level 3 Barbarian aside and marched toward Takeus. The Theban hoplite swung his +4 Sling of Eye Piercing and put a stone into the hulking warrior's left eye.

The giant kept coming.

Tak switched to his Spear of the Myrmidons, took two steps forward, and cast.

The spear flew true, striking the giant below the heart. He yanked the spear loose and threw it on the ground.

Takeus drew his +2 Spartan Short Sword and readied his Silver Shield of Athena.

What does it take to drop this guy? Did his mother dunk him in the River Styx?

The short Theban darted under the massive club and slashed the giant's wrists. The giant dropped the club, but laughed as his arms healed instantly. He drew a curved dagger and attacked.

Tak parried three cuts, but the fourth opened her shoulder.

Tyler of Silver City leaped into the fight and caught the giant in a bear hug. "I'll hold him. Get him!"

Takeus stabbed the bearded creature in the throat. The sword opened a gash, but again it healed. When the giant struggled to break Tyler's hold, Tyler lifted him off his feet.

The colossus screamed. His body withered, pounds of muscle falling away from his thrashing limbs until Tyler clutched a skinny little man. Takeus scooped the studded club from the ground and smashed the man's skull in.

Tyler dropped the corpse. "Wow."

The body shimmered for a moment, then sank into the dirt and disappeared.

Takara leaned on the club. "What a jerk! It's too bad this game is ending. We just earned a ton of Experience Points. You'll probably jump a level or two." She slapped the big barbarian on the shoulder. "We make a good team."

"Thanks. That's why my parents home school me. Because of bullies like him." Tyler handed Tak her spear. "What was that guy?"

"An earth giant. They're really strong, but if they lose contact with the ground, they turn weak. Hercules killed one."

"I've never met him." Tyler stared at a smoking temple on the outskirts of the city below. "Last time I played, I went down there."

"Why?"

"To see the mummy girls," Tyler said.

"The mummy girls... Oh, do you mean the oracles?"

"I don't know. They're kind of naked, except for a bunch of Band-Aids. They tell you the future for 50 gold pieces."

"Did they tell you Athens would burn and monsters would eat them all?" Tak laughed.

"No, I didn't ask about that." Tyler looked away.

"Then why'd you give them 50 gold? What did you ask?"

"I asked about my mom and dad and their church."

"Oh." Takara didn't know much about religion in America. She thought all Americans were Christians. The few quotes she'd read from Jesus seemed to advise everyone to be nice to each other. American tourists she'd encountered in Tokyo were nice, but as a country, they fought a lot of wars.

Tak spotted a pack of dire wolves running in their direction. "Let's climb a tree. Most of the monsters can't climb."

The two warriors ran to the edge of the forest and scrambled up a birch with plenty of low-hanging limbs. Twenty feet up, they had a better view of the burning city.

When the cyclops knocked the last row of pillars out from under one of the temples, the building collapsed in a whirl of gray dust that formed a momentary, miniature mushroom cloud. Tak shuddered. Maybe the game developers thought that was funny, but a lot of people in Japan would not. Fortunately, there were only two people around to see it, and she guessed the mushroom cloud meant nothing to Tyler.

"So what did the oracles tell you?" Tak asked.

"I don't know. Nothing they said made any sense. It's like those jokes you're supposed to guess."

"You mean riddles?"

"I guess so."

"Do you remember what they said?"

"Some of it. It was hard to listen. A bullman ran in and tried to eat my head," Tyler said.

"Minotaurs, I hate those sons-of-... I hate those guys. The trick is to take out their knees and then stay back and finish them with arrows."

"I stuck it in the eye."

"That works, too."

"The mummy girls talked about a mountain and a cave."

"A mountain? Where?"

"She didn't say."

"What else did she tell you?" Tak asked.

"She said to run away from the light."

"That's vague."

"I didn't even ask about a light, but the brown-haired girl said to run away from it."

"Oracles are a scam. The one at Delphi costs 100 gold and she makes even less sense. Guys only go to her because she's pretty. I think she's an idiot."

"Maybe." Tyler examined his broken spear. "I ran away from the light. Maybe that girl was right." He took off his helmet. "Are there other places like this?"

"Other online games? Sure, there are several. Fantasy games, space games, social ones where people build stores to sell you stuff and everyone can fly. You ought to try them out when this one ends." Tak wondered if Tyler might be interested in buying a pre-leveled character for a new game.

"I'd like to see those, but I won't get to."

"Why? Will you get in trouble if they catch you playing online?" Tak asked.

"Yeah. I only play when they're gone to meetings at our church. Now..." Tyler shrugged. "They're gone so I can play."

"Damn, that's weird."

"What?"

"My hit points are dropping. Fast." Tak held up her arm. The gash in her shoulder glowed green. "That dagger must have been poisoned. Do you have any anti-poison potions?"

"What color are they?"

"Orange. The purple healing ones won't stop poison."

Tyler dropped to the ground and turned his pack upside down to sort through the items. "No orange. Crap."

Takara climbed down beside him. "Tyler, my character will be dead in seconds, so--"

"Takeus, I really am lost!" Tyler kicked his empty pack. "We went out in the desert and Silas said to go to the light and I saw the blinking lights but I didn't want to go to heaven. And dad and mom said it was time to get on the spaceship, but I ran and Silas chased--"

Takara disappeared in a burst of blue light.

Minutes passed. Athens burned.

Tyler sat under the tree and watched smoke drift up to the stars.

* * *

Damn it.

Monsters rampaged through Thebes.

At least it isn't on fire. Yet.

Takara drifted up the steps into a white, marble temple. An acolyte came forward, his face calm.

"Ghost of a fallen hero, do you desire rebirth?" the robed man asked.

Tak deposited five hundred gold in the temple coffer. "Yeah, hurry. You're going to have monsters in here taking your head off in a minute."

The acolyte continued at the same slow, maddening pace. "The mercy of Zeus be upon you." His hands glowed and disappeared into twin globes of golden light.

Takara's avatar solidified from a gray, translucent ghost into the short, colorful hoplite she was used to.

"Thanks," Tak called over her shoulder as she ran down the steps. A screeching harpy dropped out of the sky, claws extended. Tak ducked and slammed the edge of her shield into the creature's stomach.

The harpy flew into an obelisk and fell to the ground. Tak raced past it and down a narrow alley. She stopped and scanned the area around her.

As soon as she was certain no monsters were close enough to follow her, she activated a portal orb and jumped to Athens.

Come on. This needs to work.

A long second later she tumbled out into a rocky slope above the burning metropolis. Using her map feature, she ran to where she'd left Tyler, but even at full speed it took her three minutes.

Tak skidded to a halt and searched the tree line. Something glittered in the tall grass beneath a wide oak tree. She hefted her spear and crept forward.

A bronze helmet lay among the fallen acorns. But Tyler was gone.

* * *

Chapter 8
Tokyo, Japan
Day 2

When Takara woke, the sun was high but her aunt's door was shut. Takara stood at the bathroom mirror and peeled back her lower lip. The inside was split where her teeth cut the flesh from Jiro's knee strike. She touched the spot with her tongue and winced. It wasn't as bad as the time she came home with a black eye and received well intentioned but misguided lectures on abuse from her aunt, Mr. Saito and a random woman on the metro.

By the time Tak came out of the shower, Aunt Shiori was up. Shiori sat on their tiny patio, sipping hot tea while rain trickled out of the sky and dripped off the edge of the roof.

Kameko, their neighbor's round orange cat, padded out from under Shiori's chair and butted Takara's shin. She reached down to scratch his back. The wet cat arched for a moment, then thumped down on her slippers. "How was the supermarket inventory?"

Shiori yawned. "Long. So long I lost my appetite. Your lip is swollen."

"I missed a takedown."

"Jiro?"

"Yeah."

"That boy." Shiori warmed her hands on her teacup. "There's more tea. I hear Jiro's mother is bad again."

"I thought she was in remission."

"It came back. She's in the hospital." Shiori sighed. "You know she's my age?"

"No, I didn't." Takara eased into the other chair. The cushion was covered in long, orange hairs. "Jiro seemed stressed out."

"And what about you?"

"Me?" Takara lifted Kameko into her lap. The cat purred like an air filter on a fish tank. "I'm fine. I met this...person online."

"A man?"

Takara winced. "No, Auntie, not a man. A boy. At least I think it's a boy. You never know online."

Shiori put down her cup. "Why don't you try meeting a man in real life? Not this pretend stuff. You'll turn 30 next year, you know."

"I know when my birthday is. We've had this conversation before." Takara crossed her arms and Kameko frowned up at her. "I don't know what to make of this boy. I think he might be in trouble."

"What sort of trouble?"

Takara shrugged. "I'm not sure. The whole situation was confusing, and monsters kept attacking us. He told me his parents belong to some church that believes the Internet is evil."

"There are dangerous people on the Internet," Shiori said. "People who take advantage of others, especially children. Has he asked you for money or pictures?"

"No! Well, not yet. I thought it might be a scam, but it didn't feel like one. He asked me for help. He said he is lost, and he didn't mean in the game." Takara stood and deposited Kameko in her aunt's lap. Rain slipped from the edge of the roof, drop by drop. When the next drop fell, she lashed out and punched it. Takara held up her fist. Water ran off her knuckles.

"Quick hands. Like your mother. I don't think I ever beat her at table tennis. I used to get so mad I'd throw the ball out the window so we couldn't play anymore." Shiori finished her tea. "What will you do?"

"I don't know. I don't know this boy. He is not my responsibility."

"The Buddha spoke of 'right action.'" Shiori smiled. "I believe he also mentioned something about 'right livelihood,' but that's for another day."

* * *

New Mexico, USA

At dawn, Tyler poked his head out of the cave and scanned the wilderness. During his escape, he'd climbed into a range of hills thick with trees and crisscrossed with dry streambeds and canyons. The cactus and ocotillo shrubs of the lower lands were gone. At this elevation oaks and junipers ruled, while above the cave ponderosa pines grew tall.

He needed to pee, but he made himself wait until he was sure he was alone. Then he ran to the nearest tree and relieved himself.

The cave was halfway up the slope of a hill, with a clear view of the land below.

It's like a secret hideout for kung fu monks.

He sat inside the entrance, watching for Silas or wandering Gila monsters. His chin didn't hurt anymore, but it was sticky and when he rubbed it, dried blood came away and it stung again.

Tyler cast a stone down the hill. It bounced off a tree and cracked against a rock. He thought of his parents going off the cliff and wondered how they hit when they landed. His head spun. He curled up and lay on his side in the wind-driven sand inside the cave.

Was I wrong? Was the oracle wrong? Did Mom and Dad really get on a spaceship?

No. That can't be right. They'd never leave me behind. Silas lied.

But what if they're up there, on the ship, looking for me?

Or maybe Silas, with his soft voice and creepy purple eyes, still searched for him.

The boy shivered and pulled up the collar of his dusty sport coat. His mouth tasted like paste and he wished he had a cup of milk or one of those Capri Sun juice bags his father always brought back from town. He found a peppermint in the inside pocket of his coat, but the red and white candy only made him more thirsty.

He stood and walked back and forth in front of the cave, but he didn't see any ponds or streams or the road. Tyler knew he had to find the road in order to get out. However, finding the road meant finding their car and the cars of the other families.

Tyler thought about what it would be like to look over the cliff in daylight and see all those people at the bottom.

His family and friends twisted up and extra dead.

The trees spun and he shut his eyes. Tyler staggered back to the cave and sat in the shade with his head between his knees. After a while the dizziness passed and he decided not to think about the cliff anymore. At least until he was back in Silver City and sitting in a police station. Maybe the cops would order pizza.

The thought of pizza made his stomach knot. Even the idea of a big glass of plain water washing away the paste taste in his mouth made Tyler stand and work his way up the hill.

He scared up a frog with red spots on its back that made a single leap into the nearest scrubs and disappeared. Tyler stopped and sat on a rock. The sun soaked through his coat and into his shoulders, chasing away the lingering morning chill.

There was no sign of Silas or the others. Or any others. No people, no cars, no houses, no roads.

A big sky. A big wilderness.

A big empty.

Tyler thought of his parents. His chest went tight.

He sat on the rock in the sun while tears filled his eyes.

* * *

Chapter 9
New Mexico, USA
Day 2

Silas touched the brake and steered onto the unpaved road leading to the group's compound. The road had not been graded in a while and his Jeep Patriot shook.

The stereo skipped and Silas cut his speed. He rolled with the windows down, left arm propped on the door while his right hand held the bottom of the steering wheel.

Morning sunlight warmed the Jeep, soaking into the cold leather seats and through his suit coat. Silas loosened his tie. The wind on the cliff slung a great deal of dust and his suit needed dry cleaning.

He glanced left to right at the dozen single-wide trailers arranged around the dirt cul-de-sac. The compound was tidy. There wasn't much landscaping, but the few scrubby shrubs were clipped, and plants in colorful pots made the trailers' steps cheerful.

Silas switched to a simple set of Dickie's work clothes and put on a pair of bright green rubber gloves. He took a plastic tub of cleansers, a lightweight vacuum and a push mop out of the back of the Jeep, and carried them into the first trailer.

Inside, he vacuumed up hair from the carpets, wiped fingerprints off doorknobs and the refrigerator handle and the control pad for the microwave oven. He forced himself not to derail into the minutia, but to give the trailer a basic cleaning.

He finished the first trailer in 53 minutes and figured he'd erased any evidence of himself. Silas went outside to the Jeep and drank a bottle of water.

When he carried his tools to the second trailer, Silas circled around a covered well.

The families had boarded the old well up so their children wouldn't fall into it. Silas smiled. In Jonestown they put children in the well on purpose.

As he cleaned the second trailer, he thought of nights he'd spent in the well. Once for throwing firecrackers. Three times for stealing food. The well wasn't full of water. In fact, there didn't seem to be much water around Jonestown and the farmers struggled. But kids that misbehaved were put into the well over night, and Silas had spent several nights there, crouched deep in the earth as spiders crawled across his bare arms.

After 74 minutes of cleaning, he moved on.

The third trailer, owned by the Coles, caught the brunt of the morning sun due to its position in the cul-de-sac. The air inside was warm like a shower stall. Motes of dust floated in the yellow rays of light shining through the windows.

Silas stood still, a can of Pledge in one hand.

Empty.

The people were gone, but their things were still there.

Silas blinked. "I am a fission bomb. Flesh is destroyed, but furniture remains. Wood, brick, glass. All still here."

He smiled at the poetry of it. The imagery. Silas imagined a city, Chicago or Houston, full of people. Noisy, dirty, filthy people. And then a new day. A dawn. All the people gone. Just clean lines left. Clean, straight buildings, clean sidewalks, clean, orderly streets. Quiet. Sunny.

Clean.

"I must scale this. This was small. It could be large. Like Jonestown, but clean."

He thought of that morning in November of 1978. He'd spent the night in the well, but when the sun rose, no one came to get him. He heard people moving about the camp, and later gunshots. When the sun was overhead, Silas tucked his toes into the dead tree roots lining the well and climbed out.

There were bodies everywhere. Hundreds of bodies, most of them lying face down in groups. So many he couldn't walk down the path without stepping around them, or over them. Or on them. Bodies that reeked of voided bowels.

The boy Silas tried to move them off the path, but they were too heavy. The camp was a mess. Filth everywhere. His head spun and he ran toward one of the huts, tripped and fell onto a corpse. A dirt, filthy corpse.

Silas the man shivered.

"No bodies here. None."

The compact man moved through the trailer, bringing cleanliness. When he got to the master bedroom, he sat on the edge of the bed and looked at the photographs on the nightstand. A girl in a cap and gown. A long dead grandfather, wearing a straw hat and holding some dripping, slimy fish. A boy with the start of a mustache sitting on a dirt bike, smiling at the camera.

Silas opened the drawers of the dresser and tidied up the clothes inside. Under a stack of socks he found a handgun. A revolver. The gun was small and stubby. Instead of a hammer, it had an odd camel's hump. The word "Airweight" was etched in perfect cursive into the finish on one side.

He picked it up. Indeed, it felt light in his hand. He pushed the release and swung the cylinder open. There were only five chambers, all loaded.

Silas put the revolver in his pocket and began to vacuum.

Eventually, someone would find the bodies. It would be smart to be far away when that happened.

He estimated it would take him the rest of the day to finish cleaning the trailers. A few minutes to pack the Jeep and he could leave.

But before he left New Mexico, one detail remained. A ten-year-old detail in an ill-fitting sport coat.

While he cleaned, Silas collected items he would need for a hike into the wilderness. A nylon backpack, matches, pull-top cans of pork-and-beans, a plastic spoon, and a map of the Gila National Forest. His straw cowboy hat and Garmin GPS were in the Jeep. Silas decided against carrying a tent. A tent would be heavy, and he hadn't found one anyway. The alternative was driving into Silver City, where he would have to enter a store and interact with a clerk to buy one.

Silas stayed out of town. He always sent group members in for groceries and conducted his business by phone or Internet.

The only sleeping bag he could find was a thin, pink Hello Kitty model designed more for slumber parties than wilderness survival. He unrolled the bag and held it longways--it just reached his collarbones. Silas shrugged. He could take a heavy jacket and the sleeping bag would have to do.

Silas shut the door of the trailer and carried the equipment to his Jeep. The sun cantered into the west and he still had four trailers to clean.

* * *

Chapter 10
Tokyo, Japan
Day 2

"All right Tyler of Silver City, what's this spaceship you're talking about?" Takara muttered as she sat down at her computer. She heard her aunt in the kitchen, washing dishes while she watched the little television on the counter. Takara took a mouthful of tea and flinched when the hot drink found the cut in her lip.

She used her favorite search engine to look up UFOs and UFO religions. For twenty minutes cargo cults of the Pacific sidetracked her, but soon she was back among articles about the Aetherius Society, Raelism and the Unarians. She was surprised to find Mormons believe in aliens on other worlds.

She spent forty minutes on Scientology and concluded it was an elaborate scam designed to separate gullible, needy Hollywood stars from their money. They seemed the most dangerous of the groups until she read about the Heaven's Gate cult and the mass suicide of 38 of its members in 1997. The cult leaders, Marshall Applewhite and Bonnie Nettles, convinced their followers that a spaceship, hidden behind the comet Hale-Bopp, would arrive to take them away.

Takara sat back from the computer monitor.

Tyler said a spaceship came to take him to heaven. This kid is highly confused. Where the hell are his parents?

* * *

After lunch, Takara got an umbrella and splashed down the street to the koban police outpost on the corner. Outside the small building, a young officer gave directions to a deliveryman. Takara looked in the window and waved to Sergeant Shimada. He opened the door and took her umbrella. Inside the cramped room, two officers chatted while they ate their lunch.

The big cop motioned her to a chair, and then squeezed around his desk to sit.

"Don't tell me." Shimada shut his eyes and put one meaty hand to his forehead. "Your neighbor's fat orange cat stole your aunt's scooter and is loose in the city."

Takara laughed. "Aunt Shiori says hello. And Tameko wouldn't be so big if you didn't give her treats every time you patrol."

Shimada spread his hands. "I can't help it. She begs. I had an orange cat when I was a kid, you know. What's up?"

"I have a problem. A mystery."

"We fix problems. We solve mysteries."

"I think a young boy I met online in a game might be in trouble," she said softly. She looked over her shoulder, but the other cops were talking on their radios.

Shimada frowned. "What sort of trouble? Bullies at school? Maybe shoplifting or alcohol?"

"No, no, he seemed very nice. And young." Takara took a deep breath. "I think his parents are in some sort of extreme religious group. A cult. He talked about spaceships and heaven like he'd been brainwashed. I'm worried his parents might hurt him."

Shimada tugged open a drawer and fished out a list of phone numbers. "I know a gal in Investigation at the Station. I'll call her and--"

"I don't know if they've actually hurt him, yet."

"Oh? Hmm. Okay, I went to the academy with a guy who just moved over to Crime Prevention. We'll stop this before it ever starts." Shimada reached for his phone. "What building does the boy live in?"

Takara watched the other two officers go out. When they opened the door, rain blew in on the floor. "I don't know. He lives in America. It's a place called New Mexico, but it's in America."

"Is he Japanese?"

"I think he's American."

Shimada put the phone down. "Takara, we'll do anything to help a kid, but if he's not a Japanese citizen and he doesn't live in Japan, there's the question of jurisdiction."

"Isn't there some way?"

"I don't know. I'm not sure there is much we can do from here."

Takara leaned across his desk. "After the earthquake, you didn't quit on Akira."

Shimada looked down at his big hands. "No, we dug for 15 hours straight. But we were too late for him. And your parents, too."

"The failure was mine, not yours," Tak said. "I couldn't reach him. My point is that you tried. Can't we at least call the police in New Mexico to make sure the boy is okay?"

"We can try. We will try." Shimada dug in his desk again and came up with a business card. "This is my pal Kobayashi in Crime Prevention. Call him. I doubt there's anything he can do, but he has great connections. He'll know who to talk to at Prefecture Headquarters. It may take time, but they'll find the right person to contact over in the United States."

"Thank you, Shimada-san. I just want to know he's okay. Thank you." Takara got up and retrieved her umbrella.

"Keep me updated on what happens. If Kobayashi can't do something, we'll find someone who can," Shimada said as he opened the door for her. "Oh, and please tell your aunt I said hello."

* * *

New Mexico, USA

When the sun made it too hot to sit on the rock, Tyler stretched and pushed himself up. Further down the hill a scrawny rabbit with a black tail hopped around looking at things.

Tyler wondered if he could follow the rabbit to a water hole. The rabbit had to be thirsty, hopping around in a fur suit.

He held a stone in his right hand just in case the rabbit was mean.

I'm a ninja.

When the rabbit hopped away, the boy slid over the rocks and into the woods like a melting ice cube. He tried to keep the rabbit in sight, but it was hard. He lost track of the creature, and finally rose from his crouch to look.

The rabbit's head swiveled, and Tyler saw its black tail blur. It disappeared.

Stupid rabbit.

Tyler started to throw the rock, but checked his pitch. He might need the stone for real enemies. The boy bounced the rock in his hand and realized it wasn't much of a weapon.

As he zigzagged back and forth down the hill, he picked up fallen tree limbs one at a time and threw them away. On the fourth one, he found a keeper.

The stick was as tall as a seventh grader. He stuck one end in the ground and leaned on it. The stick was sturdy. Tyler decided it was oak.

He broke the twigs off and then rubbed one end against a flat rock. His arms burned with effort, but soon he'd filed the end to a point. The stick was now a spear.

Tyler shouldered his weapon and hiked back toward his cave. He stepped over a log and his shoe sank in a pile of wet, black beans.

Tyler hopped on one foot and smelled his shoe.

It's crap. Gross.

While he scraped his shoe off, he noticed tracks leading away from the fresh dung. The prints were shaped like butterflies--sharp at one end, dull at the other. When he looked closer, Tyler saw the tracks were doubled, one on top of the other. Two on the left, two on the right, but staggered.

Something with four legs that poops black beans. A deer.

Sometimes Tyler's mom made black beans and rice. She put sour cream on top and if he was good she let him use corn chips like spoons to scoop it up. His dad put hot sauce on it, but Tyler didn't.

The corn chips always made him thirsty. As thirsty as he was now.

Tyler figured if the deer ate black beans it must be thirsty, so he followed the tracks.

The woods grew so thick he had to crawl on his hands and knees. He lost the tracks four times. Tyler began to mark the last track he found with a rock and then circle around it until he found a new track going away.

Lizards darted past. A squirrel clung to the side of a tree and scolded him. A branch poked him in the ear and he bruised his hand on a sharp rock.

Tyler duck walked along the narrow trail and almost pitched headfirst into a ravine. Using his spear like a cane, he scrambled down between the cool rock walls. He descended into a path of smooth, oval stones running down the hill and away. The earth between the stones was dark and moist.

This was a stream. It had to be. Smooth rocks come from rivers. But it's dry.

Tyler kicked a rock. The stone flipped and its bottom was wet, but water didn't fountain up into the air like a garden hose.

Stupid deer.

The hike back to the cave seemed a lot longer. Once Tyler stopped and looked around. For a horrible moment, he wasn't sure he was going the right way.

His heart shook in his chest. His hands trembled around the haft of the spear. Then he saw the deer tracks and smelled the poop and knew he was close.

When he arrived at the cave, Tyler threw a stone into the darkness just to make sure there wasn't a monster inside. He heard the stone strike rock, not ribs, so he went in and sat in his spot against the wall.

He wasn't too hungry, but his head hurt and the paste taste in his mouth was worse. He took off his sport coat and folded it into a pillow. First he lay with his head near the sunlit entrance, but he figured he couldn't see anyone coming that way, and if he fell asleep, the first thing a monster would bite was his head.

Tyler turned around and put his feet in the sun and his head on his coat in the cool black shadow of the cave. When he stretched out, his shoulder hit something hard and flat.

The computer.

He sat up and flipped open the little notebook, put his finger on the power button and hesitated.

Was that real? Takeus of Thebes and the burning city and those monsters? Those monsters aren't real. Is Takeus? Can I trust him?

Tyler rubbed his temples hard with his thumbs. He closed the computer and leaned back against the cool wall, the spear within easy reach.

I need to think.

But soon his heavy eyes fell shut.

* * *

Chapter 11
Tokyo, Japan
Day 2

"Did Sergeant Shimada help?" Aunt Shiori asked.

"He gave me the number of a man in Crime Prevention at the station house," Takara said while she wriggled out of her raincoat and shoes.

"Did you tell Shimada I said hello?" Shiori asked as she sat checking her email on her laptop.

"Of course. He said to tell you hello."

"Did the other officers hear you?"

"I don't know, Auntie. Why should it matter?"

"I just don't want people in the neighborhood to talk, is all." Shiori toyed with the optical mouse.

Takara sat to change her wet socks. When Shiori didn't say anything, the younger woman stared at her with raised eyebrows.

"Come on, out with it."

Shiori looked away. "You should be a police officer. You could interrogate criminals."

"Auntie?"

"One morning I came home from work and I saw Tameko rolling around in the grass and went outside to give her a treat. Shimada was on patrol, taking a loop of the building. We talked. While I was petting Tameko, he reached down to scratch her back and our hands touched." Shiori blushed.

Takara cackled.

Shiori glared. "Have you looked at his shoulders? Shimada was a noted wrestler in his youth. He's quite a handsome man. All the ladies in the building say so."

"You've got a crush on Shimada." Takara fled to her room. She called out, "I better not come home and find you ironing his uniforms."

"Takara!"

Still laughing, Takara pulled on dry socks and then woke her computer. Shiori came and leaned on the door. "Are you calling Crime Prevention?"

"I will, but first I want to talk to Tyler again." Takara tapped in her password. "I'll give him a chance to admit if this is a hoax."

"And if it's true?"

Takara shrugged. Shiori went out. Takara heard the refrigerator open, and then her cell phone rang. She flipped it open and checked the number. It was Game Mania. Maybe Saito-san was calling her in to cover for someone.

Takara tossed the phone onto a pile of clothes without answering.

She logged into *Lair of the Hydra.*

* * *

Lair of the Hydra

Takeus of Thebes stepped out of the portal into the cold, still, stale air of a crypt. A single torch burned, sending black, sticky smoke up the granite wall and across the ceiling.

A rectangular, marble box rested on a dais in the middle of the floor.

The ceiling was low enough to make the short Theban stoop. Tak ducked under the torch, careful not to catch the horsehair crest of his helmet afire.

As he stepped into the pool of flickering light he realized the lid of the casket was missing. Takeus turned sideways to ease by the marble shell. His hip bumped something and the warrior glanced down at a bare foot. A slender, bare, mocha-colored foot.

Takeus eased his short sword free and leaned over.

The woman lay on her back, her robes torn down the middle. Her eyes were open, but rats had already scooped out the soft meat with their sharp, little teeth. Her mouth was open in a silent, perpetual scream.

Her legs were splayed, ankles resting on opposite sides of the casket. Blood smeared her smooth, brown stomach and thighs.

Takeus sheathed his sword and unpinned his wool cloak. The Theban draped the cloak over the woman's midsection, careful not to touch her cold flesh.

He turned to the door and examined the rusting iron bands. Three brass levers were set in the wall, with unfamiliar sigils above them.

He pulled the levers in order, left to right, but the door did not budge. Takeus tried the second, third, then first lever, but again, the iron-bound door remained shut.

Takeus heard a rustle and turned. Something moved beneath the cloak.

The fabric collapsed inward, concave for a moment, then the woman's knees shifted. The cloak swelled. Fresh blood soaked through the heavy weave. Her toes twitched.

Takeus rammed the edge of his shield between the door and the frame. The torch flickered. The room dimmed.

Takeus heard a gurgle, then the sound of fabric tearing.

He shoved the shield sideways. The door split open.

Takeus bolted outside and froze.

Beasts roamed the graveyard, digging corpses out of their cold beds and plunging red jaws deep into sawdust-filled stomachs. In the streets survivors fought in small knots, back to back beside overturned chariots and in the doorways of burning houses.

A fawn-colored dog ran past Takeus, shaking its head so hard spit slung from the sides of its mouth. The shaking dog ducked under a wagon and bit the back of a shopkeeper's leg. The man whirled and buried a rusty hatchet between the dog's ears.

The hatchet stuck.

The man put his bare foot on the dog's head, braced himself, and yanked on the hatchet. The dog's head melted and became a tan, syrupy pool shot through with streaks of green and black. The syrup washed over the man's foot to his ankle, sank through his skin and pulsed up his leg.

He screamed.

His face melted.

Takeus ran.

A three-headed lion staggered into the street in front of him. Takeus raised his spear, but the big cat fell over on its side. A fourth head, plastic faced and gaping, morphed out of its ribs. Another head sprouted from its back. Heads burst out all over the creature and it writhed, a mass of gaping mouths.

Takeus dodged a blue-painted barbarian with an axe, and raced out of the city. The short Theban planted his back to the wall of a farmhouse and dug in his pack for the portal orb.

"Where would Tyler go? Someplace safe. A high place where monsters can't get him. Easy to defend."

Tak activated the orb.

* * *

Moonlight bathed the coarse brown sand and sent a wide, yellow path across the sea. Lazy waves washed up, carrying a milky layer of foam. Takeus trotted away from the open beach and into a series of dunes. The crests of the dunes shimmered when the wind blew through the sea oats.

A shadow drifted across the ground. The Theban looked up and saw an immense owl, cruising the air currents off shore.

Takeus crouched in the shoulder-high sea oats.

The owl continued its hunt, drifting down the coast toward the burning city.

Tak looked for a bright sliver on the far side of Syracuse's outer harbor. The lighthouse. A high place, built of stone, with a narrow entrance a single warrior could defend.

Tak nodded and slipped through the dunes. The thirty-foot walls of sand cut the wind and even the noise of the waves. The shadowy canyons were silent except for the crunch of his sandals.

A short hike around the curve of the shore and Takeus crawled to the edge of a dune and looked up at the lighthouse. The stone tower was intact, but unlit. Piled blocks barred the entrance.

Tak scanned the top of the tower and saw movement.

The Theban slid down the dune and called, "Tyler?"

A splash made her turn.

Half a dozen figures shambled out of the surf. They swayed in the wind, faces rotted away, spears gone, but still carrying wicker shields.

"Takeus?" a voice called down from the tower.

"Yeah, it's me! The door is blocked." Tak pulled a clay pot of Greek Fire from her pack, lit the wick, and threw it.

The jar shattered on the lead creature's chest and the jelly erupted in flame. The thing howled and stumbled backward into the water.

"I'll lower a rope," Tyler yelled. "Hang on."

"Hurry!" A second peltast, a Thracian by his dress, staggered out of the foam, one arm extended, fingers reaching.

Tak rammed her spear into the Thracian's knee. The leg folded and the man went down, but he crawled toward the short warrior.

A thick knot of rope hit Tak's helmet. She turned and went up the side of the tower, pulling hand over hand.

When Tak reached the top, the long-armed Hyperborean seized the straps of her cuirass and hauled her over the crenels.

"What are those?" Tyler asked.

Takara looked down. One Thracian floated face down in the ocean, his back still on fire. The others stood at the base of the lighthouse, moaning with the wind.

"Dead peltasts. But not dead enough." Tak turned. "I was looking for you."

The blonde barbarian leaned against the stone wall. "I was looking for you. I need your help. I'm lost and--"

"Tyler, wait. If this is a scam I want to know. I'm sick of playing games."

"What?"

Tak drew her short sword. The heavy blade gleamed in the moonlight. "I'm not kidding. Whatever you're after, it isn't funny anymore. I talked with the police."

The lanky barbarian backed toward the door. "The police? But I didn't do anything wrong. It was Silas. I didn't want to go on the spaceship. Mom and Dad got on, but I didn't want to and...I didn't do anything."

Tak raised her sword. "I don't normally get into this player versus player crap, but you tell me your real name or I take your head."

"Tyler Burroughs."

"Were do you live?"

"I told you! We live near Silver City, in New Mexico. In America. I'm thirsty."

"What's your address?"

"I don't know. We live in a trailer. It's white."

"What's your telephone number?"

"I don't know. Dad got rid of the phone. He said we didn't need it. He said we were living off the griddle."

"You're lying." Tak sheathed her sword. "I'm leaving. I don't get your scam and I don't want to."

"I'm lost. Takeus, I'm lost."

The Theban pointed. "Syracuse is right over there. If your portal orb is messed up, go to one of the temples of Mercury. You can jump anywhere you want--"

"Not here! In New Mexico. I'm lost. In the desert. Not like a sand desert, there are trees and everything but I can't find any water and I feel dizzy. My head hurts."

Tak held a portal orb. It glowed blue in her hand, but she stopped. "How are you accessing this game?"

"My dad's notebook computer. Like I did before."

"Where are you?"

"On a hill above my cave. I found a cave. It's a really good cave because it's empty. And it's mine."

"Your laptop has a wireless card?"

"I guess so."

"Listen to me. If you're truly lost, why don't you just use the computer to reach the police? Find the website for the station in Silver City and email them your position."

Tyler slumped. "I can't. I don't have email."

"Okay, first shrink the game window and look at your desktop. What icons do you see? What little pictures?"

"There's only three. *Lair of the Hydra*, HP Director and Adobe Reader."

"Where's your email?" Tak asked.

"I don't have one. My dad had an email address but he got rid of all that stuff before he let me play with the computer. He said it was to keep me safe from predators."

"So you can't email. How about instant messaging?" Tak asked.

"I looked, but I can't find it."

"Okay, wait, you're in the desert? Are you on batteries or are you plugged into a car?"

"I don't have a car. The cars are at the cliff. I don't want to go to the cliff."

"So you're on battery. How much battery life do you have left?"

"I don't know."

"Damn Tyler, do you know anything about computers?"

"I'm ten! I've never been to real school. I'm in the woods by myself and there are Gila monsters and I don't have any water. Tell me what to do." The barbarian paced the narrow walkway.

Takara blinked.

"You need to use the Internet to get help. Use a search engine. You can look up ways to find water and all that. Look up 'survival' or 'desert survival.'"

"I can't."

"It's not that hard, Tyler. Just open Internet Explorer or Firefox and bring up Google."

"You don't understand. I don't have those. Mom and Dad got rid of them."

"Hell." Takara smacked the stone wall with the flat of her hand. "I have no idea what the hell is happening." The short Theban leaned on the wall and looked up at the moon. "This is too damn weird. Tyler, I don't know what to say. You haven't asked me for money. You haven't asked me for pictures. I don't get your game. Maybe...maybe you're crazy. Maybe you're a prisoner or a mental patient with access to a computer. Maybe you're sitting in your pajamas somewhere laughing at me."

"I'm wearing my good clothes. My mom made me put on a sport coat. My dad tied my tie." Tyler opened his hands. "I don't need money. I need water."

Takara bit her lip. "Tyler, do you feel safe in your cave?"

Tyler shook his head side to side. "Sort of. I haven't explored it all yet. Just the front. But it's better than outside. I don't like it when it's dark."

"Okay, you have to find water but try to stay near your cave. I'll talk to the police here again. They'll talk to the police in Silver City and they'll come find you, okay?"

"I guess. But what if Silas--"

"Tyler, you have to conserve your battery. It'll run down if you stay online too long. When I leave, exit the game and shut the computer down. Tomorrow when the sun goes down, log on and I'll be here in *Lair* and we'll meet at this lighthouse. Okay?"

"Okay."

Takara activated her portal orb. "I'll see you tomorrow at sundown."

* * *

Chapter 12
New Mexico, USA
Day 3

Silas parked the car, switched off the headlights and drank the last of his hot chocolate. The dawn air was cool and he rolled his sleeves down. He was a short but compact man and he slung the pack crammed with water bottles, pistol, and Hello Kitty sleeping bag over his shoulder without effort.

He marked the location of his car with a handheld global positioning system, and then tucked the unit in his pack.

Silas fussed with the straps of his pack as he walked, but the weight bit into his shoulders. He was trim, though, and in good health, and he reeled off mile after mile of semi-desert as he worked his way south toward the cliff.

Hours passed, the sun rose, and he emptied a bottle of water.

When he reached Horse Mountain, where he'd sent his group to their deaths, he wished he'd brought a pair of binoculars. He lay in the dead, brown grass for half an hour watching for forest rangers or the Border Patrol.

Tyler Burroughs is Erwin Schrodinger's cat. A cat in a box, possibly alive or possibly dead. But if the box remains shut, then both states are of equal probability. Tyler is alive, sitting under a tree eating manna from Heaven. And yet simultaneously, Tyler is dead, lying in a gully while vultures pick his bones.

The only way to find out was to follow the tracks and open the box. He pushed through a thicket and walked up the slope toward the cliff.

There were many shoe prints in the dirt leading up the trail. Silas shuffled with his head down, examining each mark.

"Hey, mister!"

Silas froze.

A young couple rushed hand in hand down the trail toward him. Silas reached into his pocket, and realized the pistol was in his pack. He waited.

The two slid to a halt, panting and pale. The woman was thin, with a long nose that would have dominated her face if not for her enormous brown eyes. Her hair was long and thick, and her legs tan. She looked like a Greek princess.

Silas turned to the young man. He was tall and reedy, with dirty blonde hair and a billy goat's beard. His right forearm was in a blue cast, but not a sling.

The two carried walking sticks and frame packs with glow sticks and charms jangling from them.

"Do you have a cell phone?" the young man asked.

"No."

"We have one, but I can't get a signal."

"What's wrong?" Silas took off his sunglasses so he could see the actual color of the girl's eyes. They were a rich, chocolate brown that would have looked just as natural on a deer.

The man leaned over with his hands on his knees. "We were hiking along the cliff and Chelsea looked down and saw--"

"We thought people had thrown garbage over the cliff," the girl said. "You know, like old clothes and stuff. But when we looked, we saw a leg, then a head, then--" The young woman vomited, choking so hard she fell to her knees. The man held her long hair out of the way like he'd done it before.

Silas slipped his pack off one shoulder and dug in it. He pulled out a bottle of water. "Here, take this." He looked at the man. "What are you going to do?"

The woman took a bandanna from around her neck and wiped her face. "We need to find our way to a road. Flag down a ranger or someone with a phone. Will you help us?"

"Of course." Silas hefted his pack back on his shoulders. "Oh, no!"

"What?"

"What if someone is alive down there?" Silas asked.

"Oh God, we didn't, I mean, we should have checked but we panicked," the man said. He looked as sick as his girlfriend.

Silas touched her arm. "Look, before you go for help, can you two show me the spot where you saw the people? I used to be an EMT. If there are survivors, I'll climb down and help them."

The young man took the woman's hand. "Okay, let's go."

The couple led Silas back up the ridge and walked parallel to the cliff edge. The young man pointed. "It's a little further. Around that pyramid-shaped rock the cliff curves and then there's a smooth part."

"Okay," Silas panted as his short legs struggled to keep up.

"It's here. This is the spot." The couple stopped well short of the edge and shucked their packs and walking sticks.

Silas considered.

The gun will make a lot of noise. The sound might carry for miles.

"I'm sorry." He rubbed his face. "My eyes aren't too good anymore. Can you look and see if there's anyone moving that needs help? Then while you two run to the road I'll find a place to scramble down and aid them."

The girl glanced at the boy. Now he looked ready to vomit. "I'll do it." She stepped forward but he grabbed her hand.

"I'm okay. We'll do it together," the young man said.

She smiled. Holding hands, they marched to the edge and looked over. He pointed. "Okay, see that square rock? Next to it is a lady in a dress. And above her, is a guy in a gray suit."

Silas picked up a walking stick and moved behind them. "I think I see them." Silas jabbed the young man with the stick and pushed him off the cliff.

The girl's grip broke as her boyfriend dropped over the edge. She turned, confused.

Silas stared into her marvelous brown eyes as he speared her with the stick.

The heels of her boots slipped over the edge. She grabbed at empty air and fell.

Silas leaned over in time to see the young man snap against a sharp rock. He watched the woman bounce twice and thump onto a jumble of stones.

He took a bottle out of his pack and swished the warm water around his mouth before swallowing. No noise. Not even any screaming. He'd expected screaming. There was no disappointment. It was like ordering a hamburger and finding cheese on it. Not what he'd expected, but it was fine.

He leaned over for another look, and his boot sent a marble-sized stone over the edge. Silas stared at the bodies one hundred feet below.

The girl moved.

Silas jumped back from the edge. His heart rate spun up and he bent over, dizzy for a moment.

He dropped to his hands and knees and crabbed forward for another look.

The young man lay split nearly in half, red bones lancing up at the sun. The girl was intact; a halo of blood soaked her long brown hair.

Her arm moved.

"Shit." Silas twitched and another tiny stone bounced down the cliff. He watched it for a moment, then scooted back from the edge.

He picked up a fist-sized rock, brushed the loose dirt from it, stood at the edge and let it drop. The slope of the cliff was not quite vertical, and the rock tumbled as the degree of incline changed near the bottom.

Silas found a second stone. This time he lobbed it. It struck the rocks five feet from the girl and bounced.

The cultist frowned. He considered the physics of it, the clean precision of angle and velocity and feet per second.

He threw a third stone. It hit her in the stomach. She convulsed, sat half way up and fell back.

Silas thought he heard her moan, but with the wind swirling around the cliff it was difficult to be certain.

He went back for more rocks.

He used an octal system. Piled eight rocks at a time, cast them, then gathered eight more.

Of the first eight, one rock, the third, hit. One in eight, or 12.5 percent. Silas nodded to himself while he ran the numbers in his head.

In the second group of eight, he also hit once, but in the third group he hit twice or 25 percent. And in the fourth group, three times.

His shoulder tired and he rubbed it while he looked down at her. She'd rolled over onto her side and somehow dragged one broken arm up to protect her face.

After 32 stones, Silas found a circular rock the size of a bowling ball. He carried it to the edge, raised it above his head with both hands, and threw.

The stone hit her hip.

She screamed.

Silas looked around, but didn't see any one. No other hikers, no park rangers, nothing.

He picked up the next rock.

The wind carried a noise to him, a steady, droning noise. Silas listened. It was above. Since Horse Mountain was the highest point in the area, he knew the noise came from the sky.

He replaced his sunglasses and squinted. Silas didn't see anything for a full minute, and then he caught a brief, metallic flash. For a second the sun hit something just right and he saw a machine so high in the air it was just a silver sliver.

Silas ran for the bushes.

* * *

Chapter 13
Tokyo, Japan
Day 3

Takara took the phone out onto the patio, then decided she didn't want the neighbors listening, and went back inside.

Shiori was out shopping, and Tameko had returned to his actual home for lunch.

Tak held the business card and dialed with her thumb. The phone rang once.

"Crime Prevention, Kobayashi speaking. How may I help you?"

"Sir, this is...my name is Takara Murakami. I need help and your friend Sergeant Shimada-san gave me your number."

"Ah, Shimada!" The man's tone warmed. "How is that old wrestler? We have lunch together the first week of every month, but we missed this time."

"He is well. I spoke to him yesterday at the koban and he suggested I contact you. This may sound strange, but I met a person online. A person I believe is a young boy, and he told me very odd things about his parents and I think he may be in danger."

"Oh?"

Takara waited, but when Kobayashi said nothing else she continued. "Shimada-san warned me this might be difficult because the boy isn't Japanese. In fact, he isn't even in Japan. He's in New Mexico, in the United States."

"Hmm." Takara heard the sound of a chair creak. "Perhaps you'd better explain how you met. Start at the beginning."

Takara told him about *Lair of the Hydra* and was surprised when Kobayashi said his nephew played online and he was familiar with the concept of thousands of people sharing a fantasy world.

"I'll be frank with you, Miss Murakami. It sounds like a scheme. This person may be a dangerous pervert."

"But if he is a boy..."

"Yes. If. Okay, give me the boy's name and location. Whatever you have."

Takara told him what little she knew and listened to him type it in.

"Okay, I'll notify Prefecture. I can't start calling agencies at random in a foreign country without permission, but I'll get started right now."

"Thank you, Kobayashi-san. Thank you. Please call me as soon as you learn anything."

Takara squeezed the phone for a moment, then dropped it in her lap. *Tyler said he needs water. He must be thirsty in the desert. Akira was under the rubble for hours. I heard him coughing. He must have been very thirsty.*

* * *

After she slurped a bowl of noodles, Takara sat down at her computer.

She started with *Lair of the Hydra*. She didn't know Tyler's father's given name, but she knew his surname so she searched the player profiles for 'Burroughs.'

The search results turned up players in California, Florida, Texas and three states Tak had never heard of. That was just the results for the United States, and *LOTH* had players all over the world.

Next she used a search engine to find the telephone white pages for Silver City, New Mexico. There was not a single Burroughs listed.

Tyler Burroughs, where are you?

She recalled Tyler said he lived outside of Silver City, not in it, so she searched the listings in Grant County, but had no luck.

Takara sat back and sipped a can of Coca-Cola. Rain beat on the window. A chill ran down her neck. She pulled one socked foot up under her in the chair and leaned forward.

Lair of the Hydra was the one connection she was certain of. She went back to their homepage and found the number for technical support. She called the support number in Austin, Texas, but the recording repeated the message on the site about *Lair's* imminent closure.

She went to the contact form and sent them an email marked "URGENT!" but Takara didn't have much hope. If they weren't manning their own phones, then the tech supporters weren't reading their email either. They were probably cleaning out their desks and auctioning the office furniture.

Takara considered calling the police in Silver City, but she reasoned Kobayashi would get better results. Cop asking cop, rather than random nut asking cop.

What else? Tyler doesn't have a phone number or an address. But his parents must. They have to have an Internet provider to log onto the Internet. So his parents have an account with either a phone company or a cable company. And an account has to have contact information.

She went to the refrigerator for a can of Mountain Dew. The cola hit the spicy noodles in Tak's stomach and she winced.

Damn it, Tyler, you're making this hard. What does everyone in America have? Water, electricity, cable television, two cars, a dog, a cat, a gun, maybe a boat.

Takara spent half an hour finding the telephone number for the water company in Silver City. She input the country code, then called and explained to the person in her rusty high school English that she needed the address of the Burroughs family in or around Silver City.

The water employee told her she couldn't give out that information because there weren't any Burroughs in their database. Tak hung up.

What do they drink from, a well?

Takara went back to Internet providers. If it was a local company, she would have to track them down one by one. A national cable provider that sold bundled television, phone and Internet service would make more sense. Or a phone company, assuming Tyler's parents had a landline at some point.

Social engineering time. Takara finished her Mountain Dew, cleared her throat and picked up the phone.

A voice answered, "Hello, Monology Cable. This is Kevin. How can I help you?"

"Hello, I want more TV. More channels."

"Are you a customer or would you like to switch from your current provider?"

"Customer. I am customer," Tak said, intentionally emphasizing her accent and making her English worse.

"Okay, great! So you want to upgrade your service?"

"Yes. Upgrade."

"Can I get your account number please?"

"Oh, no. My husband moved bill. Cleaned the desk. It was here this morning." Takara leaned the phone by her desk and shuffled a stack of magazines. "Cannot find now. My name is Mrs. Burroughs. B-u-r-r-o-u-g-h-s. Grant County, New Mexico."

"Okay, that's no problem. We can use your telephone number or your street--"

"Street address change. We moved. One week ago. Do you have the new address? Old address was Fortune Street, maybe still in database?"

"We have an old listing for--wait, I'm sorry, what did you say your home phone number was?"

"We use cell phone only. No landline."

"Okay, then I'll need your cell phone number."

"Account is under husband's name." Takara wiped a drop of sweat from her lip.

"Okay, can I have your husband's cell number, please?"

"I don't know. He switched companies. New number."

"You don't know your husband's phone number?"

"New number. I have not learned it yet."

Kevin sighed. "Ma'am, I can't help you without an account number or a phone number or street address. Something. This call is being monitored for quality assurance purposes and if you're not pleased with my service, I can forward you to a manager."

Takara bit her lip. If Kevin didn't fall for it, the manager wouldn't either. "No, thank you. Goodbye."

She sat back in her chair and rubbed her eyes. Tak opened a desk drawer, took out a vial of eye drops, tilted back and splashed relief into her eyes.

She flicked her cell phone and made it spin on the smooth desktop. It slowed until the stubby antenna pointed right at her.

It all goes back to Lair of the Hydra. The information is there. They had to pay their account with a credit card. If I can get the credit card information, I'll have an address, a phone number, everything.

She stood and paced her narrow room. *I need someone to crack the LOTH customer database. Fast.*

Takara picked up her phone.

* * *

Chapter 14
New Mexico, USA
Day 3

Tyler scooted closer to the sunlit entrance to the cave. He leaned back against the cool wall and rubbed his temples with his thumbs. He put the back of his hand on his forehead, like his mother did when he got sick.

His skin was hot and dry.

What will Mom say when I get home? No, wait, she's on the spaceship, going to heaven. No, she's at the bottom of the cliff.

I'm lost.

And Takeus of Thebes thinks I'm a liar.

Tyler picked up a rock and threw it against the wall of the cave. It ricocheted into the deeper area he had not explored. Tyler threw another rock.

This time he heard a noise. A noise like a tap on a window. Just once.

The boy took his spear in both hands and edged forward. He shuffled into the darkness. Five steps. Ten.

His left shoe met air and he stumbled. As he fell, Tyler knew he'd stepped off a cliff.

But his right foot, then his knee, and then his elbows hit rock and he lay still and listened to his own heart.

It's just a step. A big step.

He got up and used the spear like a blind person he'd once seen cross a street. Back and forth, tap, tap, back and forth.

Tap. Tink.

Glass.

Unable to see, Tyler squatted and felt around with his left hand while his right held the spear. His hand touched something cold and smooth. He picked it up and eased back until he found the step. Tyler scrambled up over the step and hurried back to the sunlit cave mouth.

"It's a bottle."

He sat to examine his find. The cap was gone and not even a smell remained. The glass was dark brown, too dark to see through. Tyler dumped sand and a dead bug out of the bottle. The neck was narrow, but the base was wide. His small fingers found a seam along each side of the bottle, and a pattern around the edge of the bottom. A few numbers were raised in the glass, but they meant nothing to him. A faded bit of paper clung to the side, but the only word on the yellowed label he could make out was "Spirits."

Tyler lifted his arm to throw it back into the cave like Takeus had thrown the bottle of Greek Fire. The Greek Fire had burned the zombie even after he fell in the water.

Water.

Tyler's tongue swelled in his mouth at the thought. If he found a stream, he could fill the bottle and bring it back to the cave.

The boy stood and left the cave. The bottle was too fat to put in the pocket of his sport coat, so he carried it in one hand and his spear in the other.

He'd tried the deer tracks on the hill above, and chased the rabbit to the right, so Tyler decided to turn left.

He staggered along a second deer trail, pushing plant limbs aside and ducking tree branches. The trail led down and away from the cave, and walking downhill was easy.

The boy thought about marking his way with stones or by scraping the bark off trees, but he didn't have the strength. He planned to follow his own tracks back to the cave.

Tyler stayed on the trail until he reached the top of a short ridge. He poked his head around a tree trunk and looked down. Below he saw an open stretch of sand curving around the base of the ridge and running on down the hill. Smooth stones littered the sand, and the sand itself looked brown. Wet.

A squirrel hopped out into the wash, unaware of the boy above. It dug in the soft sand, then dropped an acorn in the hole.

When Tyler shifted to get a better view, the creature caught the movement and leapt into the green bushes of the bank.

I wonder what he tried to bury? It'd be cool if he was burying a magic ring.

He followed the deer trail until it descended and ran parallel to the dry streambed, then he cut over. The sand was mushy under his sneakers.

Tyler found the squirrel hole. There was no magic ring in the hole, just an acorn.

But the acorn was floating.

He squatted and stuck his finger in the water. Tyler set aside the spear and bottle, and dug. He tossed rocks aside and worked until he had a hole as long as the bottle, and twice as deep.

Water seeped into the hole. Slow but steady.

Tyler sat in the shade with his spear across his knees. The sun crept behind the mountains and shadows grew long in the ravine while the hole filled.

He shook the last grains of sand from the bottle, crept forward and sank it sideways in the hole.

Before it was even half full, he yanked the bottle up.

The water was warm and gritty.

And fantastic.

Tyler chugged. Streams ran down his cheeks and onto this neck. He closed his eyes and pressed the cool bottle to his forehead. He put the bottle back in the hole to refill, then lay back with his head propped on a warm stone.

Later, when he opened his eyes to check if the hole was full, Tyler froze.

It was dark. Pitch black night.

* * *

Chapter 15
Tokyo, Japan
Day 3

Takara paced while the phone rang five times. She knew Kyle never answered.

When the phone went to voicemail she said, "Hey, it's me. I need some computer work. Call me." Takara hung up.

While she waited for Kyle to call back, Tak went online and found a map of the world's time zones. She opened a second tab with a map of the United States and found New Mexico. A third search told her what time the sun set in the Silver City area.

Time to visit the lighthouse.

She logged onto Lair of the Hydra, and took a portal directly to the lighthouse, but it lay empty. Even the zombies were gone. Tak got up and paced the floor of her room, shadow boxing and sipping Mountain Dew.

Damn it, Tyler. You should be here. And if I leave to go look for you, sure enough you'll show up and I won't be here.

She glanced down and the screen and resumed pacing.

Thirty minutes later her cell phone rang. She looked at the screen. It wasn't a number she recognized, but then, it wouldn't be.

"Kyle?" she asked.

"Yeah. What's up?"

"You want to earn some cash?"

"Sure. My usual rate applies."

"Where should we meet?"

"Can you be in Shinjuku in an hour?" Kyle asked.

"Yeah."

"Kinokuniya Book Store, sixth floor."

"Got it. See you." Takara logged out of *Lair*, and ran a brush through her hair. Her eyes stung too much to fool with her contact lenses, so she grabbed her glasses, scribbled a note to her aunt, and left the apartment.

Shinjuku was south, but she had to backtrack east on the Mita metro line to reach the connection at Sugamo. There she switched to the Yamanote line and rode it south a half dozen stops to the big interchange at Shinjuku Station.

It was not far from the northern exit of the station to the bookstore, but the crowded sidewalks slowed her.

Fifty eight minutes after hanging up, she reached the sixth floor of the book store and found Kyle in the English language section.

Kyle spotted her the moment she approached. His face was pale and his clothes looked like he'd slept in them.

"What did you tell your parents?" Takara asked.

"Told them I was going out."

"You never go out. They'll be suspicious."

Kyle smiled. "I go out. You don't know, but sometimes I go out. I told them there's a new *Cowboy Bebop* DVD I had to get."

Takara nodded. "Good thinking. Look, about the job, I need--"

"Do you want coffee?"

"What?"

Kyle ran one hand over his unshaven chin. "Starbucks. They have coffee."

"I know Starbucks has coffee." Takara stared at the anime-obsessed young man. "Are you feeling okay? I know you don't like crowds."

"I don't! I just...you know, I thought maybe we'd have coffee." Kyle looked away.

Takara pushed one finger under her glasses and rubbed her eyes. "Maybe next time. This is a priority job."

A short, buck-toothed kid holding an *Appleseed* manga stared up at Tak, smiled and scooted closer.

Takara glared.

The kid scurried away, the comic pressed to his chest.

Kyle shook his head. "Same Tak. Okay, what's the job."

Takara made sure no one was near. "I need you to crack the customer database for *Lair of the Hydra*."

Kyle blinked. "Tak, this isn't like running down the IP address of a client that cheated you. You're talking about--"

"*Lair* is shutting down in a matter of days. There isn't much time. Here." She held out a paper folded into a neat square. "That's all I know about the person. I need their credit card information and everything that comes with it. Home address is top of my wish list, but I'll take mailing address, phone numbers, whatever you can get. I'll pay double the usual."

Kyle looked at the paper and stuck his hands in his pockets. "I don't know."

"You can't do it?" she asked.

"Don't work the pride angle," Kyle whispered. "I don't have any left."

"You want more money?"

"Always nice, but I have to weigh it against the risks. I steal a credit card number and it becomes a crime. I wouldn't do well in prison."

Takara bit her lip. She pictured him in a small, dark room by himself for twenty-three hours a day, eating plain food at regular intervals and reading stacks of manga.

I don't think prison would be much different than your regular life.

"This isn't about stealing credit card numbers. It's about a kid. He's in trouble and I'm trying to track him down. I already called the--I called in some favors to find him, but no luck." Takara breathed in deep. Mention of the police would send Kyle running.

"Did you tell anyone you're hiring me?"

"Of course not."

Kyle took the paper and put it in his pocket. "I guess you already tried the social engineering angle. That's your thing, right? Manipulating people?"

Takara pressed her lips together.

"I'll start with their web site," Kyle said. "Run some port scans against their servers, see if there's anything easy. I doubt there will be. I'll try to get internal addresses and find usernames and log ins. Maybe I'll get lucky."

Tak nodded. "I need it fast."

"Okay."

A couple drifted by, not holding hands but walking close together and laughing. Kyle watched them for a moment and smirked. "I'll call you when I have something."

He slinked away.

Takara went toward a different exit.

Down six floors she stepped outside into a sea of dark heads bobbing on the sidewalk like survivors of a doomed ship. Thanks to her height, Takara could see above most of them. She let the crowd carry her toward the metro station.

* * *

New Mexico, USA

Tyler climbed out of the dry streambed onto the ridge above. If there was a moon, clouds had tackled it and pushed it into a gym locker. There were a few stars, but they seemed faint, covered in mist or fog.

Even if I'm lost, the water was worth it.

He wedged the neck of the Spirits bottle in his belt so he could grip his spear with both trembling hands.

He couldn't see his own tracks from earlier in the day, but the deer trail formed a rough tunnel through the undergrowth. Tyler wondered how the deer walked without getting their antlers stuck in the branches.

The boy moved as slow as he could force himself to. He held his spear vertical to clear away spider webs.

As he crept through the darkness one shaky step at a time, he scanned the trees to either side of the trail. Something moved on his left, a fast, skittering sound, like sneakers on concrete.

Tyler crouched.

His eyes stretched so huge he thought they might pop out of his head. He gripped the spear until his fingers ached.

He tried to count to twenty, lost track at fourteen and started over. Hunched over, he skulked away from the noise.

As he worked his way parallel to the ridgeline Tyler wondered what made the noise and considered his possible enemies.

Silas, bears, Gila monsters, snakes, except garden snakes, spaceship aliens, coyotes, Silas and pirates.

He considered other creatures he might encounter on the trail that would be friendly or at least not try to eat his head. *Squirrels, dogs, raccoons, birds, chipmunks, ferrets, rabbits, monkeys, lizards, ants, crap. I forgot insects. Spiders bite, scorpions bite.*

As his eyes adjusted to the night, he moved faster. The incline of the slope increased and the boy stopped to catch his breath. The cold air pierced his shirt--he'd left his sport coat in the cave. Tyler looked down at the thin white cloth; it almost glowed in the dark.

Stupid. You are so not ninja.

Something howled. A long, plaintive wail. A cry into the void. Was it pain and loneliness, or hunger and rage?

Tyler pressed himself to the rough bark of a tree and searched for lower limbs he could climb.

It's just a dog. You like dogs. Dogs lick and sometimes they jump on you, but it's just a dog.

He tried to imagine his neighbor's dog Rufus. Tyler squeezed his eyes shut but he couldn't picture the dog. All he could see was a gaping mouth and long, white teeth.

The creature howled again.

Tyler ran along the trail.

In the dark he almost passed the cave, but spotted the patch of black against the hillside and turned.

He scrambled inside, panting.

The howl sounded again from the hilltop above him.

A second howl answered the call from below.

* * *

Chapter 16
New Mexico, USA
Day 4

As soon as it was light, Tyler crawled out of the cave and shook the night's chill from his bones. The coyotes had kept him awake for hours, but they never came near the cave. His stomach felt like it was eating his other organs. But thanks to the water, the pain in his head was tolerable.

While he waited for the sun to climb over the mountains, he searched for a stone to cap the Spirits bottle. He threw away seven, kept three that were good for throwing, and settled on a thumb-sized, brown rock that fit the neck of the bottle without sliding down into it.

He started up the hill above the cave and the trees around him swirled. He leaned on his spear until the dizzy spell passed.

Tyler shielded his eyes and looked in all directions, but he couldn't see the cars or the cliff. The country was so choppy that the vehicles might have been over the next hill.

I have to find my way back to the cliff. The cliff leads to the cars. The cars lead to the road. But...

The boy sucked in a deep breath of air.

They're just dead people. Ninjas aren't afraid of dead people. Ninjas make people dead.

But what if Silas is there? I can't outrun him now. I could wait until it's dark so he can't see me. No, I can't wait. I'm hungry. I'm thirsty again.

First he went back to the dry streambed, following the same route he'd established the day before. Animals moved into cover as the sun rose and warmed the ground. Tyler heard them in the trees and gripped his spear.

During the night, water had seeped into the hole he'd dug. He filled the bottle and drank it down, and then tried to refill it but there wasn't enough. He held the brown bottle up to the sun, saw it was less than half full, and carefully capped it with the brown stone.

He hiked back to the cave, retrieved the notebook computer, and stood ready.

Which way?

He closed his eyes and threw a rock straight up. He heard it thump in the dirt behind him.

Uphill? Crap.

Tyler tucked the notebook in his belt, held the bottle in one hand, his spear in the other, and marched.

After the crest, the downhill should have been easy, yet his legs hurt. He tried to recall if he'd run up the hill during his escape from the cliff, but he couldn't remember.

I don't want to think about it. I just want to find the cars and road without seeing any dead people.

Once he found the road, he could follow the car tracks just like he'd followed the deer's track. The road was dirt, so it would be easy. When he reached the highway, he'd walk until a police car or a fire truck gave him a ride.

It's a good plan.

The day grew hot. The sun seemed to rotate around him, always on his neck and in his eyes. Tyler tried to hike in the shady ravines, but as he hiked down out of the hills the land became flat. The trees shrank to stubby, gnarled things. The oaks disappeared, replaced by ocotillo shrubs. Tyler stopped and stood swaying. A cactus rose at his feet.

The boy stood in something like desert.

He shucked his sport coat, wrapped it around the notebook and bottle, tied the sleeves together and slung it over his shoulder.

Tyler turned a slow circle. Desert, sun, hills, his tracks leading away, desert again, and the way forward. Forward looked the same as it did the last time he looked up.

Something about seeing his tracks in the dirt made him shiver.

The wind would blow, rains would come and his footprints would melt away. Like the butterfly-shaped deer tracks. The deer had been there, but it was gone now. A ghost.

Tyler rubbed his nose. He drank the rest of his water, even the cloudy grit at the bottom of the bottle.

Without a watch he didn't know how long he'd been walking, but the sun was straight above him, a huge yellow ball cooking his brain.

I need a break for a while. Someplace shady.

Tyler turned toward the hills on his left. There would be a canyon, a ravine, something. Maybe even a stream.

He aimed for a notch between two hills, leaning on his spear, the paste taste thick in his mouth again.

A few hundred yards short of the notch, Tyler heard thunder. Faint at first, but then he was sure. Thunder from the hills. Then a strange tremble beneath the blue soles of his Spiderman sneakers.

Dust billowed at the entrance to the canyon. The thunder became steady. Tyler stopped and looked around. He didn't see a tree to climb or a rock big enough to crawl under. He squatted in the dirt.

A swarm of creatures burst out of the canyon. Snorting, thundering, raising dust to the sky. Tyler threw himself into the dead grass, his hands pressed over his ears.

The dust parted and a giant brown horse galloped toward him. Twenty or thirty horses followed. Taller than cars, their massive alien heads coated in dust. Wild eyed and shaggy.

Tyler trembled.

These were not the horses in *Lair of the Hydra*. Those horses carried packs and pulled wagons and stood still when you told them to.

These horses were chaos. Long tailed and long maned. Smelly. Huge hooves and teeth.

And awesome.

Tyler stood.

The horses veered. The big brown led them by, the smaller horses running behind him.

One ran by Tyler, so close he felt its unshod hooves strike the earth. Smelled its sweat. Tasted its dust in his nose and mouth.

The horse shimmered gold in the sun, with a white mane and a streaming white tail.

It was the first beautiful thing Tyler saw since his last look at his mother's face.

Tyler ran after the horses.

The notebook slapped against his back and he changed his grip to run with the crude pack under his arm.

Dust filled his eyes until tears started. He choked on the sand, gagged on his dry tongue. He ran, then walked, jogged, and ran some more.

He fell behind.

The dust thinned. The horses went over a hill. Something on his right side under his ribs made a fist and the boy bent over. Tyler rubbed the spot and took deep breaths of the hot August air. He trotted up the hill, the spear dragging in the sand behind him, a long line stretching back into the past.

Tyler stumbled down the hill. The horses stood in a cluster at the base of a rock wall, their heads down.

The boy smelled water. Smelled it even though he thought water didn't have a smell.

Tyler ran down the hill.

The horses turned. The big brown with the black ears tossed his head and stamped his hooves. Tyler pulled up, tripped and fell. When his body went horizontal he got so dizzy he lay stretched in the dirt.

The thunder began again. He felt it through his palms and elbows and knees.

When he raised his head the horses were gone. The golden horse was gone. The magic golden horse that might have carried him to Silver City and pizza and Capri Suns and Butterfinger candy bars.

Tyler staggered forward. Under the rock wall he found a narrow gully with mud as thick as peanut butter crushed by a thousand hoof prints.

All the water was gone. The horses were gone.

Tyler fell to his knees and cried.

* * *

Chapter 17
Tokyo, Japan
Day 4

Game Mania was busy throughout the morning. Mr. Saito came in the shop and he and Takara spent hours going over inventory and ordering items for next month.

When Saito-san finally left, Takara told Yoshi to watch the register and retreated to the tiny office. She checked her phone for texts or voice mail, but there were no messages. She picked up the landline phone.

"Crime Prevention, Kobayashi speaking. How may I help you?"

"Kobayashi-san, this is Takara Murakami. We spoke yesterday about the boy. I hate to bother you, but have you had any word?"

"Ah, of course, of course. I remember."

Tak heard him shuffling papers on his desk. She hoped it was neater than hers was.

"Here we are," Kobayashi said. "I called Prefecture. Prefecture called Regional Command. Regional contacted the embassy."

"The American embassy here in Tokyo or the Japanese embassy in the United States?" Takara asked.

"Honestly? I don't know. I got this second hand from a friend at Prefecture. Someone at Regional is supposed to get back to her in the next three to five days."

"Five days? Tyler is lost in the wilderness. In five days he could be dead." Takara took a breath. "I'm grateful for your effort, Kobayashi-san, it's just I hoped..."

"I understand. People want matters resolved quickly. But the officers at Prefecture expressed the same concerns I have. Is this person real? Is it a prank or a scam? Speaking of which, have you had further contact?"

"No, I was supposed to meet him in the game last night, but he wasn't there. I'll look for him again tonight. If this is a prank, why is he still at it? And if it's a scam, why hasn't he asked for money or something?"

"I don't know," Kobayashi admitted. "The whole situation is odd. If you talk to him, see if you can get him to reveal more information about himself and his location. In the meantime, I'll call my friend at Prefecture again."

"Okay, thank you Kobayashi-san. I appreciate your help."

"It's my job. I'll call as soon as I hear something."

Takara hung up the phone and stared at the screensaver on the desktop monitor. The screensaver was a cat chasing, but never quite catching, a mouse. A twenty-second animated loop. Tak watched the loop three times.

Can I wait five days to hear from the police?

Can Tyler?

* * *

New Mexico, USA

When his cell phone rang, Border Patrol Agent Brian DeWitt was trying to open a microwavable tray of rice and vegetables without scalding his hands.

"DeWitt here, hang on."

He flicked the thumb stud on his pocketknife, slashed the cellophane covering the food and stepped back. The tray emitted a cloud of steam normally associated with an active volcano.

"Freaking microwave. We have got to get a new one."

He put the phone to his ear. "Sorry."

"DeWitt? It's Warren. Hey, are you still at Deming Station?"

DeWitt searched the break room for a plastic fork, and settled for a spoon. "Yeah, why?"

"I thought you were going over to Lordsburg."

"I am. As soon as I eat lunch. Why, what's up?"

"Oh, probably nothing. Somebody from Las Cruces called and said a plane spotted some vehicles over your way."

DeWitt scooted his folding chair up to the table, held the phone in one hand and the tiny plastic spoon in the other. His stomach growled so loudly he figured Warren could hear it over the phone.

"What are the vehicles doing? Four wheeling? Offloading nuclear weapons? What?" DeWitt tried a bite. The broccoli was limp, but the sweet and sour sauce made it edible.

"I don't know," Warren said. "Report said eight vehicles on a dirt trail off Highway 15. The trail is marked as 579, but they're beyond that. Somewhere around Wild Horse Mesa."

DeWitt took a mechanical pencil from his shirt pocket and tried to scribble on a napkin, but the pencil tore the paper. "Crap. Okay, off 15, on 579. Eight vehicles. Look, Warren, we're shorthanded today and there's a lot going on. Could you pitch this over to Lordsburg Station instead? They're about the same distance away that we are."

Warren laughed. "I was going to call them, but I knew you were headed over there. So if I call them later today, I'll just get you anyway."

"Right. What's the rush anyway? It's probably some kids with a couple cases of beer. Did you get this from aerial?"

"Yeah."

"One of the Cessnas?"

"No, I think it was a Predator. Doesn't matter. I know there isn't a pilot in the UAV, but there's one sitting somewhere looking through a camera and waggling his joystick."

"I think you've been at your desk too long waggling your joystick. Why don't you drive over there? Get some fresh air." DeWitt tried to open a bottle of water one handed, and failed.

"I'm in Alamogordo. I'm not driving all the way--"

"Kidding. Look, maybe I'll call the Ranger station in Silver City. They run up Highway 15 all the time. One of those guys can detour and take a look."

"Okay, thanks. Hey, how's the diet going?"

"It sucks."

* * *

Chapter 18
New Mexico, USA
Day 4

Silas opened his eyes and stared straight up.

The sky was a washed out gray sheet hanging high above his head. Silas pushed the Hello Kitty sleeping bag down and sat up. The bag was damp, as was his hair. The morning air tickled his back and he shivered.

He rubbed his eyes, stepped into his boots and looked at his campsite.

Silas spun a complete circle, scanning the hills to make sure no one was watching, and then crouched at a stump to relieve himself.

He sat on his damp sleeping bag and ate a pair of Blueberry Pop Tarts and drank a bottle of water. His back and hips were sore from sleeping on the ground.

Silas rolled his shoulders loose, gathered his things, and resumed his search. He left the thicket and hiked back to the cliff edge. He was so intent on the ground he strayed close to the edge and sent a handful of pebbles raining down.

He shook himself.

Silas paused next to two small shoe prints. The soles of the shoes left a pattern like a spider web, with a large 'S' where the big toe would be. The wind had eroded the tracks, leaving them more like soft puddles in the sand, but the pattern was readable.

Silas tried to remember if Tyler had worn dress shoes or sneakers that night. He'd never seen the boy in anything other than sneakers, and it was possible his parents had bought dress shoes on their last trip to Silver City. However, these were the only small tracks leading away from the cliff. The rest of the children had obediently walked with their parents over the edge.

Silas replayed the events of that night in his mind and smiled.

It was so perfect, so complete. Except for Tyler.

While he followed the track he crossed a column of ants that were busy investigating a dead grasshopper. Silas stopped to watch. The ants formed a line from the grasshopper to a tunnel entrance. At a certain, hard to identify moment, the ants knew there were enough of them to lift the grasshopper. The dead insect rose, like a magician levitating his curvy assistant.

The grasshopper floated along a chitinous highway of six-legged workers, like a flower-covered float in a parade. Silas stared.

Which is it? A magic trick or a parade?

Silas counted ants. *How many workers does it take to carry a grasshopper eighteen inches over smooth ground?*

He stared without blinking. After five minutes he rubbed the bridge of his nose and looked away.

Stop moving.

He looked down. The ants were almost to the mound entrance. It yawned beneath him, a vast black hole spiraling down into the earth. Silas hurried to count the ants before they disappeared.

Clusters of three were too slow. He counted by sixes, by eights, by clusters of five, by tens. Tens were too hard to maintain in cohesive groups.

Slow down. Stop moving. Stop moving.

The grasshopper's head reached the pit, the servitors beneath it cheering, clashing their mandibles together. Silas heard the roar. He put both hands to his temples and squeezed.

He stomped.

His boot smashed and scattered. Workers and warriors flew off the ground. More ants boiled up but he crushed the mound and sand filled the tunnel. He smeared the grasshopper and the workers clinging to it across a rock.

Silas stomped so hard pain shot up his shin to his knee. He staggered. His eyes closed and he lost count.

When he opened his eyes he saw the sky above. A blade of dead grass tickled his neck. Silas sat up and wiped tears from his cheek.

He found his straw hat and pushed it down on his head, and stood. And resumed tracking the boy.

* * *

Tokyo, Japan

In Game Mania, Takara checked the store for customers, saw that it was slow, and pushed the door to the office half shut. The door was a folding plastic contraption like something from a phone booth. Half shut it blocked eyes, but still let light and air in. Ever since the earthquake, Takara avoided dark, enclosed spaces.

She hooked up her USB drive, opened Firefox and clicked on *Lair of the Hydra's* homepage. Someone had graffitied the site, expressing their displeasure at the game's end. Tak laughed. Just as she was about to log in and teleport to the lighthouse, she decided to run a search for Tyler's account.

She went to the list of servers, picked the Cerberus server they'd met in before, and used the Search function to see if any Burroughs were logged in.

The search returned zero results.

Damn. Unless he's logged onto a different server somehow, he's not here. I thought since he missed our meeting last night he might try again today.

Or maybe I have the time zones wrong. In the browser, she brought up a map of the world's time zones and pushed her finger across the screen. *Let's see, there's an eight hour time difference, but we're a day ahead of them, so...* Takara pulled her hair. *This is ridiculous.*

Okay, think. If it turns dark later in the evening because it's summer, then maybe he's running late. But it's morning of the next day here, and I just got to work, so for him, it's what? Midnight?

Takara clenched her fists. A fat blue monster with buckteeth sat on the desk. Tak punched it in the mouth. The stuffed creature fell over.

Maybe he already logged on and I wasn't there? Hell. Maybe his battery went dead. She doodled on a sticky note. "His notebook might have anywhere from two to five hours on battery. He's probably used 90, maybe 120 minutes. That's assuming it was fully charged. So at best, with a five-hour charge he has--"

"You're talking to yourself."

"What?" She looked up. Yoshi's bushy head squeezed through the gap in the doorway. He looked like a trophy hunter had shot him and mounted his skull on the wall.

"You talk to yourself a lot," he said.

"It's the only way I can have an intelligent conversation at work."

Yoshi blinked. "Why do you wear your glasses all the time? Don't you have contact lenses?"

Takara minimized the windows on the screen. "Do you have a work-related question?"

Yoshi shrugged. "Not really. It's slow out front."

"Yoshi, do you know what a Gila monster is?"

"No."

* * *

The store stayed quiet. A man came in at late morning and kept asking if they had a room in back for special videos until Tak chased him off. Yoshi talked a pair of middle-aged ladies into buying a Nintendo Wii and the fitness board that went with it.

Tak checked the *Lair* servers again for Tyler, but he was not online. She went outside to pace but it was too hot, so she paced the aisles inside, drinking can after can of Boss coffee.

Just before noon her cell phone rattled. Tak thought it might be her aunt calling to meet for lunch. Instead it was a number she didn't recognize.

"Hello?"

"It's me," Kyle whispered.

"Oh, hey--"

"Don't say my name! They could be listening."

Takara rolled her eyes and stepped into the tiny office. "What's up?"

"It's about the job you gave me."

"Okay, what did you find out?"

"Not on the phone. Don't you read the links I send you? They track everything now. Email, online gambling, pornography habits, medical records. Yesterday I read a story about--"

"Where do you want to meet?"

"Meet me at the Starbucks on...well, you know which one. In fifteen minutes."

Takara hung up and stared at her phone. Tokyo had many Starbucks coffee shops. But for Kyle, there was only one. The one where he met a girl and talked to her for 108 minutes before she left, having agreed to meet him there the next day. When she got home, the girl received notification she was not accepted into the college she'd dreamed of. She hung herself.

Two years later and Kyle still wouldn't talk about it.

Kyle asked me to get coffee when I met him last night at the bookstore. Did he mean that Starbucks?

She tucked her phone away, picked up an umbrella and left the office. Out front, Yoshi leaned on the counter, reading a baseball magazine. Madoka had called in sick, and Atsushi was on the floor between two aisles, fast asleep.

"I'm going to run an errand and pick up some lunch. Do you want anything?" she asked.

Yoshi dug in his pocket. "Can you get a couple of bento lunch boxes for Atsushi and me?"

Takara waved her hand. "I'll get it. Good job on the Wii sale this morning." She pushed through the door.

Yoshi smiled. "Thanks, Takara-san. I'll watch the shop. Thanks!"

The sidewalk was crowded, but Takara could see over the heads of most of the people. She stretched out her long legs and hit the door to the Starbucks in seven minutes.

The scent of coffee and hot chocolate and Tollhouse cookies filled her nose, but it was hot outside and she'd already drank about 10 liters of canned coffee. Kyle sat at a table the size of a pizza, his hands in his pockets.

After the barista sold her a cold bottle of water, Takara zigzagged between tables and sat with the thin young man.

"So what did you come up with?" Tak asked.

Kyle bit his lip. He had dark rings under his eyes, which lay stark against his pale face. "Nothing."

"Nothing? I came down here for nothing? Great!"

Three girls sat at the next table. Their heads turned in unison.

Tak glared at them. They looked away and whispered among themselves.

Kyle slid so low in his chair his chin nearly touched the tabletop. "I had difficulties."

Tak breathed in deep through her nose. "What happened?"

"I got in, but *Lair* is a mess. No one is maintaining it and it's falling apart."

"That's evident from the game. But surely their credit card database is still stable," she said.

"Yeah, it is. But their security is better than I thought." Kyle looked around the shop, sat up and leaned over. "My software wasn't up to it. I tried something new, a crazy wildcat program I bought from a Russian guy, and it crashed my computer. Fried the hard drive."

"Damn. Sorry about that. I didn't think it'd be that tough." Tak sipped water.

Kyle looked away. "I'm not really that great a hacker, Tak. I mean, I talk about it a lot, but I don't write my own stuff. I've downloaded some scripts, cracked a few things, but..." He stirred his coffee for long minute.

"So did you find anything before your computer crashed?"

"Nothing about their credit card. I did find where an F. Burroughs registered for a chance to win a free T-shirt. Lion of Nemea gave out *LOTH* shirts to the first 100 people to enter."

Tak sat forward. "That could be Tyler's father. Where did they send the T-shirt?"

"No idea. The spreadsheet was corrupted. All I pulled was a list of zip codes. This Burroughs was in 88022. I looked it up. It's New Mexico," Kyle said.

"That's great! Why didn't you tell me that when I sat down?"

"Tak, it doesn't prove anything. All this means is that there is a guy in New Mexico who plays *Lair*. Big deal. Without the credit card data we don't have a phone number, or an address or anything." Kyle sighed. "I know I failed. You don't have to pay me."

"No, you tried so I'll pay. It may be a few weeks before I can get you the money, though." She watched the three girls next to them look at pictures on their cell phones and giggle. "I may need my paycheck for an airline ticket."

"To?"

"United States."

Kyle stared. "You're going to find this person, aren't you? I know you, Tak, you never let things go."

Takara capped her water. "I haven't decided. It depends on some other factors." She didn't mention Kobayashi in Crime Prevention because that would send Kyle into his bedroom for a month.

"Listen to me," Kyle hissed. "This guy is probably a serial killer. As soon as you're alone with him he'll drug you, and you'll wake up naked in his basement. Then he'll come down the stairs and--"

Tak grabbed Kyle's forearm and squeezed. "I said I haven't decided. And it's not your business what I do next." She let go and stood. "I've got to pick up some bento boxes for the guys at the shop."

She left him sitting at the table, staring at the empty chair.

* * *

Chapter 19
New Mexico, USA
Day 4

Silas hiked north, deviating a little to the west. The tracks were soft and sometimes difficult to spot, but he was able to follow them if he focused.

The short man was so intent on the ground three steps in front that it was after noon before he noticed the hills rising around him. Silas thought about the night at the cliff and remembered that when he and the other adults reached the hills he'd called off the search because the people were afraid the spaceship would leave them behind.

He'd almost told them not to worry, there was enough gravity for everyone.

Several times along the trail he crossed sets of animal tracks. Each time he stopped and walked a few paces along the new track, then clenched his fists and went back to Tyler's prints.

During a water break, Silas sat with his back to a rock and examined an interesting track. The prints were small, with two close together, and then two prints set apart. Silas stared at the track of the creature and figured it was a rock squirrel. One set of prints had four toes, three palm pads and two heel pads. The other had five toes, four palm pads and two heel pads. He wasn't sure which were the front feet and which the back.

Silas screwed the cap back on his water bottle.

He left the squirrels behind and followed Tyler's prints into the shallow, rolling hills. Even at four or five thousand feet, the day grew hot.

Sweat ran down his shirt between his pack and his spine. The nylon straps cut into his shoulders. His feet hurt from stepping on sharp stones.

Silas lost the trail.

He stood for a moment, looked around and realized there were trees and thick brush springing up ahead.

When he couldn't find a new track in the rocky soil, Silas went back to the last track he'd found. He walked a circle around it, found nothing, and started a second, larger circle.

This time he found a scuff mark on a rock. Half of a heel print in the dirt. A line that looked like the toe of a small shoe.

Silas knelt for a moment to look at the heel print. When he looked up, he saw right into a black hole in the side of the hill. From any other angle, he might never have seen the cave.

The compact man slipped his pack off and dug in it until his hand found the pistol.

He rose, then stopped and went back into his pack for his flashlight. He left the pack by the heel print and moved forward as quietly as he could.

Silas had made no effort at stealth during the day, but now he was aware of every sound. His boots crunching sand, his dry throat swallowing, his heart thumping in his chest.

He tipped a marble-sized stone as he went up the hill and froze when it bounced down behind him. At first he went straight up the hill, but then he angled to one side so the boy would not see him coming.

At the cave's low entrance he had to duck and crawl on all fours. He sniffed the air, wondering if he'd find a decomposing ten-year-old with a mouth full of flies.

Inside the cave he rose to his knees, brought up the pistol, and activated the flashlight. He flicked the beam back and forth.

Rock walls, loose sand, cool air. The ceiling sloped up and he stood and shuffled forward. He spotted the drop off just before the toe of his left boot went over it. Silas recovered his balance and stepped down.

The wispy yellow beam of the flashlight played over a jumble of stones and broken glass. He prodded the glass but everything was covered in dust and half buried in the sand. He wasn't certain, but the site felt old.

Ten more steps and the cave narrowed and ended. Silas went back to the entrance, worked the flashlight back and forth, and smiled.

There was a shoe print with a spider web pattern and an 'S' at the big toe.

Silas nodded and stepped out into the hot air. The sun eased down into the west.

* * *

The boy sat in the shade of the rock wall and watched the sun. Gray clouds piled into a fat wall and rolled toward him. The sun, his morning friend and afternoon enemy, fled.

Tyler wondered if God stacked up the clouds like he stacked up his Legos. He looked at the land beneath the clouds and thought he might die there, just as surely as if he'd jumped off the cliff with his parents.

Tears blurred his sight. He wanted to open the notebook and talk to someone, anyone. But Takeus told him to wait until sundown. If he went into the *Lair* before that, there would be no one but monsters.

"Monsters in there, monsters out here," he whispered, his own voice strange to his ears. He touched the notebook and then ran his dirty hand across his face.

The God that made that golden horse wouldn't talk to someone like Silas.

And God doesn't tell people to jump off cliffs. There is no spaceship. Mom and Dad aren't on their way to heaven. They're dead at the bottom of the cliff, with dirt in their mouths.

Tyler kicked a stone. It bounced until it hit the mud.

The storm closed. The clouds spit blue-white spears of electricity at the ground. The boy almost went to meet the storm. To tempt the lightning to hit him.

He thought about a story he'd read where a man, a Greek warrior or maybe an Indian brave, put his spear against the ground and threw himself on the sharp end.

Tyler shook his head.

God hadn't come out of the clouds to carry him to Silver City, but maybe God sent the Golden Horse to lead him somewhere. Somewhere important.

The boy stood, took up his spear, and walked.

With clouds covering the sun, the air was cooler. He smelled the rain and felt the wind catch him and carry him up the hill.

At the crest he paused to study the land. Trees dotted the way ahead, and whole thickets and woods covered the hills. He noticed a spot that was greener than the rest of the dull brown landscape.

As he examined the spot he noted that the green continued, snaking up the hill the way a river or stream might. Tyler smiled, and went down the hill.

It was a long walk. At times he jogged to stay ahead of the storm. The thought of rain on his face was delicious, but he knew water would kill the computer.

His legs ached as he pushed over the last hill separating him from the green line. The clouds were close. Lightning stabbed the crest of the nearest hill.

Tyler trotted on dead legs, his feet numb as they slapped the rocky ground. A blister swelled on his right hand from carrying the spear. His tongue was thick in his mouth. His vision narrowed to the ground two steps ahead of him.

He ran into a thicket of pinon pines, heedless of Gila monsters. Surely the storm had scared them into their holes. As the first fat drops of rain hit his back, Tyler pulled up at a short drop, maybe twice his height.

Grabbing handfuls of dead grass and tree roots, he slithered down into the ravine. At the bottom a stream ran--a gray brown ribbon of actual running water.

Tyler wedged the notebook under the crumbling overhang of the cliff, then ran and plunged his face in the water.

He drank until his stomach swelled and the lightning chased him under the outcropping. Tyler sat smiling and trembling a little as the storm raged above him.

Lightning struck a tree across the stream and he watched a squirrel leap away. The squirrel jumped just as the bolt struck, like he knew it was coming. He hung in midair for a moment, limbs spread, then the light burned Tyler's eyes and he blinked and the squirrel was gone.

A part of him, the stomach part, almost wished the lightning had caught the squirrel and cooked it. Tyler had never eaten a squirrel, but if a fully roasted squirrel fell out of the sky he wouldn't ignore it.

The thought of smoking squirrels falling out of the air made him grin, but only for a moment.

After the clouds stampeded away toward the mountains, Tyler went to the stream and drank again. His headache eased.

He considered crossing the stream, but with the rain it ran high and fast now, and he decided to wait. Instead, he followed the creek up into the hills, walking along its bank, stepping rock to rock and scrambling over tree trunks.

When he stopped to drink again he saw a shadow in the water.

Tyler squatted on a rock and watched the fish. It had speckles on its sides and a short mouth that looked like it was frowning. But it was just the right size for a plate.

There will be other fish upstream.

He kept hiking and his clothes dried and the storm clouds became distant gray lumps. The air stayed cool, though, and when he breathed deep into his chest his lungs seemed to swell.

Tyler had learned that night came fast in the outdoors. He found a spot where the walls around the stream were worn down and climbed out and into the woods. He didn't want to stray far from the water.

He pushed through a patch of thick, low-hanging limbs and caught a spider's web in the face. The white, clingy stuff stuck to his eyelashes. Tyler dropped his spear and batted the web away. He rubbed his face clean but shivers ran down his spine. He untucked his shirt and shook himself.

Holding the spear in front of him, he pushed forward until he ran into a steep wall of rock that ran almost straight up.

He backed up to see how high the wall was and saw a dark spot amid a cluster of brown plants. A hole in the wall.

Tyler followed the rock wall and soon found an easy slope, a sort of rough ramp of loose dirt and stones. He scampered up as night fell.

He was anxious to put rock walls between himself and Silas, but Tyler made himself slow down. He held his spear in front of him and pushed it into the cave.

The wooden tip met stone.

Tyler squinted. He ducked and put out one hand and found cool rock.

Not a cave. It's a crack in the mountain. Like the mountain's butt.

He jabbed around with the spear again, but there were no hidden side tunnels, just a fissure in the rock that would barely keep him out of the rain.

The boy figured even a crack in the mountain was better than trying to sleep in a tree and waking up on the ground. He thought about the fish in the stream. Tomorrow he would eat.

As he crawled into the fissure, Tyler imagined himself standing in a big wrestling ring, clutching a microphone and yelling to the crowd, "Tomorrow, the fish is going down. I'm taking his belt and I'm going to eat him."

Then a big fish running down the aisle and leaping into the ring and the crowd hooting and yelling.

Tyler smiled.

He powered up the notebook, and kept it turned away from the entrance. In the dark, the screen was very bright and he didn't want Silas to see it.

He pushed his dirty finger across the touch pad and clicked on the sword and spear symbol for *Lair of the Hydra*. Tyler signed into his father's account without thinking about the cliff, but then the game stopped and an error message popped up. It said there wasn't a signal and apparently he needed a signal to play.

Tyler wondered if the batteries were dying, like when a remote controlled car makes a whining noise and goes really slow. Or maybe that had nothing to do with the signal.

He thought about it. One time in the car while his mother drove, his father checked his email on the notebook. It cut out in a valley between two mountains, but when they got to the top of a mountain, the computer worked again.

Tyler thought about Takeus waiting for him in the lighthouse, fighting off monsters by himself. But climbing to the top of the hill at night to get a signal would be scary and maybe stupid.

Tyler shut the computer off, wrapped himself in his sport coat and sat against the wall with his spear across his knees. He watched the stars come out.

He watched for monsters.

* * *

Chapter 20
New Mexico, USA
Day 5

As soon as the morning light was strong enough to see by, Silas pushed his gear from the entrance to the cave and crawled out. He shouldered the pack, which was lighter since he'd drank some of the water.

The short man clicked on his flashlight, but the sun soon pushed over the hills and lit the ground. Silas followed a set of tracks away from the cave, angling slightly down from the hill.

He noticed that the 'S' of Tyler's sneakers pointed one way in some of the prints, and the opposite in others.

When he perched on the rough trail above the dry streambed, Silas nodded. He reasoned that the boy searched for water, didn't find any, and was now even weaker.

He scouted the area, but the tracks only led back to the cave. One set was sharper than the other was and he figured the boy walked to the dry stream at least twice.

Satisfied, he marched back to the cave. There were two sets of prints leading up, but this time, only one leading back down.

Silas hiked up the hill and stood on the crest to look for signs of the boy. Signs like circling vultures.

After a water break, he followed the prints down the hill and into flat country broken by thickets of oak and shallow arroyos.

Beneath the brim of his hat, his purple eyes darted from print to print, picking them out with increasing ease.

Silas walked faster.

And tromped into a field of hoof prints. He paused and looked around.

The path was a mess. Now he looked at deep marks left by dozens, maybe hundreds, of hooves.

His heart thumped in his chest. Silas inhaled and retreated to Tyler's last clear print. He shut his eyes, let the sun's heat soak into his shoulders, and then searched for the next track.

The surprise was that the boy had trekked alongside the hoof prints, instead of directly behind them. Had Tyler mingled his steps with the horses' trail, he would have made it very difficult for Silas to follow.

Silas tried to imagine why Tyler pursued the horses. He wondered if the boy was mad. He'd read stories of sailors on lifeboats at sea who'd gone insane from thirst.

Judging from his parents, Silas estimated Tyler's intelligence to be below average. His refusal to go off the cliff was more the product of some back-brain reptilian self-preservation instinct than any logical process.

The compact man hiked in quick, economical steps. When his left boot came down next to one of Tyler's shoeprints, he noticed his next footstep landed several inches beyond Tyler's right print. Silas nodded. It was simple mathematics. He took longer strides, covering more ground than the boy did. If he continued, it was inevitable he would overtake Tyler.

And there was the fatigue factor. Tyler was hungry, thirsty and weak. Whereas Silas had slept well in the cave, eaten breakfast, and drank plenty of water. The boy would tire, and Silas would overtake him like a train catching a horse.

Silas liked trains. The precision of arrivals and departures at appointed times. The lack of steering. Trains followed tracks.

If Tyler had followed the track Silas laid down for him like his parents had, his life might have had meaning. Instead, he would die alone in the desert, dehydrated and raving. Silas would find his corpse, nod and walk away.

Silas consulted his map. The wind caught it, and wrapped it around his face. He thrashed for a moment, trapped by the heavy paper before he could pin it to the ground and weight the corners with rocks.

Assuming most tourists stuck to established trails and attractions in the park, Silas believed he would not have a problem like he'd had with the two hikers at the cliff. Silas thought about the look on the girl's face as she'd snatched at empty air as she went backward over the edge. He cherished the memory, although it was crude to shove someone, even with a walking stick.

If he found Tyler alive he would have to kill him, but he didn't want to touch him. The thought of the boy's blood or saliva spattering him made Silas shudder. As he hiked, he thought about possible ways to end the boy's life.

Talking was out of the question. Even at the age of ten, Tyler possessed insufficient reason to understand deep ideas. If Tyler was near the end, Silas figured he could watch the boy until he died of thirst or exposure.

If Tyler was able to run, Silas figured he could chase the boy until he collapsed or trapped himself in a canyon. Then he would close to ten paces from the boy and fire one bullet from the pistol. If he missed, he would advance two paces and fire again. If he missed, he would advance two more.

Silas drank his bottled water. The method seemed clean and sensible. Now if Tyler would simply cooperate.

* * *

At dawn, Tyler yawned and crawled out of the crack in the rock. *If this is the mountain's butt, what does that make me?*

He thought of the neighbors' dog, Rufus, who would poop in front of anyone without a thought, squatting with a broad smile while logs tumbled like bombs from a plane.

He tied his coat back into a pack for the computer and the Spirits bottle and hiked down to the stream.

The night before he wasn't sure what he would do, other than find the road and get help. Now it seemed obvious. Follow the stream. Follow the stream until he met fishermen or a family camping or found a forest ranger.

Fifty steps short of the stream, he ducked low and crept into the bushes.

Ninja. Always ninja.

He scanned the area and saw a bee, a lizard and one bird, but no bears or Gila monsters. Or Silas.

The boy slipped down the bank and checked the stability of a flat rock with his spear. Reassured, he perched on the rock where it jutted into the stream. He rinsed the Spirits bottle, filled it and drank, then refilled it and capped it.

While he drank, a fish the size of his hand darted out from under the rock, hit the faster flow in the middle of the stream, and shot downstream.

Tyler crouched and watched the water. The rock was still cold from the night, but as soon as the sun was high enough to shine down into the ravine, it would be a warm spot.

It was tempting to stay. To make a camp in the crack in the rock wall and drink cool stream water and catch fish. But that meant giving up on the road and the police and the chance to ever reach Silver City.

The boy put the notebook, the Spirits bottle and his sport coat up on the bank. He peeled off his dusty shirt, even though it was still chilly, then ditched his shoes. His socks were filthy, so he scrubbed them in the water, and then lay them on the rock to dry.

Spear in hand, Tyler waded into the water until it reached his knees. He wasn't afraid to go deeper, but he couldn't see a fish in waist deep water so the boy saw no point in it.

He held his spear ready, and waited.

He missed the first fish twice. Later a clutch of tiny fish swam by, but they were too small to hit. As he shuffled his feet along the streambed, a frog surfaced and kicked hard into the weeds.

On the seventh try a fish darted toward him and Tyler almost jammed the spear into his own foot.

On the eleventh try he pinned a long, brown fish to the rocks, grabbed it by the tail and slung it up onto the bank.

He splashed through the water, ran across his half dried socks and stopped. The fish lay on the ground, gasping. Its mouth moved like it was whispering some final secret.

Tyler watched for a moment, and then rammed the spear into the fish. The fish spasmed once and died.

The boy had no matches. No birthday candle lighter. No magnifying glass. No fire crackers. He had a vague idea about rubbing sticks together or waiting for lightning to set a tree on fire, but he'd smelled rotting fish once and the thought of letting his beautiful catch rot in the sun while he waited for an afternoon lightning storm made him shudder.

His first bite was tentative.

He tasted blood. The boy gagged for a moment, opened his mouth, and waited for the reflex to stop.

The second bite was easier. Tyler pulled a piece of skin from between his teeth and flung it away, but swallowed the cool flesh.

He was careful with the thin white bones, but he crunched one on accident. He spit it out and kept eating.

When the fish was gone except for the head and the spine, he dug one of its eyes out and held it up to the sunlight. The eye was bright. It sparkled. Tyler examined the jewel for a moment, and then put it in his mouth.

It burst when he bit it. But it had less taste than the thin-blooded flesh. Tyler flipped the fish over and ate the other eye.

He washed his face and hands in the stream, and scrubbed the tip of the spear with wet sand.

He held the sharp branch up. "You killed a fish. I should name you," he murmured.

The boy sat on the rock and watched the stream drift by while he tried to think of the right name for a spear. It was harder than he expected.

Poker. Stabber. Killer. Sharpie. He touched the filed end and shrugged. *Not that sharp. Fisher. Lancer. Cutter. Or just Lance.*

The sun rose high enough to send long yellow beams across the creek bed, but his socks were still wet. Tyler put on his shoes, and tied the wet socks to the end of his spear. He'd seen pictures of knights who had flags on their spears when they went out looking for adventures.

While he paralleled the stream, walking opposite the direction of the current, Tyler imagined himself a knight. Not a rich knight, but more of a country knight with two blue socks tied to his lance, and riding a giant golden horse.

He thought about the golden horse and where it might have gone, and what its tribe was doing. Tyler played the memory over and over in his head. The dust clouds drifting up into the hot air, the thunder of hooves, the gold horse running hard on legs taller than his head.

The morning passed away while the boy hiked north. The sun grew hot. He switched his improvised pack from one shoulder to the other. When he stopped to put on his socks, Tyler found a blister on his big toe.

As he laced his dusty Spiderman sneakers, Tyler worked his tongue around his mouth. He could still taste the fish. Drinking water helped, but he thought cooking the next fish might help more.

He reached out and picked up a fallen tree limb, broke up a section of it and rubbed the two pieces together. Tyler worked at it for few minutes, but nothing happened.

He threw the sticks away. *It's never this much trouble to light a torch in Lair of the Hydra.*

The boy sat up.

He'd never paid much attention to the action during the game--he just clicked the 'light torch' button. Tyler called up the sequence in his mind. His warrior always dug in his pack, knelt down and banged two small objects together.

Tyler scooted into the shade of an oak and opened the notebook. The computer hummed to life and Tyler clicked on the *Lair of the Hydra* icon. He didn't sign on because he knew Tak wouldn't meet him until sundown. Instead he brought up his character's page and checked his inventory.

Bronze dagger, iron sword, broken spear, Traveler's Orb, flint and steel, healing potion. Flint and steel. *That's the fire maker. That piece of metal and that gray rock.*

Tyler shut the notebook. He examined the buttons on his sport coat--they were gold colored and fragile. His belt buckle, however, was a sturdy steel square.

He grabbed a rock at random and struck it against the buckle. Tyler tried twenty rocks before he remembered the road.

If I find the road, I won't have to cook my own fish.

He set off.

Lizards skittered from his footsteps and birds launched out of the trees when he passed, and once he heard something in the bushes above the creek, but Tyler marched on. His stomach felt weird and he stopped to move his bowels several times.

Was it the raw fish or the stream water?

Tyler rubbed his flat belly as he walked.

There is a road. We drove in on a road. I can walk out on a road.

Tyler repeated the words in his mind, over and over.

Sometimes the canyon around the stream narrowed to where he had to walk the water's edge, and other times it was wide with a sandy patch and bushes and trees. While he hiked, Tyler picked up rocks and smacked them against his belt buckle.

The river stones were nice and smooth, but he figured a wet rock wouldn't make sparks. He ignored the blue rocks, and the reddish ones, and the ones with speckles or lines in them. He tried a lot of gray rocks.

He wondered how many sparks a flint rock might make and pictured his pants catching on fire and having to jump in the stream. Tyler shook his head, figuring that would be just his luck.

The sun was directly above his head, shooting hot little needles into his skull, when he found the mountain.

The mountain was wide and tall, with patches of trees scattered across it like a dog with mange.

Tyler uncorked the Spirits bottle and drank while he surveyed the mountain. Instinct told him it was too big to go around.

The boy retied his shoes. His toe hurt but he didn't take off the sock to look at it. The stream appeared to climb the mountain, so he stayed with it.

It wasn't bad at first. The slope was gentle, and he was strong from the fish breakfast, but as the day wore on, Tyler slowed.

The mountain was mean. It fought him. His legs hurt. He bruised his heel jumping between two stones. Once he slipped and scraped his palm. The creek bed got so deep he decided to climb out to see where he was going.

Tyler had to pull himself up with both hands, but he couldn't with the spear. He cast it up over the lip, and then worked his way up using a stunted tree's roots. The moment he was over the top, Tyler looked for his spear, but didn't see it.

His hands shook. The boy darted forward a few steps, paused and spun around.

There!

He yanked the spear out of a bush and clutched it to his chest. Tyler closed his eyes for a moment and took deep breaths.

Clouds gathered around the top of the mountain. The temperature dropped under the shade of the storm. The higher he climbed and the darker it became, the more he noticed the cool air on his neck and face. There were plenty of trees and rocks, but Tyler searched for another crevice to get under when the rain came. He knew he had to keep the computer dry.

He kept his head down, watching his own feet as they churned uphill. Suddenly the ground leveled out and he stumbled. Tyler stood at the summit.

He rotated, looking for houses or ranger stations or roads, but all he saw were more canyons, hills, and trees. Brown, green, and tan, but no black ribbons of roads. No white houses.

Tyler put his back to a rock and watched the clouds form an angry mob. He sat with his legs splayed, feet aching, and sipped from the smooth glass mouth of the Spirits bottle.

The air around him was heavy and moist and he knew it would rain any minute. He forced himself up.

Marching downhill was easy until his knees began to hurt. It rained, but he was in an area of thick, interwoven aspens, firs and spruce trees, so most of the raindrops never reached him.

He passed down into pines and junipers and without the heavy network of foliage the rain hit harder. Tyler found a jumble of rocks and wedged himself and his gear under an overhang that extended just past his shoes.

The ground turned from dry to damp to muddy. Water soaked into the seat of his pants. Tyler sipped from the Spirits bottle and waited.

Twice his bowels cramped and he ran through the rain to the nearest bush, but it didn't stop him from drinking more stream water. And after a while, his stomach settled.

* * *

Chapter 21
Tokyo, Japan
Day 5

Takara sat on one of the coveted seats next to the doors on the Yamanote circle metro line. Customers had kept her busy through the afternoon and when she took a moment to dart into the office and look on *Lair* for Tyler, he wasn't there.

At the Komagome stop an elderly couple boarded the train. Tak got up and they sat with a smile. They were both small. Tak marveled at the old woman's tiny feet.

She held onto the overhead rail as the train accelerated. Her feet ached from standing all day, but she only had to wait until the next stop at Sugamo to change lines.

Her phone rattled and she pulled it from her pocket without snagging the charms. It was a text from Aunt Shiori.

"Meet for dinner at the Sisters?"

Tak's thumbs tap danced over the keys. "On my way."

When she left the metro station, streaming out with all the others heading home after work, the first fat warm drops of rain hit her shoulders. One hit the crown of her head so hard it almost hurt.

Pop. Pop. Pop, pop, pop. Spring-loaded umbrellas snapped open all along the sidewalk. Cars turned on their headlights and a few vehicles even slowed down.

Tak thought of the white plastic umbrella she'd taken to meet Kyle and couldn't remember if she'd left it in Starbucks or Game Mania.

She tried to walk fast, but the rush hour crowd slowed her. Raindrops fell more quickly. Tak turned on a side street, spotted the lights of the Sisters' diner and ran the last fifty steps.

The diner was a narrow room squeezed between neighboring buildings. A counter split the room down the middle, with eight stools on one side and the two sisters cooking on the other. There had been three, but the middle sister died, and so now only two old women in clean blue aprons greeted Takara when she dashed inside.

Rain dumped out of the twilight sky and the sidewalks cleared.

Tak joined her aunt at the counter and sat down. A salaryman perched near the entrance, sipping a tall can of beer and slurping udon noodles. He checked his watch and then his phone. A shop girl and her husband sat on the middle stools, talking to the youngest sister, a 70-year-old with the energy of a hummingbird.

"How was work?" Shiori asked.

"The same. Slow in the morning, busy in the afternoon. Yoshi sold a Wii so I didn't call him names for at least an hour."

Shiori chuckled. There were circles under her eyes. Tak watched her and thought her mother's youngest sister looked older than her 44 years. "When will they give you a better slot, Auntie? You're a manager. You shouldn't have to stay up all night for these inventories."

"It's difficult to inventory a store during the day. They pay us to perform this service, so we try not to disrupt their business." Shiori sipped a cup of green tea. "Someone has to guide the crew at night or they won't finish."

"You've been with them a long time. They should give you an office job. During daylight."

They ordered rice, miso soup, more green tea and a small plate of pickles. Shiori smiled. "I asked them to prepare unagi. It will give us energy."

The eldest sister brought Shiori broiled eel on a bed of rice. Takara had cold somen noodles with strips of shrimp and sesame dip. She told the old woman, "I accept," before she began to eat.

The salaryman near the door paid up and dashed out into the rain.

Shiori lifted a piece of pickled eggplant with her chopsticks. "Did you find out any more about the boy?"

Tak slumped on her stool. "Not much. The officer from Crime Prevention hasn't called me back and I can't find the boy online. I asked a friend of mine to look into it, but he only found a reference to a person who might be the boy's father."

"Hmm." Shiori poured soy into a dipping saucer. "What will you do?"

Tak watched raindrops shatter against the concrete outside. "I have some leave time saved up at work."

Shiori chuckled.

"What?"

"You forget, Takara. I may only be 15 years older than you, but I've known you since you were born. You're impetuous like your father, and stubborn like your mother. I knew you would not let this matter alone."

"Auntie, you always speak about 'right action.' Isn't that what your Buddha advises?"

"Yes, and he's your Buddha, too."

"I feel obligated to help this boy."

"Why?"

"Because no one else has."

Shiori lowered her voice. "And not because of your brother?"

"Akira was nine. Tyler is ten."

Shiori stared at her for a moment. "The boy needs your help. Perhaps you need help to aid the boy?"

"I will contact the local police when I arrive. They may not even be aware he's missing. Once they know, we can resolve the situation quickly. I'll only be gone three or four days."

"Why don't you take a couple of the young men from your martial arts club?"

"Auntie, I can take care of myself. A woman can travel alone without--"

"I meant in case you fell off a mountain, or needed an interpreter. When was the last time you practiced your English?"

"I use it online all the time. Mostly written for sales and in-game chat, but I can still speak basic sentences," Takara said.

"If this boy's parents tried to take him on a spaceship, they may be crazy. Or drug addicts."

Takara pushed up her glasses and rubbed the bridge of her nose. She felt in her pocket for her eye drops, and then remembered she'd left them on the desk at work. "Who would I take? Kyle?"

Shiori laughed. "No. How about Shoda or Jiro? They're both strong."

"I'm not going there to kidnap the boy. I just want the authorities to intervene before he is hurt." Takara ate a slice of cucumber. "Shoda is busy at his father's bicycle shop. And Jiro...Jiro's mother is sick."

"Yes, she is. But if Jiro is away for three days it will not hurt. She has a husband and two daughters to care for her. And Shoda could ask his father for a few days off." She touched Tak's arm. "At least consider it."

Takara nodded. "I will. Looks like the rain is slowing down. Let's go home."

Aunt Shiori bowed to the two sisters behind the counter. "It was a banquet."

* * *

Tak walked her aunt home and went inside just long enough to brush her teeth and grab an umbrella. "Auntie, I'm going out to recruit for my journey."

Shiori reached up and tugged Takara's collar straight. "Why don't you put in your contact lenses?"

"Why?"

"You look prettier than with your glasses."

Tak snorted. "I'm not going to seduce them. I'll pay their airfare and meals."

"As you like. Though it never hurts to negotiate from a position of strength." Shiori handed Tak an umbrella. "Who will you pick?"

Tak paused, hand on the doorknob. "I'm not certain. Shoda is stronger and more stable, but..."

"But?"

"In a fight, Jiro is fierce. Almost vicious."

Shiori smiled. "Maybe you should take both. To balance each other. Besides, they can share a hotel room. I'll help you with the money."

Tak nodded, her throat suddenly tight. "Thanks, Auntie."

She left the apartment and walked fast through the rain. When she ducked under an overhang to descend to the metro station, she caught her hair in the umbrella spines.

The metro was less crowded now that rush hour was over. There was no direct way to Toranomon Hospital from her neighborhood, so she had to change to the Ginza line to reach the complex.

Tak managed to scoot across the wet road without being crushed by traffic, and hurried up to the hospital. Jiro worked from late afternoon to midnight as a security guard at the medical complex. To Tak, who'd worked for years at the same store, Jiro seemed to change jobs every few months. She suspected he'd only stayed at the hospital because his mother was a patient there.

Jiro and another young man stood near the main entrance in yellow slickers, their shoulders hunched beneath the rain.

"Hey, Jiro," she called.

"Tak? Hey. Oh, this is my pal, Himura. We've been partners since we took the first aid class together."

Tak nodded to the other man. She looked at the blue cap covering Jiro's head and smiled. Normally, he was fussy about having his hair perfectly spiked.

Jiro's eyes rose under the bill of the cap. "We have to wear these. Part of the uniform. The ladies like them, though." He elbowed Himura in the ribs.

Tak stepped aside as a man limped past, holding his belly and moaning as he went in the automatic doors. She shivered.

Jiro looked away from the sick man, his eyes flat. "Hey, Himura, can you watch the door for a few minutes while we go inside?"

"Sure, nice to meet you." Himura waved.

Tak collapsed her umbrella and followed her dripping friend inside. "Is your mother seeing visitors?"

"Some days. My sisters were here earlier."

"That's good."

"Did you come to visit her?"

Tak took off her glasses and wiped raindrops from the lenses with the edge of her shirt. "Sure. Hey, have you ever been to America?"

"No."

"Okay, this will sound weird so don't interrupt. I met a boy online." Jiro's mouth twitched. "Don't smirk. This American boy is ten years old and his parents are crazy. They want to take him on a spaceship to heaven. He's in danger. The police here tried to talk to the police in America but it's taking too long. The boy used a notebook computer to contact me and he told me he's lost in the wilderness in a prefecture called New Mexico. I'm going there to alert the authorities and look for the boy." Tak took a breath.

Jiro took off his cap and finger combed his hair. Without the spikes standing straight up, he looked more conservative. Almost normal. Tak watched him for a moment, then continued.

"His parents may be involved in a cult. They might be drug addicts. I don't intend to confront them myself but rescuing the boy could be dangerous."

"Ah, that's why." Jiro smiled. "I suppose I'm flattered. I'm surprised you didn't ask Shoda. In sparring he's almost my match."

Tak stepped back against the wall as a blocky young man marched past. A white mask covered the lower half of his face, but his eyes were intense.

"I'm going to ask Shoda, too," she said.

Jiro shrugged. "You know my mother is sick. How long will this take?"

"A day there, a day back, and a day or two to convince the local authorities the boy exists and must be removed from his parents." She tapped one foot. "I'll pay your airfare, of course, and food, lodging. Any gifts you buy are up to you."

Jiro snorted. "Maybe I'll bring my sisters cowboy hats." He looked at the rain outside. "Are you going up to visit my mom?"

"Yes, my aunt asks about her. She'd come, but her work schedule is even worse than ours."

"Of course." Jiro put on his cap and moved toward the exit.

"Where are you going? This place is huge," Tak said. "Show me where her room is."

* * *

When they stepped out of the elevator, Jiro said hello to the nurse behind the desk. She nodded in recognition.

He led Tak down the corridor, his slicker dripping on the floor. When they reached the end of the hallway he pointed at the room on the left. "She's in there." Jiro turned. "I have to get back to work."

Tak grabbed his arm. "At least go in and make sure she's up to seeing visitors. I don't want to barge in there."

Jiro started to pull away, but stopped. "Pushy as ever, Tak." He tapped on the door. "Mom? It's Jiro."

Tak heard a faint reply. Jiro opened the door and called, "Takara Murakami is here to see you."

He pushed her ahead. Tak took three long steps into the room and stopped. "Hello, Mrs. Yukimura."

Jiro's mother lay propped up in bed. There was an IV drip connected to her arm, and an electronic monitor on one finger. Her hair was gone and her color awful.

Tak stared. "My Aunt Shiori sends her prayers that you'll recover. Soon. She prays a lot."

Mrs. Yukimura smiled. She turned her head and looked at Jiro. "Your sisters were here earlier."

He nodded. "I know."

Tak sat beside the bed. "Those flowers are lovely." She leaned to smell a bouquet on the table.

"From my husband. He wanted to bring me a plant, but I told him a plant might outlast me. So he brings flowers." Mrs. Yukimura grunted a little laugh.

"Mom," Jiro said.

Tak looked over her shoulder. Jiro stood by the door, wringing his hat with both hands. The overhead light cast a pale halo around the sick woman's bed, but Jiro remained in the shadows.

He opened the door. "I have to get back to work."

"Jiro?" Tak said.

He went into the hall and closed the door behind him.

Mrs. Yukimura's fingers brushed Takara's hand. "He won't come near me. Won't touch me."

A tear ran down the woman's cheek.

Tak gripped her hand.

* * *

Chapter 22
Tokyo, Japan
Day 5

Takara found a seat on the metro and dozed on the ride to Shoda's family's bicycle shop.

She walked past the dark construction site; its wet plastic tarps were quiet for a change. The lights were on in the bicycle shop, but the front door was locked and the laminated sign on the door read, "Closed, please come again tomorrow."

Tak dug her cell phone out of her pocket. One of the charms came loose and bounced off the sidewalk into the gutter. The stream of rainwater carried it away.

"Damn it." She tapped buttons, and put the phone to her ear while balancing her umbrella on her shoulder.

"Hello?" Shoda answered.

"Are you still at the shop?"

"Yes, I'm--"

"Come open the door." Tak hung up.

A minute later Shoda opened the door, but only a few inches. "Tak, what's up?" A smear of white paint ran across his cheek.

Tak pushed the door open. "It's raining. Let me in."

"Watch the cat!"

A gray bullet shot toward the door. Tak blocked with her feet like the soccer player she'd once been. The cat collided with her sneaker, bounced off and ran back around the counter.

"Have you tried picking it up when you open the door?" Tak asked.

Shoda shrugged. "It claws."

Tak collapsed her umbrella and dropped it in the umbrella stand. "It looks like a rat."

"Don't say that around my dad. He loves the thing." Shoda stroked the cat's back, then walked behind the counter to the shop in back. A sheet of plastic lay beneath one wall, along with a pail of paint, two brushes, a can of spackling, and a piece of scrap wood. "I'm patching the hole my clumsy cousin made."

"How's he doing in his new school?"

"Great. He joined the tennis team and he's had two dates. I can't understand it." Shoda laughed. "He'll ask you out if you're not careful."

Tak watched her stocky friend smear spackling over a piece of pine glued into the hole in the drywall. Shoda tried to smooth it with a putty knife, but the wall looked like the surface of the moon. "Did Kyle tell you?" Shoda asked.

Tak sat on a workbench, put her hand in wheel grease and jumped up. "Yuck. Tell me what?"

"I have an interview. At a bank. For a real job." Shoda beamed.

Tak waved at the shop. "This is a real job. There's nothing wrong with working in a--"

"I know. But, hey, if my dad didn't own this place, I probably wouldn't even have been hired." Shoda exchanged the putty knife for a paintbrush and slathered white paint onto the wall. The spackling was still wet and the combination formed a slurry mess.

"You might want to let that dry first," Tak said.

"What?"

"Never mind. When's your interview?"

Shoda stretched his back. "Next Tuesday at eight. Tomorrow, I'm going to buy a new shirt and tie. Maybe you like to come shopping with me?" Shoda looked at her. "You know, to help me pick out something appropriate."

Takara counted days on her fingers. "Shoda, have you ever been to America?"

"No. I've always wanted to see the Grand Canyon, though. Why?"

Takara paced the room while she explained the Tyler situation. Shoda sat on the plastic sheet and listened. Takara detailed her efforts with the police, and why she thought any action they took might come too late to save the boy.

When she stopped for breath, Shoda raised one finger. "These people sound dangerous. If you can afford a third ticket, maybe we should bring--"

"I already asked him." Tak smiled. "So you'll come?"

"Him? Who, Jiro?"

"Yeah, isn't that who you meant?" Tak asked.

"No, I was thinking we should ask my old judo teacher. He could probably get leave from the fire station for a few days. Or how about your aunt's friend, Sergeant Shimada?"

"What's wrong with Jiro? He's fierce."

Shoda scraped spackling from the putty knife with his fingernail. "Kyle thinks Jiro is bipolar. I'm starting to think he's right." Tak began to speak, but Shoda held up his hand. "I'm not saying it's his fault. It's an illness. But with the stress of his mom's cancer and their money problems, he's getting worse. One day I see him and he's excited about everything. The next time he's so depressed he barely talks."

Tak rubbed her eyes. The cat peeked around the corner at her, but didn't enter the room. "I know they're having trouble paying the bills. His sister just took a second job. I still think he could help, though. Shimada is a good man, but he'd have no arrest authority in America and I doubt he could even bring his gun. And I can't wait for him or your teacher to apply for leave. I'm going to buy the tickets online tonight and hopefully leave tomorrow."

"It's your decision, but we'll have to keep an eye on Jiro. He might be as much a danger as these cult people." Shoda put the lid on the paint and tapped it shut. "Let me know what time we're leaving. I'll be ready."

"Thanks." Tak smiled. "Now come grab the cat so it doesn't get out the door."

* * *

Takara tilted her desk chair back, squeezed a drop into each eye, and shut her lids for a moment. She put the bottle next to the keyboard, woke the computer, and searched for airline tickets.

Three adults, round trip, Tokyo to Albuquerque, leaving tomorrow. She clicked buttons for her preferences, waited for the next page to load, and gasped at the prices.

"Damn." The trip would wipe out half of her accumulated vacation time at Game Mania and all of her savings. *When I get there I'll have to use credit cards. Great.*

She considered logging into her game accounts to make some last minute sales, but she hadn't even started to pack her suitcase yet.

Takara picked up her phone and thumbed a text message to Shoda and Jiro. "meet bike shop 1pm. flight @ 3:35" The ride out to Narita airport would take an hour, depending on traffic, leaving them 90 minutes to pass through security and find their gate.

Takara slumped onto her futon.

* * *

New Mexico, USA
Day 5

The boy spent the night in the rocks. His legs were wet from the rain and he shivered in his sport coat, even with the collar up and his hands deep in the pockets.

He remembered how hot the computer got when it was on and he considered powering it up and holding it to his chest until he warmed, but he knew the batteries would run out soon and he wanted to talk to Takeus of Thebes again.

The rain gave up and went away.

Tyler drifted into a half sleep with his arms on his knees and head bent. During the night when the clouds were long gone and the stars bright, Tyler stretched his cramped calves and staggered to the nearest tree to relieve himself yet again. When he buckled his pants he had to push the belt in a notch. He pinched himself and realized he was getting skinny.

As he walked back to the rock pile, Tyler saw a flash in the sky high above and looked up.

Red lights crept across the black night. The lights blinked.

The airplane was so high he couldn't hear it or make out its size or shape. And he reasoned the people sitting on the plane couldn't see him so far below.

He watched the winking red lights and thought about his mother and the smell of hand wipes and the way she finger combed his hair when he got up in the morning. He thought about his father's belief in the spaceship and his trust in Silas.

Tyler rubbed his dirty forehead.

That wasn't real. There was no spaceship. Silas made them jump off the cliff. It was just lights at the bottom. Just lights.

But he wondered. He sat under the rock with his arms wrapped around the spear and wondered if he'd made a terrible mistake.

* * *

Chapter 23
In Transit
Day 6

The first leg of the flight took Takara, Shoda and Jiro from Narita Airport, outside Tokyo, to Los Angeles, California.

Onboard, the crew distracted people from the fact they were speeding 30,000 feet above the world's largest body of water with constant food service. And drink service. And more drink service.

Tak watched the passengers and crew. The alcohol was tricky. To keep people happy and relaxed, the attendants kept the alcohol flowing, but not gushing. Too much alcohol and people might get unruly.

She estimated half the people on board were drunk.

Every time more than three people lined up at the restrooms, the captain came on the public address system and told them to stop loitering and return to their seats for security purposes. If someone stood to pace or stretch for more than a minute or two, a flight attendant zipped down the aisle and asked them to return to their seat and keep the aisles clear--for security purposes.

The seatbacks each had a small screen inset in them so she could watch television shows or movies, or listen to music, or stare blank faced at an animated map of a tiny plane making its way across the Pacific Ocean.

In the window seat next to her, Jiro muttered, "I'm sick of 'security purposes.' Every time the bathroom door opens, someone beats me to it."

When the attendants dimmed the lights in the cabin, Jiro crammed a pillow into the gap between the wall and his headrest, and went to sleep.

In the row behind them, Shoda finished the last of his neighbor's snack cake and leaned forward between the seats. "Wake me if they bring more food."

Takara nodded and went back to studying a list of useful English phrases she'd downloaded to her laptop while waiting in the airport.

"That's a clever idea."

Tak turned to the woman in the seat next to her. She was Japanese, very old, and quite small, but her eyes were bright behind their glasses. She sipped a plastic cup of ginger ale and nibbled Melba toast. "I'm going to visit my first great grandchild," the old woman said.

Takara nodded. "Congratulations. You must be proud."

"I am. They live outside of Los Angeles, in Palmdale. According to my grandson, it's very warm there." The old woman wiped her mouth with a napkin. "What takes you to America? Are you an athlete?"

Takara smiled. "No."

"You're so tall, I thought you might play volleyball or basketball."

"I did in high school, but not since."

"Yes, I suppose the Americans have tall girls of their own. Like those girls in the Olympics in China, playing volleyball in the sand." The old woman took the cellophane cracker wrapper and folded it up inside the napkin and put it to one side of her tray. "This is my first flight. I think I prefer trains."

"Me, too. At least from a train you can see the countryside. And trains don't drop out of the sky into the sea."

The old woman shut her eyes. "Don't say such a thing. I can well imagine crashing into the cold sea. It makes me shiver."

Tak touched the woman's arm. "Sorry. I'm just sick of being trapped in this metal tube. I'm ready to jump out and swim the rest of the way."

"Even a Kappa drowns sometimes," the old woman murmured.

"A water goblin drown? That would be strange."

"I'm surprised you know what a Kappa is, young lady," the woman said. "That's an old saying. I heard it when I was a girl. What's the farthest you ever swam?"

"A kilometer, in a university pool."

The old woman shook her chin. "A pool is not the ocean. A pool is like a soup bowl. The sea is a living thing. It holds many souls. When the foam slides up the sandy beach the sea mutters, but when the waves crash, it screams with the voices of the dead. The sea is to be feared, especially at night."

Takara smiled, but she pulled the collar of her jacket up around her neck.

The old woman sipped her ginger ale. "When I was a girl, I lived in a town on the coast called Yaidzu. At Yaidzu, people are fishermen, taking bonito from the sea."

"The shore is very rocky, and the sea is rough. But you could see Mount Fuji from my grandfather's house. The fishermen used to put charms on the prows of their boats, asking Fuji for protection and good fortune." She shifted in her seat toward Takara. "Some still do."

"Everyone in the village could swim. I learned so young I have forgotten learning. There were many strong swimmers among us, but we never swam at night."

"Because of sharks?" Tak asked.

"You are more likely to drown in the waves, than get eaten by a shark. And there are other things in the ocean as bad or worse." She folded her wrinkled hands. "No, we did not swim at night because of the Hashima girl."

"Who was the Hashima girl?" Takara asked.

"The daughter of a fisherman. When she was about your age, maybe a bit younger, she met a man from Ajiro--the village across the bay. They became lovers. At night he would light a lantern and put it on the shore in front of his house. She would swim across the bay to be with him, and then swim back in the morning."

"How far was Ajiro from Yaidzu?"

"Several kilometers. One night while she was swimming across, the lantern went out. Maybe he fell asleep and the wind extinguished it. Who knows? But without the light to guide her, she lost her way and drowned. She probably swam in circles for hours, searching for the light."

"That's awful." Takara shivered beneath her coat.

"Yes, a sad tale. Whenever I visit the village, I hear her voice in the waves and I pray for her."

Takara shoved her hands deep in her pockets. "Maybe I won't jump out and swim after all."

The old woman smiled. “It would be a long journey without a lantern to guide you.” She shut her eyes and leaned back in the seat.

Takara watched the tiny white plane on the screen creep toward the distant shore.

* * *

Chapter 24
New Mexico, USA
Day 6

In the Gila National Forest, Andrew Rowbury tugged loose the flexible rod that held up the entrance to his tent. It snapped back and whipped him across the shin. "Son of a--"

"Daddy!" His nine-year-old daughter, Flower, held her hands over her mouth and laughed.

He kicked the tent as it collapsed. "Took me an hour to put that up, and two seconds to bring it down."

Flower sat on her pack, reading a map of the Gila National Forest. "What's a petro glyph?"

Andrew stood stretching his back. "It's a picture. On a rock."

"Are we going to Whitewater Canyon?" Flower asked.

"Not today. Today we're going to leave the tent here in the car, and hike south. See some real wilderness." Andrew struggled to fit the tent back into its tube-shaped nylon bag.

His wife, Emma, came back from the campground restrooms, a towel over her shoulders, and her toothbrush in her hand. "Honey, did you fill the canteens?"

"Not yet. Maybe Flower can help you." Andrew knelt to roll up their sleeping bags.

A white pickup truck rolled into the parking lot and a park ranger got out. She took a moment to put on her hat and settle it, and then walked to their camp.

Andrew waved. "Good morning."

"Morning folks," the ranger said. "Heading out?"

Emma nodded as she and Flower retrieved empty canteens from their packs. "We're going hiking today."

"If I find an arrowhead, can I keep it?" Flower asked.

The ranger smiled. "I tell you what, if you find one, bring it by the Visitors Center and we'll see if we can tell how old it is."

Flower nodded. "Okay."

"Just be aware that we get some afternoon storms this time of year. The rain won't hurt you, but careful of the lightning," the ranger said.

Andrew looked up. "Is there a storm predicted for today?"

"We might get one this afternoon, but tomorrow is looking like a big one." The ranger glanced up at the hot blue sky. "If it does rain, stay out of the arroyos. They fill up very fast and people have drowned."

"Will do," Andrew said.

"Have a good hike," the ranger called over her shoulder as she walked back to her truck.

Emma pushed the map into Andrew's pack. "I'm glad we brought ponchos."

* * *

In Transit

Tak, Jiro and Shoda passed through Customs and changed their yen to dollars in the Los Angeles airport, and then caught the connecting flight to Salt Lake City.

"I think the winter Olympics were here one time," Shoda said when they landed.

Takara nodded, and pushed her glasses up. Her hair was a mess, her face felt greasy, and she was sick of the stale air inside the plane. "I think we should take a ship home. Or walk."

Jiro checked his watch. "I have no idea what time it is here. Or what day. I know we have one more flight, so let's find it and get this over with."

They flew the last leg to New Mexico, and landed at the Albuquerque International Sunport just before five in the afternoon.

"Why is it a Sunport? Do they have trips to the sun?" Shoda asked.

Jiro groaned.

"Who cares. I need coffee," Tak said. Their arrival gate was at the very end of the 'B' concourse. She staggered like a brain-hungry zombie toward the food court.

Jiro pointed at shops as they passed. "Earth Spirit. Thunderbird Curio. What is a curio?"

"I don't know," Tak said.

"What's a thunderbird?"

"It's a car," Shoda said.

"Oh."

"Pizza, Mexican, ice cream. Damn it, where is the coffee?" Tak asked.

Shoda stopped to look at a map. "This says there's coffee by the rental cars."

"Which way?"

They followed the crowd down to the Level 1 terminal and the baggage claim area. Takara looked for the old woman, and then remembered she'd gotten off in Los Angeles. Takara blinked.

"After we get a rental car, can one of you drive for a while?" she asked.

Jiro shook his flattened spikes. "Sure."

"It's 230 miles to Silver City. Are you confident you can drive in America?" Shoda asked.

"I drove a delivery truck in Tokyo for five months, so I think I can handle Albuquerque, or however you say it." He mangled the name, but they understood him.

"Praise the Buddha," Tak said.

"What?" Shoda asked.

"Coffee." She sprinted to the Black Mesa Coffee and Bakery. Minutes later she thanked the barista and walked away with an extra large to-go cup. "Okay, now I can function."

They retrieved their baggage, just one bag each, and followed the crowd outside. Some people walked away, while others milled.

Takara approached an older woman in business clothes. "Excuse me, please. Where are the rental cars?"

"Oh, they aren't here. You have to take the shuttle. There's a shuttle every five minutes," the woman told her.

"Thank you very much."

The three Japanese lined up beneath the tall metal sign for the shuttle. The Americans formed a loose mass and when the shuttle arrived, swarmed aboard.

Shoda laughed. "I guess they don't queue up here."

"I guess not," Tak said.

The shuttle took them to a long row of nine or ten rental car companies. Shoda stared at the colorful signs. "Avis, Hertz, Alamo. Do you know what any of those names mean?"

"The Alamo was a fort for the Americans when they fought Spain or Mexico or someone," Tak said.

"Did they win?"

Tak shook her head. "No, all the defenders died."

Jiro winced. "Hmm. Maybe we should try Enterprise, like in *Star Trek*."

"Okay."

At the Enterprise counter they filled out the paperwork and Tak handed over her Visa card. The man behind the counter was not concerned that she was Japanese, but he asked twice if she was 25 years old.

Jiro lobbied for a pickup truck on the argument that they might be on desert trails, but Tak rented a sensible and familiar Nissan Sentra with automatic transmission. The man at the counter assured her it had a powerful air conditioner.

Minutes later, Jiro steered them onto Interstate 25, heading south.

Tak was surprised to see that Jiro was a capable, and even conservative, driver. They passed through places with strange names--Los Lunas, Socorro, Truth or Consequences. At Caballo they turned west on Highway 152, and arrived in Silver City just before 11:00pm local time.

"I booked two rooms at the Holiday Inn Express. They have high-speed Internet," Tak managed to say before a massive yawn nearly split her head open.

Shoda smiled. "So which of us do you want to room with?"

* * *

New Mexico, USA

In her hotel room, Tak brushed her teeth and then plugged in her laptop. She sat cross legged on the bed with a pillow on her lap and the computer perched atop.

She emailed Aunt Shiori to tell her they'd arrived safely. Takara almost wrote about the old woman on the plane, but she decided to wait and tell Shiori the story in person.

After she clicked 'send,' Tak logged into *Lair of the Hydra*.

The site was still running, so she tried searching for Tyler's father's account. The search feature ran. And ran. She retyped the name and clicked it again. Nothing happened. The feature was dead.

Tak rubbed her glasses clean with the pillowcase and leaned forward.

Back to the lighthouse.

* * *

Chapter 25
New Mexico, USA
Day 6

In the morning the boy finished the last of the Spirits bottle, crawled out from the rocks, and went in search of the stream. He hiked down the mountain, using his spear as a staff.

Even though it had rained during the night, the ground was already dry again. Tyler put down his gear and climbed up onto a rock as tall as a school bus. The sunlit top of the rock was hot to the touch. A lizard darted away.

He wasn't surprised not to see a road or houses. Tyler knew he'd missed the road.

The boy shielded his eyes with his hands like he'd seen golfers do on television. His dad told him that once he'd played golf with his grandfather. Tyler thought driving the cart might make the game fun.

He noticed a thick line where the bushes were greener, or at least less brown, than the rest. The trees were different, too. He recognized sycamores because they had three at his old house and it was tough to rake up all the leaves. Once you got past the bare part of the trunk, the sycamores were good for climbing, though.

Tyler slid from the rock and trooped downhill to the fat green line.

He smelled the stream before he saw it. Pushed through the thick scrub, looked down, and smiled.

Keeping ninja discipline, he watched for a while before he climbed down into the shallow canyon. The water was cold and sweet. He drank and then filled the Spirits bottle and capped it with the rock.

Speckled, silvery ribbons slipped through the current in the middle of the stream. Tyler put the laptop and bottle well back from the water, ditched his socks and sneakers, and waded in for breakfast.

This section of the creek was deeper than he thought. He couldn't find a big fish, so he settled for two small ones. They were bony, but the blood didn't bother him as much this time.

While his breakfast settled he washed his face, and his socks again. He squeezed his socks and draped them across a sunlit rock.

Tyler sat with the laptop on his knees while he waited for his socks to dry. He wanted to open the computer and tell Takeus about the fish, and his spear, and the golden horse, but he worried about wasting the battery.

He decided to continue his march alongside the stream, and camp near the top of a mountain so he could enter *Lair of the Hydra* at sunset and find his friend.

Tyler followed the creek. His sport coat, slung over one shoulder, held the laptop and Spirits bottle. He carried his spear in the opposite hand, switching sides when he grew tired.

At the base of the mountain the land leveled out, but it was still higher than the semi-desert he'd started in. He passed under oak trees and waded through knee-high patches of juniper that clung to his pants legs.

Sometimes animals scattered when he approached, but Tyler was surprised at how often he crept up on them before they noticed. He hefted his spear.

It's killed three fish and I still haven't named it.

When he grew thirsty, the boy stopped and sat in the shade of a huge, old ponderosa pine. The top of the tree soared fifty feet above his head. Tyler leaned against the red brown bark and drank from the Spirits bottle.

He watched a squirrel dig in the loose soil and then dash off as if it had something important to do. Tyler picked up an acorn near his shoe.

He peeled off the acorn's tiny helmet and tossed it away. He put the acorn in his mouth and chewed.

"Yuck." Tyler spit the pieces out, but the bitter taste remained. He spit again, then washed his mouth with water and spit once more. Two squirrels watched him from across the clearing. "How do you eat these things?" he whispered.

The squirrels shrugged and went back to work.

Tyler wiped his mouth on his sleeve and tilted his head back against the bark. In the shade, the air was still hot, but not burning. He closed his eyes. A faint western breeze carried the sweet smell of junipers. The low, green plants smelled like the wooden box on his mother's dresser. Once she'd opened it and showed him a silver bracelet she said was white gold. Tyler didn't know what white gold was, but he remembered the scent of the box.

The boy opened his eyes and crawled to the nearest spread of junipers. Blue-colored berries hung from the tips of the green limbs. Tyler plucked a berry and rolled it between his fingers. A thin, white wax covered the berry. Tyler scratched it with his fingernail until the berry was clean and then put it in his mouth.

Rather than eat two dozen berries and die a horrible death from poison, Tyler decided to sit against the tree and see if just one made him sick.

He tried to think up names for the spear, but nothing seemed right and finally he dozed in the heat.

Something skittered through the pine needles on the ground. Tyler's eyes popped open, but he didn't move. An oak leaf crackled.

Tyler's right hand slid down and found the haft of his spear. The weapon seemed to quiver in his hand.

A foot-long light brown lizard slipped out of the junipers. A black ring circled the lizard's neck.

Tyler sat still.

A second lizard emerged. Its skin was blue green, but it also wore a black ring around its neck. Both lizards had round heads and powerful-looking legs with long toes.

The second lizard crept toward the first. The brown lizard darted toward Tyler, and then stood up on its hind legs and ran.

The blue lizard reared up onto its back legs and chased the brown into the juniper thicket.

Tyler sat wide eyed. "Baby dinosaurs," he muttered. "Awesome."

He watched the junipers rustle and waited for the lizards to come back. After a few minutes, he rose and gathered more of the waxy berries and put half of them in his pockets and half of them in his mouth.

He thought about the lizards and why they were different colors although they were the same otherwise. Once he'd seen a litter of puppies and they were all different colors but they had the same mom.

If those are babies, how big is their mom? He backed out of the junipers, picked up his gear, and trotted to the stream.

As the sun reached its peak, Tyler watched the sky. Rain clouds gathered far to his left, dark and puffy like week-old birthday balloons. He ate a pocketful of berries and refilled the Spirits bottle.

Tyler looked for a mountain. A series of hills rose in column straight ahead, but to his right stood a solitary peak at least as high as the one he'd climbed the day before.

The boy went to the mountain. At its foot he paused to survey the ground ahead. Tyler put a berry in his mouth, took up his spear, and climbed.

He marched at a steady pace but the mountain was steeper than it looked. Tyler pushed himself up the incline, knowing he needed to climb high enough for the computer to get a signal before sundown. Deer trails formed rough switchbacks, but he went straight up, legs pumping until he had to lean against a tree to breath.

Tyler hung his head and stared at his battered Spiderman sneakers. When his breathing slowed to the point where he didn't think he'd throw up the juniper berries, he scanned the countryside.

Above the mountain was green with spruce and firs, split by red and brown rocks, and short, crumbling cliff faces.

Below the land was more open, with solitary trees and clumps of juniper. Tyler rested against the tree and stared at the path he'd taken. Looking down at the spread of land behind him, he smiled. He'd walked that land, eaten from it, and sheltered in it.

A fleck caught his eye. A white fleck.

The boy squinted, shaded his eyes with his hands. The fleck bobbed and rippled in the hot air.

Tyler waited. The fleck drew closer and he decided it was gray or blue like a pair of faded jeans. It definitely moved toward him.

Soon he could make out a figure. A single figure hiking along the stream.

The boy slipped behind the tree trunk. He couldn't shimmy up the straight-sided pine, so he moved to a drooping oak. He set his gear on the roots and swung up into the branches, climbing high so he could see far.

When he looked, he couldn't spot the figure. Tyler bit his lip and waited. The hiker climbed up out of a ravine and stopped and bent over the ground like he was reading it.

Tyler watched the man. From such a long distance, it was hard to tell if he was tall or short. But he could see the man moved toward him. And he took the same route Tyler had taken.

He's tracking me.

The boy slithered down from the tree, grabbed his pack and spear, and ran up the mountain.

He stabbed the butt of the spear into the ground and propelled himself forward, over and over, until sweat coursed down his face and his legs quivered.

When he reached the summit, he ran across it in a crouch so as not to be seen. The sudden flat space felt strange to his legs, but it ended quickly. Tyler was aware of clouds sailing fast above him, but he was too tired to raise his head to watch.

The rain began as he started down the far side of the mountain.

He staggered to a rock and sat hunched, trying to keep the notebook dry. As he studied the mountain to figure out the easiest way down, Tyler spotted a thicket of spruce trees.

He pushed the spear into the ground and went down the slope. Between the clouds, a sliver of sun glimmered as it sank into the hills. While there was still light to see, he scampered the last few hundred yards and stopped at the spruce trees.

A large, recently fallen tree formed a lean-to against a living tree. A mix of green and brown limbs hung to the ground. Tyler looked over his shoulder at the slope above. The rain came down harder.

He squatted and crawled under the dead tree.

The ground beneath was dry, and only a few drops of rain leaked through the thick canopy. Tyler put his back to the standing tree trunk and watched. His spear lay across his aching shins.

The wind slung the rain across the mountainside. Tyler wondered if it would wash away his tracks. He unwrapped the computer and put his sport coat over his head like a hood.

As soon as it was dark, he turned on the notebook.

* * *

Chapter 26
Lair of the Hydra
Day 6

The lighthouse was shadowy and quiet. After the blue glow of the portal orb died, Takeus of Thebes lit a torch and placed it in a wall sconce. He pushed through the wooden trapdoor to the walkway on top and quickly shut it to keep the light from attracting monsters.

Outside, the moon waxed full, so bright Tak could see thin streamers of clouds high up in the atmosphere. Stars coalesced into constellations and spun across the blue-black bowl of heaven. Part of the night sky was so clear he was able to pick out tiny Lyra between Cygnus and Hercules.

Waves rolled in from the wine dark sea. Figures stood in the surf and on the sand, but something was wrong.

The figures sixty feet below did not move. They stood like statues on the rocky shingle. Then a tall figure stepped between a cluster of unmoving monsters.

Takeus readied his Spear of the Myrmidons. He twisted the leather thong on the shaft around two fingers and drew back, ready to let fly.

Moonlight glinted on tattered armor and filthy yellow hair.

"Tyler?"

The barbarian looked up from the beach. "Takeus?"

"Yeah, stay there. I'll be right down." Tak bounded down the curling stairwell two steps at a time. The banded oak door that was barricaded the day before stood open, with moonlight pouring in.

"Tyler, where have you been?"

The tall warrior looked down at her. "Here. I was looking at these stone people."

"No, I mean, why didn't you log on last night like we agreed?"

"I tried. But I was in a crack in the hill and the computer said it couldn't get a signal. I thought about going up on the hill to get a signal but it was dark and there's Gila monsters and Silas and bears. I killed a fish."

"What?"

"I found a stream. A full stream. So I drank a gallon of water and killed a fish and ate it." Tyler took an unlit torch from his pack and placed it on the sand. "Do you know how to make fire?"

"Here, or in meat space?"

"Um, not here. I mean in the other...in real space."

"You need matches or a lighter. Do you have either?"

"No. I have a spear and a Spirits bottle." The big barbarian knelt. "I thought about this a lot, so I want to test it."

The warrior drew two small items from his belt and struck one against the other above the torch. Sparks flew and the torch lit instantly.

"It works! This one is steel," he said as he held up a small metal rod. "And this must be flint."

Takara leaned on her spear. "You better throw that torch in the water." She scanned the line of dunes. "We don't want to attract monsters."

"Okay," Tyler said. He waved the torch back and forth. "I never paid attention to that before."

Takeus grabbed the torch and plunged it into the wet sand at the water's edge. She handed the smoking stump back. "Do you have anything made of steel?"

"My belt buckle. I think it's steel. It isn't gold colored. It's metal color."

"Okay, so you need to find a flint rock."

"What do they look like?"

"Hold on, I'll wiki it." While Takeus stood still, Tyler wandered into the surf where three figures stood. The stone creature on the left was long and serpent like, with multiple heads on long necks, and mouths full of fangs, and bare breasts. The monster on the right was massively fat, bent over to vomit after gorging himself. Caught between the two was a petite, beautiful woman with a slender waist, and delicate scales along her forearms and calves. Her hair hung to the small of her back, and it was tangled with leaves like seaweed. Her mouth was open in a scream as one of the serpent's heads clamped its teeth down on her bare shoulder.

"It's a mercy she was turned to stone before they ate her," Tak said as she joined him. Cold saltwater swirled above the thongs of her sandals.

"I guess." Tyler shook himself and walked back up the beach. "Did you find flint?"

"Yes, they're rocks that are usually gray, and are fine grained and very hard. If you break one the edges are super sharp. People used to make arrowheads and knives out of them. If you strike it against steel and sparks come off, then it's flint."

"But how do I find one?"

Tak shrugged. "I'm not sure. I guess you could pick up gray rocks and hit them against your belt buckle." Tak raked her spear along the statue of the fat creature. No sparks ignited. "I guess this isn't flint. Maybe we should focus on how I can find you?"

Tyler whirled around. "Are you looking for me?"

"Yes. I'm in Silver City." Takara watched the over muscled barbarian leap in the air.

"That's awesome. Thanks, Takeus of Thebes. Thanks!"

Tak waved her hands. "Okay, okay. Let's figure this out. Where are you now?"

"Lost."

"Okay, what are you doing?"

"I spent all day walking. I followed the stream to get to the road, but I can't find the road. Now I'm under a tree near the top of a mountain because it's night time."

"Good, that's smart. What can you see?"

"Some other hills, and trees and stuff. It's really dark here."

"Can you see a road or lights from houses or anything?"

"No."

"Is there something special that stands out near you? Like a big canyon, or a dam, or a bridge?"

"No. It all looks the same." The tall warrior threw his torch at the wall of the lighthouse. "How can you find me if I don't know where I am?"

"Okay, we have to conserve your notebook's battery. After you leave *Lair*, turn off the computer. In the morning try to find some flint. Then go up on top the highest hill around you and light a fire." Takeus looked up at the lighthouse. "A signal fire, just like the lighthouse. That way the police and I can find you."

Tyler shook his head. "If I light a fire Silas will see it."

"Tyler, who is Silas?" Tak asked.

"A bad man. He told everyone to jump off the cliff and when I didn't, he chased me. He has creepy purple eyes."

"Do you think he's still chasing you?"

"Yeah."

"Are you sure?"

"Today when I was climbing the mountain I looked back and I saw a man. He was following me. It has to be Silas."

"Why do you think that?"

"Because everyone else I know is dead."

* * *

Chapter 27
New Mexico, USA
Day 6

In the hotel in Silver City, Tak shut her laptop and sat back against the headboard. She squeezed her burning eyes shut for a moment, and then put her shoes back on.

She went down the hall and knocked on Shoda and Jiro's door.

Jiro opened it immediately. He had his cell phone pressed to his ear. His eyes were swollen and red.

"Just a minute." He held one hand over the phone. "What?"

Takara stood in the doorway. "Is that your family?"

He nodded. "Shoda's sound asleep. You want me to wake him?"

"No. I talked to Tyler online. He's under a tree out in the wilderness. I don't think we can wait until morning to--"

"He's in a tree? What is he, a monkey? This guy is ridiculous. I can't believe you fell for his scam."

"If you don't believe there's a boy in trouble, then why did you come? Never mind. Talk to your family. I'm going to the police." Tak shut the door harder than she meant to. The doors to the rooms on either side shook.

Tak went downstairs, the car keys jingling in her hand. The lot was full of cars but no people. Although she rarely drove in Tokyo, driving in Silver City at night was easy. Her laptop rested on the seat next to her to display the route she needed.

She found Cooper Street, and pulled into the Grant County Sheriff's Department. Tak smoothed her hair, pushed her glasses up and went inside. The foyer was well lit; a deputy stood behind a desk stirring a cup of coffee. Tak noticed the cup said Black Mesa Coffee and smiled.

"Can I help you, ma'am?"

"Yes. My name is Takara Murakami. I arrived today from Japan. I need to find a boy named Tyler Burroughs. I believe he is in danger."

The deputy nodded. He was tall, taller than Tak by at least four inches, with long, corded arms burnt brown by the sun. "Perhaps you'd better sit down and explain."

Takara sat and folded her hands so he wouldn't see her twisting her fingers.

The deputy wrote on a yellow legal pad. "You said the boy's name is Tyler Burroughs? Okay. Do you have an address?"

"No, sir."

"Phone number?"

"No, sir."

"That's all right, we have a directory to look up his parents. How old is this boy?"

"Ten."

"What's the nature of the situation?" He held the pencil ready.

"I believe the child's parents are involved in a cult group that intends suicide."

The deputy's lower lip disappeared beneath his mustache and he chewed for moment. "All right. When will this suicide take place?"

"I think it already has."

The deputy blinked. "Ma'am, I'm confused. Are you reporting a homicide?"

"Homicide? I don't know that word."

"A murder?"

Takara sat forward. "No, I mean, I don't know. Tyler is alive. I think his parents are not. They told him they were getting on a spaceship but they jumped off a cliff. He ran away into the desert or forest."

The deputy tapped his chin with the pencil. "So we have a possible suicide, plus a missing child." He nodded. "How did you come to find out about this?"

"I met the boy online." Takara watched the deputy's eyebrows rise. "In a game. The boy was frightened. He told me his parents and their group were leaving on a spaceship." She took a breath. "I went to the police in Tokyo, where I live. Then I spoke with an officer in Crime Prevention, and he agreed to contact the police here in America. But it was taking too long and the boy is lost, so I came here to ask you to find him."

The deputy nodded. Takara noticed his nametag read 'Kane.' "Deputy Kane, this boy is lost. He used his father's notebook computer to contact me, but when the battery runs out, he will have no way to do so."

Kane stared at her for a long moment. “Okay.” He swiveled his chair to his computer. Tak couldn’t see the screen from where she sat. A moment later his fingers stopped typing and he looked up. “We don’t have a Mr. and Mrs. Burroughs in our computer for Grant County, but they might have moved here recently or not have a phone. There’s folks living in trailers out in the desert that don’t show up in the database.”

He twirled a pencil between his fingers. “Are you sure about all this? I mean, are you sure this isn’t a man pretending to be a boy? We’ve had inmates in prisons try that sort of thing. Or perverts at home. Has he asked you for money or to meet him?”

“I told him I would come and find him.” Tak bit her lip. “Tyler is real. I know it.”

“Hmm. And where is he now, since you said you spoke to him online after he ran away from his parents?”

“He doesn’t know. He is lost. They lived near Silver City. Then they went into the wilderness with their group to a tall cliff, and Tyler ran away.”

Tak’s eyes burned and she wanted to stop and put some drops in, but she didn’t want to do it in front of the deputy.

“Did Tyler mention if his parents use drugs? Might be meth heads.”

“He did not say.”

Kane sat forward. “Do you have your laptop with you? We could contact him now.”

Tak nodded. “In my car. One minute, please.” She went to the car and retrieved it, powering it up as she walked inside. She sat back down. “I doubt he will be here because we agreed he must conserve his battery, but I’ll try.”

She put the laptop on the desk and Kane moved his chair to watch. In the background, Tak heard radios crackle and snatches of conversations between deputies.

She went to the *Lair of the Hydra* homepage and pointed at the search feature. “Normally we could look for him here, to see if he is logged on, but the game is ending and maintenance is not performed.”

Kane looked blank, so Tak logged in and moments later Takeus of Thebes stood beneath the lighthouse, his spear and shield ready.

"This is *Lair of the Hydra*. The game where we meet."

"How come he doesn't just Facebook like everyone else? Heck, my granny Facebooks."

"Tyler's parents disabled many of the computer's functions." Tak pointed at the lighthouse. "We meet here."

"Your, uh, character appears to be male."

Takara nodded. "Oh, yes. Many people play as different races or genders."

Kane nodded. "So is it possible that Tyler is pretending to be something he isn't? Is it possible that he is a man, not a boy, and that he is not lost?"

Takara breathed out. "It is possible. But I do not believe it is the case."

"Okay. I see some statues and water and such, but no Tyler."

"No, he is not here."

"Yeah. Thank you for showing me that." He scooted his chair back around his desk. "Here's what we'll do. When my lieutenant arrives in the morning, I'll talk to him about it. He'll talk to the Sheriff and we'll call around to the Silver City PD and the Gila Rangers and the Border Patrol."

"Oh! Gilas. Tyler mentioned them. I saw Gila Forest on the map of this area. He must be there. We should search."

Kane put his palms up. "Let's hold our horses. First we'll see about locating his house, and we'll send somebody out to talk to them. If no one is home, we'll look wider."

"Can't we start now?"

"Ma'am, you need to understand a few things. The Grant County Sheriff's Department has 18 people in our Traffic and Patrol Division. Have you looked at the size of Grant County on the map?"

"It is big."

"Yup, it is big. The Silver City Police have about 35 people. I don't know how many Rangers are stationed at all of the parks around here, but I know the Gila National Forest is 3.3 million acres. That's huge. Before we rouse all available hands to look for Tyler, we need to be sure he exists. If we determine he does exist, we'll find him. We'll get the Border Patrol to help--they're good at finding people in the wilderness. But we need to do this step by step."

Takara opened her mouth, closed it, and stood. She bowed. "Thank you for your efforts."

Kane stood and made an awkward, reciprocal bow. "Are you staying here in town?"

"The Holiday Inn Express."

"Okay, I'll call you tomorrow. Thank you for bringing this to our attention."

"Thank you." Takara walked to the car. When she sank into the seat, she shut her eyes. The drive back to the hotel took all of her energy. The moment she was inside her room she flopped on the bed and slept.

* * *

Chapter 28
New Mexico, USA
Day 7

In the morning, Takara rolled over and sat up in her dark room at the Holiday Inn. When she stood, the floor swayed beneath her like she was walking the aisle on a plane.

She slid open the curtains and hissed as blinding white light filled the room. Tak closed the curtains and covered her eyes until she reached the bathroom.

After a shower, she took her old college backpack out of her luggage. Small charms swung from the zippers, and a few pins with funny phrases or environmental messages clung to the nylon shell.

She shook it out and sniffed it. It smelled like failure.

I should have finished. Two more years and I would have had my degree.

She zipped the bag shut, locked her room and went down the hall to knock on Shoda and Jiro's door.

On her second tap, the door snapped open.

"Morning!" Jiro was bright eyed and spike haired, dressed in a black T-shirt and green camouflage pants. "Let's go eat, then I'll show you the equipment place we found this morning."

Shoda came out of the restroom, drying his hands on a washcloth. He wore his stained mechanic's clothes from the shop and an Orix Blue Wave baseball cap. "Morning, Tak."

As the three walked downstairs to the parking lot, Takara asked, "What is this place you found?"

"An equipment store. It has surplus military goods and knowledgeable clerks. And guns!" Jiro spread his arms. "Lots of guns."

"Jiro, we need tents and sleeping bags, not machine guns."

"I bought a machete!"

"What?"

"Yeah, it's a beauty." Jiro smiled. "I hid it in my room. We'll get it before we leave for the forest. It's okay. I told them I'm a security guard back home."

Takara looked over her shoulder at Shoda.

Shoda shrugged. "I bought a walking stick."

"Not you, too." They marched across the parking lot. Takara squinted. The sun always seemed brighter with her contact lenses in. She slipped behind the wheel of the rental car. "Okay, we'll go to this store you found, but coffee first."

* * *

Border Patrol Agent Sam DeWitt looked through his windshield and muttered. Fat black clouds hung in the sky and he smelled rain in the morning air. Usually the storms didn't come until the afternoon.

He drummed his fingers on the steering wheel. "If I stop for a breakfast burrito, by the time I get there it'll be raining. Damn it."

His stomach rumbled as he passed the restaurant, but DeWitt forced himself not to turn off.

"Twenty-two pounds to go. Twenty-two."

On the plus side, the temperature dropped to something less than frying hot. The air blowing in through the window almost felt cool, even though the back of his shirt was plastered to the vinyl seat.

DeWitt shifted around to get comfortable and continued north on Highway 15. A mile or more ahead a thin blue rope of lightning arced between two clouds, and then ricocheted down to the ground.

The hair on the back of DeWitt's neck stood up. "This is a great idea. I could have called the Rangers, but no, I had to get out of the office just to look at some abandoned cars. Good thinking."

He slowed down so he wouldn't miss the left turn onto the dirt trail numbered 579. His vehicle dropped down off the lip of the road, and DeWitt tapped the brakes. He bounced along the rutted road and watched lightning play over the ridges north and west.

"Wild Horse Mesa. Okay, should be right up here."

After two miles of jostling, the rough road played out and he could see the rear end of a line of vehicles several hundred yards up ahead. DeWitt stopped the truck, set the brake and switched off the ignition.

The air was thick outside the truck, but the rain still held back. DeWitt reached across the seat for his Gore-Tex jacket, but then tossed it back in. It was rain proof, but hot.

Thanks to the clouds it was dark enough for him to remove his sunglasses. He tucked one stem in his front shirt pocket and hiked through the loose sand and rocks toward the vehicles.

At 25 yards from the rearmost vehicle, a green minivan, DeWitt's hand dropped down and unsnapped his holster without any conscious thought. He took another five steps, stopped and looked around.

He wasn't certain, but the vehicles seemed like they hadn't moved in a while. Maybe days. He turned and looked back. The tracks leading in were blurry, like they'd been rained on and wind swept. DeWitt squinted at footprints around the vehicles.

One hand on the butt on his gun, DeWitt walked along the side of the van and used its side mirrors to examine the inside of the vehicle. It was empty.

He moved up and checked the compact Honda ahead of the minivan. "Empty." He followed the line of cars, and all eight were empty.

What foot tracks he could make out led west.

DeWitt stopped and rolled his big shoulders to loosen his neck. "This is weird."

The wind picked up, carrying dust across the tops of the vehicles and into his face. DeWitt blinked and spat a mouthful of grit. He thought about a mouthful of burritos and winced.

All of the vehicles were unlocked. Three had their keys still in them, five didn't. There was no sign or smell of alcohol or drugs. DeWitt had been in law enforcement long enough to have a feel for vehicles. The cars weren't kids' cars, they were family cars. He could tell by the litter and the car seats and the sippy cups tucked into the storage areas.

"It's like they came out here for a picnic and...what?" DeWitt put his hands around his mouth and yelled, "Hey, Border Patrol."

No response.

DeWitt studied the wilderness. The back of his neck itched and he loosened his pistol in its holster. After a minute of searching the area, he shrugged and followed the tracks west.

It appeared the people had moved as a group. DeWitt noticed some shoe kid-sized prints among the larger ones and continued thinking, "Picnic."

He hiked down from the mesa, wondering what the people had been up to. "I've heard of looking for the perfect spot, but this is quite a walk with kids."

As he continued to march west, a fat, lukewarm drop of rain spattered the back of his neck and ran down under his collar. The big lawman flinched.

A thousand raindrops followed. DeWitt cursed himself for not bringing the Gore-Tex jacket, or a hat. He began to turn back toward his truck, but looked down at the tracks. A hard rain would wash what was left of them away and he would lose the trail.

"Damn it. I should have stopped for burritos."

He pushed into a fast march, following the melting tracks. The rain fell harder. After a mile he dropped down into a dry streambed. While he crunched across the stones, DeWitt saw the water begin to rise and flow faster.

In a storm, the rain could fill a dry creek bed quickly enough to form a rushing wall of water and debris. He knew that every year in the West someone drowned when caught in a stream, so DeWitt hurried to scramble up and out of the arroyo.

"Coming back might not be so easy."

He pushed on. Raindrops thumped the dirt and washed the tracks away, but DeWitt saw that the group had followed a rough trail west.

The incline increased and half a mile later he began to work his way up Horse Mountain. The elevation changed from 4,000 feet to something like 6,500. DeWitt tried to picture the map in his mind, but the rain distracted him and made him keep moving.

"Okay, they went for a picnic on Horse Mountain. Now where in the heck are they?"

DeWitt followed a switchback up the slope, walking slower and breathing harder by the minute. Finally he stopped and leaned on a rock and took deep breaths. The rain soaked his eyebrows and ran down into his eyes. He blinked and tried to sort out the tracks on the ground as they deteriorated.

The tracks turned away and he followed them out to a level area near a steep drop. The wind swirled here, and DeWitt ducked when lightning crackled in the canyon below.

Footprints formed a rough circle where people might have milled, talking, and then the prints led in a straight line toward the cliff.

DeWitt followed the prints, but the rain and wind in the exposed spot had washed most all of the indentations away. He looked left and right, then took two long steps toward the edge.

Conscious of the rain softening the ground, he eased out further and peered over the edge. Rain poured into his eyes and he wiped them with his hands, but it was hard to keep them open long enough to focus.

Eighty or a hundred feet down he saw a jumble of boulders--stones the size of television sets and couches. He spotted something, a flash of color among the rocks. DeWitt blinked and leaned out a little more. His sunglasses slipped from his pocket and fell.

He grabbed at the glasses, tipped and fought for balance.

DeWitt bent his knees and sat down hard to avoid falling.

"Damn it." He stood and wiped cold mud from the seat of his uniform pants. "Oh, this is just great." He slung the mud from his hands.

The rain thinned enough so that he could breathe without sucking up a mouthful of water. DeWitt looked for the color he'd seen on the rocks and squinted.

He connected the bright blue cloth to a rock, and then to an L-shaped object. A leg. The leg connected to a body. DeWitt leaned back and took in the picture. Bodies littered the rocks at the base of the cliff. Lots of bodies.

He turned and hustled back down Horse Mountain.

* * *

Chapter 29
New Mexico, USA
Day 7

Tyler hiked along the stream. The morning was hot, but after climbing a mountain the day before, the hills he crossed were almost easy.

The boy stopped and hunkered down near the top of each crest to study the trail behind him. He didn't see Silas, but Tyler knew the creepy man could be just one ridge behind him.

He stopped to drink and refill the Spirits bottle and saw that the stream disappeared up the side of another mountain. And the peak looked higher than the last one.

Tyler sat to re-lace his Spiderman sneakers and then started to climb.

Clouds gathered like ants around a dead bird. One moment it was sunny and hot, and the next it was half dark and the temperature dropped. The higher Tyler climbed and the darker it became, the more the cool air revived him.

The boy looked back often, always watchful, but the trees grew too dense to see more than a few hundred steps in any direction.

Tyler rubbed his empty stomach, but fear drove him to put as much distance between himself and Silas as he could.

He kept his head down, watching his own knees and feet as they churned uphill. The trees thinned and he passed into a jumble of rocks. The rocks were large enough to force him to scramble over them, which was difficult with his hands full.

Tyler tied his sport coat pack to his belt and climbed with one hand while the other held his spear. He slipped and barked his knee. As he sat hissing and rubbing the spot, he realized the summit was near. Energized, he surged up the last two dozen steps and stood on a level area at the top.

Legs trembling, Tyler sat and guzzled from the Spirits bottle. Clouds collected above him. As he drank he noticed something shiny in the brown grass.

Tyler crawled forward. He pushed dead grass aside and found a metal disc the size of a dinner plate.

"New Mexico Geodetic Survey. Diablo Mountain. 8731." The first four words ran in a circle around the disc, with the mountain's name and the numbers inside them. There was a triangle with a dot in its center carved in the middle of the disc.

The metal plate was the first manmade thing he'd found since the Spirits bottle.

Tyler touched the disc. He wondered when the disc was put in the ground.

He didn't know what 'Geodetic' or 'Diablo' meant, but the rest was obvious. He touched the triangle and pulled his hand back. The triangle almost seemed a religious symbol, like a cross or a star.

The boy sat with his feet to either side of the marker while the sky grew dark. He touched the triangle again, and pushed down on it like a button, but the plate didn't pop up and reveal the head of a robot or open a door to a secret fort.

He struck his belt buckle against it. Not because he thought it would make a fire, but just because he couldn't think of anything else to try.

The air around him was heavy and moist and he knew it would rain any minute. Tyler pushed the dead grass back over the marker and ran to get his pack.

Lightning tickled the range of hills he'd crossed earlier that morning.

He pushed hard down the far side of the mountain, the threat of Silas hovering in his mind. It began to rain. Despite the thick, interwoven aspens, firs and spruce trees, the drops made their way through to hit him. The boy hunched over to protect the computer.

Tyler puzzled over the marker, but somehow just the idea that someone else had once been there reassured him.

His stomach growled again, and a headache built behind his eyes. Tyler's legs shook as he went down the side of the mountain.

The rain drove through the trees and hit his back. He tucked the notebook under his shirt and bent forward to keep it dry.

The wind slung the rain sideways, stinging his face. Tyler stood panting.

The boy looked over his shoulder to see if Silas came over the mountaintop, but the rain was too heavy to see any distance. He shook water from his eyes and searched for shelter.

A narrow deer trail took him through a thick patch of trees. Tyler watched his feet to avoid falling, but when the wind gusted into his face, he turned away from the trail.

And saw a cave.

Tyler stumbled forward, too tired to ninja. The entrance was slightly taller than his head, and wide as a car door.

Once inside and out of the storm, he followed the procedure he'd established at the first cave, sniffing the air for wet bears or Gila monsters. The cave passed the sniff test, so he threw rocks, one after the other, at all angles around the cave. Some bounced off the walls, others sailed a long way before making any noise.

He trailed his left hand along the wall and poked the dark with the spear in his right. Sand had blown into the entrance, but after eight steps the ground became rocky. Tyler threw three more rocks, and by accident, one juniper berry.

If one of the rocks hit a bear it would roar. Any monster would. Except maybe a snake. But even a snake will rattle its tail to tell you to back off.

With the computer safe inside the cave, Tyler went back into the rain. He collected several armloads of brush, and covered the entrance to camouflage it.

* * *

Chapter 30
New Mexico, USA
Day 7

The Silver City Surplus store had a glass front with flyers advertising gun shows and concealed weapons classes and pictures of camouflaged men kneeling next to dead mule deer.

The man behind the counter wore a gray beard and sported faded green chevrons on his muscular forearms. He nodded to the Japanese travelers. "Back already? I set aside three sleeping bags for you. The price is right and they're better than what you'll find at Wal-Mart."

Takara maneuvered between racks of orange safety vests and bottles of deer urine until she reached a long counter that ran the length of the store.

The proprietor stood behind the counter, cleaning a bolt-action rifle. Behind him on a desk, a portable radio played softly, and a muted television was tuned to a news channel. Takara looked through the glass counter and gasped.

Guns. Dozens and dozens of handguns. She stepped back and realized the wall was black with long guns. Rifles, shotguns, black and brown and even a few stocks that were green.

"So many." Takara blinked. She'd played online games involving firearms, and had sold many virtual guns for real money, but she'd never held or fired a real gun in her life.

The storekeeper squinted at her. "They don't have stores like this in Japan, huh? I was stationed in Okinawa for a while and I remember." He smiled. "I explained to your friends this morning that I can't sell you one, and even if I could, I don't think you could get it through Japanese customs without a big fuss."

"It's all right. We're not here to buy a gun. We need camping equipment for the Gila National Forest," she said.

"Oh?" The man nodded. "You know, I told your pal this morning that it's a forest, not a jungle, so he won't need a machete, but he was determined to buy it. For a minute, I was worried he was gonna put on a hockey mask and go look for some campers."

Takara stared. She had no idea what the man meant. "I would like to purchase sleeping bags, small tents to carry, matches, and compass. Do you have those?"

"We sure do. Let's get you started." The man limped around the counter. As he moved past her, he looked up. "You sure you're not Korean? Never seen a Jap girl so tall."

Takara smiled. "All Japanese. Jiro, Shoda."

The young men looked up from a glass case of pocketknives.

Takara waved them over. "Come pick out packs. Sir, do we need boots?"

The man piled three puffy sleeping bags on the counter and looked down at her flimsy sneakers. "Yes, ma'am, you sure do."

Over the next hour, a few customers drifted in to buy ammunition or ask directions to a fishing creek. Takara tried on several boots and settled on a black, high-topped pair that made her ankles look slender.

The old soldier sold them a map, and took the time to show them how to read it and use the Silva compass Tak bought.

He also handed Tak three shiny, silver packets, each about the size of a cell phone. "When you start out on the trail, put one of these in your pocket. It's a space blanket. It'll keep you alive, and you can use it to signal for help if you have to. For the size, the weight, and the price, there's not many things more useful to carry."

Tak examined the packet and nodded. "Thank you."

After he rang up their purchases on Takara's credit card, the old man helped them carry the gear out to the car. "I never tell folks their business, but on your way in to the Gila, check with the park rangers and tell them where you'll be camping. It's a big wilderness out there and not everyone you'll meet is friendly."

* * *

Takara sat with the Gila National Forest map spread across her bed. The landline on the nightstand rang, a harsh klaxon sound.

"Yes?"

"Are you awake?"

"Yes, Jiro. I'm awake. Do you want to get lunch?"

Takara stared at the handset. "Jiro?"

Thirty seconds later someone knocked on the door.

Takara squinted through the peephole, saw Jiro's spiked hair and opened the door. Jiro bounded into the room. He wore his new boots and his pack, with the machete dangling in a scabbard from his belt. "Are you ready?"

Tak shook her head. "I'm reading the map. We need to plan. Where's Shoda."

"In our room. Doing pushups." Jiro mimed the exercise. "We need to get moving! Let's go find this kid before he's eaten by weasels." He bounced up and down and Tak heard water slosh in his canteens. "I'm ready to go. Let's get this started."

Tak folded her long legs under her. She held up the map. "Jiro, the Gila National Forest is huge. Three point three million acres. We don't know where to start. We should wait until sundown when Tyler logs into *LOTH* and then he can tell me more details about his loca--"

The phone clanged again. Tak looked at Jiro, shrugged, and picked up the handset.

"Yes?"

"Ms. Murakami?"

"Yes."

"This is Deputy Kane. Miss, we've found a crime scene with over twenty bodies. It's possible Tyler Burroughs is among them. If you are willing, we'd like you to come down here."

Tak sank onto the edge of the bed. "Twenty bodies? But Deputy, I've never met Tyler in person. Only online."

"We realize that, but you know his age, gender, and so forth. You might know more than you think," Kane said. "And if we don't find him among the bodies, it may convince you that Tyler Burroughs doesn't exist. I think someone is playing a cruel hoax here, or maybe even planning another crime."

"Okay." Takara took a pen and pad from the nightstand. "Please give me directions."

* * *

Chapter 31
New Mexico, USA
Day 7

Takara shoved her sleeping bag into the trunk of the rental car. Jiro passed her items one at a time. "We have to go now?"

"Yes, Jiro, now." She pushed his backpack inside. "Why?"

"You said we'd get lunch."

"Ten minutes ago you couldn't wait to run into the forest and now you want lunch?"

"I'm hungry. Besides, the boy's not going anywhere."

Tak turned and stood eye to eye with him. "That's not funny. Tyler is alive."

Jiro stepped back. "Okay." He went around the side of the car and dropped into the back seat.

Shoda came out of the hotel office. "My English is still pretty good considering I haven't studied since high school. I asked directions to the highway and understood most of what the lady at the desk said."

"Good," Takara said. She handed him a page from a hotel notepad. "Here are the directions Kane gave me. You can navigate." She got behind the wheel.

They drove north out of town and up Highway 15. Takara turned on the radio, but then flipped it back off. "Look for our turn. He told me 579."

Shoda raised his sunglasses and squinted at the road map. "We should be close. A kilometer is six tenths of a mile, right?"

"I guess." Takara spotted a big sedan with a rack of lights on top, idling on the shoulder of the road. Deputy Kane stepped out of the car and waved. Tak pulled over and lowered her window.

Kane nodded. "It's a ways up this road. Follow me. Pull over when I do."

"Yes, sir."

The deputy folded himself back into the cruiser, spun the wheel and drove west along a rough road, trailing dust.

Shoda put on his sunglasses. "Is he the cop you talked to before?"

"Yes. He is a very serious man," she said.

"He looks like a cowboy," Jiro said from the back seat. He put his machete on the floorboard. "I wonder if he's ever killed a man?"

"Jiro!"

"I'm just curious. You know how Americans love to shoot people," Jiro said.

"Don't you ask him any such questions," Tak said.

"Damn, Tak, you're no fun." Jiro sat back in the seat.

Dust billowed from Kane's rear tires and Tak dropped back a few car lengths. The ruts in the road made the small Nissan bounce. Takara wanted to slow down but she was afraid of losing Kane's cruiser in the dust.

Finally his brake lights flashed and Kane pulled over. Takara parked behind him. As the dust settled she noticed other vehicles--eight civilian cars, plus five law enforcement and one ambulance.

They followed Deputy Kane on foot up the rough trail. Takara's new boots pinched. A second deputy walked past with a fat roll of yellow tape.

Kane marched up to a tall, slope-shouldered man and cleared his throat. The man turned. "Oh, Kane. Are these the witnesses?"

Kane nodded. "This is Agent DeWitt. Border Patrol." The tall deputy waved the Japanese forward. "They aren't witnesses, but this young lady may have been in contact with one of the victims. I hope she can identify him."

DeWitt frowned. "You sure you want to take her up there? It's bad. Worse than anything I've ever seen. Maybe we should wait until the medical examiner cleans them up. Or identify by their driver's licenses."

"The victim she may know is a young boy, age ten. He won't have credit cards or picture ID. She thinks he's alive and lost in the Gila. If he is, we need to know. And if he isn't, well, she'll have to deal with the nightmares," Kane said.

DeWitt blinked. "Okay, then. After you cross the creek bed there's a cut to your left that takes you to the foot of the cliff. I marked it with tape."

"Thanks." Kane tugged the brim of his hat down, and then led them around the abandoned vehicles. Takara looked in the windows of the cars she passed and wondered which one was the Burroughs'.

Kane set a fast pace, and Takara stretched her long legs to keep up. Dust swirled around the trail, coating her sunglasses. The heat soaked into her. Shoda panted and spoke in Japanese. “I wish we’d brought our packs. I’m thirsty already.”

Jiro examined the surrounding hills. “Maybe we’ll see a bear.”

“Jiro.”

“Bears are scavengers. If there’s bodies, then maybe a bear--”

“Jiro!”

Kane looked back, but kept walking. They worked their way down off the mesa into a shady saddle of land. Later they crossed a dried-up stream and hiked until Kane veered left at a piece of yellow tape hanging limp in the hot air.

“That’s Horse Mountain,” Kane said, pointing at the modest peak on their right.

Takara sweated, but it dried immediately. The heat was far worse than anything she’d dealt with in Japan. Her boots squeaked and cut into her ankles.

She watched Kane ahead of her, and eyed the gun on his hip.

I wonder if he has shot anyone?

The land was wilder than she’d anticipated. More brown than green, and riddled with a 1,000 canyons and a 100 mountains. It was vast, and hot and still. Quiet. Hugely quiet. Like standing in an empty theater.

Jiro muttered to Shoda as they hiked, but Tak did not listen. She focused on where she put her feet. And she watched for wild animals.

The trail to the base of the cliff was more up than down. Although the ground was broken and rocky, enough cops had tramped back and forth all morning to make the route easy to see.

They followed Kane up a series of switchbacks, some narrow enough to make Takara nervous. Half an hour of steady hiking left the Japanese gasping, but other than red cheeks, Kane appeared unperturbed.

The ground leveled out and Kane stopped. Tak laced her fingers together and put them on top of her head until the stitch in her ribs eased off. Shoda sat on a rock and mopped his face with the tail of his shirt. Jiro sniffed the air.

“This is the western side of Horse Mountain.” Kane pointed up. “From that point to the ground is about a hundred feet, give or take.” He ran a callused hand across his chin. “The smell is pretty bad.”

Takara scented nothing as they moved forward, then the wind shifted and the stench hit her like a wave. She gagged. Shoda held his sleeve over his mouth.

"We've found 24 bodies so far. Mind where you step and don't touch anything," Kane said.

They pushed into the invisible wall of rot. Takara's eyes watered. She swallowed hard. At first she didn't see anything but a jumble of boulders beneath a vertical rock face.

Then she spotted flashes of color. A scrap of blue. A bit of white.

The bodies lay scattered like broken toys. Limbs askew. Clothing torn. Blood dried to a thick, brown crust. Flies swarmed. Their wings created a steady drone.

Kane stood by a flat, desk-shaped boulder. "If you can check the children? There's no need to look at the adults. Coyotes and buzzards have been at them."

Takara followed the deputy from child to child. The children were well dressed, but limp and dirty and pale. Kane slapped insects away, but they only moved on to the next corpse.

When she staggered past a little girl in a blue dress, Takara had to lean on a rock and take shallow breaths until the nausea passed. She thought back to a newspaper photograph she'd seen a week after the earthquake. It had taken her a long moment to realize the picture was of her collapsed apartment building, and the people on the stretchers were her dead mother and father. And her little brother, Akira.

Sweat ran under her long hair and down the back of her shirt, but Takara shivered.

Kane stopped. Takara looked up. They were outside the ring of corpses.

"Miss, did you see him?"

"What? No, I don't think so. There were no boys his age. Tyler is ten years old. There was one boy, but he was small. Seven maybe, or eight. I don't know..."

"It's all right. Once we've sorted the families we'll figure it out. The way they landed on top of each other left them all mixed up. Everyone is dressed in their Sunday best, but we found two adults dressed like hikers. We're looking into that, too." Kane spat. "I'm sorry you had to see that."

Takara nodded. Shoda waited a few steps away, taking deep breaths.

Jiro stood in the shade, staring up at the cliff edge.

Takara sighed. “I’d like to go back to my car now.”

She took a step and stumbled. Shoda grasped her arm. “Are you okay?”

Tak nodded. “It brings back a lot of bad memories, you know?”

Shoda held her arm and they walked back to the car together.

* * *

Chapter 32
New Mexico, USA
Day 7

In the half light of the cave entrance, Tyler powered up the notebook computer. The familiar green field and blue sky filled the screen. He turned the computer away from him and directed its light to the dark rear of the cave. The glow didn't extend much beyond the range of his spear, but it was better than nothing. Tyler edged along, sniffing and listening and watching for holes.

It was hard to hold the computer and probe with the spear. Tyler moved as quietly as he could. A bear didn't leap from the darkness. A horde of zombies didn't surge up out of a hole in the floor.

Tyler tilted the laptop up to light the ceiling in case a Gila monster was waiting to drop on his back. Something on the floor caught his eye and he looked down at a long rock. The rock wasn't shaped like the other loose stones.

The boy knelt and set the laptop on the floor. The curious stone was shaped like a narrow leaf. Or a knife. He touched it. The edges were scalloped and sharp. Tyler picked up the sharp rock.

Three pale sticks lay around the stone knife. It was hard to see color in the dark cave, but the sticks looked dusty yellow gray. Two larger sticks ran away from the knife. Tyler swiveled the computer.

A skull stared at him with hollow eyes.

Tyler kicked backward, fell on his rear, and scrambled away. When he reached the cave entrance he stopped. With the storm clouds it was almost as dark outside as inside.

His left hand was wet where it held the stone.

Tyler licked a warm drop off his thumb. *Blood.* He opened his hand. *It is a knife. A stone knife.*

The boy pulled his belt out of the loops. He slapped the side of the knife against his belt buckle.

Sparks flew. Hot flickering motes so brief it was like he imagined them.

He hit the buckle again.

Sparks.

Tyler smiled, then realized he'd left the computer and his spear back with the skeleton. He held the knife out in front of him.

It's just a dead person. You're a ninja.

The boy whispered his mantra as he crept back to the computer. He recovered his spear first, and then angled the computer's light for a better look.

The skeleton wasn't very big. In fact, it looked about his size. Tyler shuddered and hurried back to the entrance, the notebook tucked under one arm. His knees shook.

Tyler shut the computer off, wrapped himself in his sport coat and sat against the wall, turning the knife over in his hands. His hand bled from the cut, but he sucked on it for a minute and it stopped. He looked left out of the entrance and watched for Silas. He looked right, deep into the cave, and watched for monsters.

* * *

Deputy Kane led Takara and her friends back up the trail, past the tape marker and across the damp streambed. By the time he sighted the cars, Kane's mouth was dry.

While the young Japanese walked to their rental car, Kane fetched a warm bottle of Vitamin Water from his cruiser. The juice was hot and sweet. He drank it in sips and watched Agent DeWitt pace back and forth, talking on a cell phone.

Kane noticed the smear of mud across the rear of DeWitt's uniform and grinned. When DeWitt passed by, Kane said, "Must have been an interesting climb this morning."

DeWitt listened to the phone for a moment, snapped it shut and turned around. "I damn near got fried by lightning. Then my new sunglasses went over the cliff and I almost went with them. I missed breakfast and lunch. And now I can't get the chopper jockeys to take off."

Kane finished his drink and dropped the bottle into a plastic bag he kept on the floorboard of his cruiser. "What about the helicopter?"

DeWitt rubbed his red face with one hand. "We can't get a vehicle to the foot of the cliff, so I figured we could use a cable and a net attached to the helicopter to haul them out. Like a Coast Guard copter pulling someone out of the ocean."

Kane moved to the meager shade of a dead tree. “Makes sense. What’s the hold up?”

“The boys won’t fly. They say a storm is coming and it’s going to be a bad one. By the time they get the Blackhawk in the air and fly here, the edge of the storm will be closing in.”

“I guess we’ll just have to haul them out on stretchers.” Kane hoisted his pistol belt up. “That’ll be some work.”

DeWitt leaned on the dead tree. “I wonder if we could use horses? Or ATVs?”

“Most horses don’t care for the smell of dead people. We could round up some mules, but it might be easier to get hold of ATVs.”

DeWitt’s phone rang and he flipped it open, listened for a moment, said, “Yes, sir,” and closed it. “That was my boss--he’s ahead of us. They already loaded a flatbed with four ATVs and five stretchers. I have to go to Deming to pick it up. Might grab a dry uniform while I’m there, too.”

Kane smiled. “Why bother? It’ll be raining by the time you get back.” He looked over DeWitt’s shoulder and saw the Japanese girl pulling her pack straps over her shoulders. “I’ll see you when you get here.”

Kane started toward the Japanese, but stopped. “DeWitt, while you’re at it, how about hitting one of your federal databases for information on the boy?”

DeWitt stood with one boot in his vehicle. “Why, isn’t his family in the local listings?”

“Nope.” Kane nodded back toward Horse Mountain. “If he isn’t here and he isn’t there, it makes me wonder if Tyler Burroughs really exists.”

* * *

Chapter 33
New Mexico, USA
Day 7

While Takara tied her sleeping bag to the top of her backpack, Deputy Kane approached.

"There's a thunderstorm coming. You all going to look for him?" the deputy asked.

"Yes. Tyler told me he ran away from the cliff when his family jumped off. He may be nearby. Hiding. So we will look for him."

Kane took off his hat and wiped his forehead on his shirtsleeve. "Agent DeWitt is heading into Deming to pick up some all terrain vehicles. I asked him to search the federal databases while he's there."

Takara pushed several bottles of water into the bulging pack. "Thank you, Deputy Kane."

Kane watched Shoda and Jiro pointing at a map on Takara's laptop computer. The young men spoke rapidly in Japanese and Kane shook his head. "Miss, the Gila is no place for amateur hikers, but I can see you're determined to find this boy. Have you given any more thought to the possibility he doesn't exist?"

Takara pulled the laces of her right boot tight, and stood up. In her boots, she was almost as tall as the deputy. "Tyler is real. He is in danger. I must find him." She took a breath. "But we will be careful. I have a cellular telephone and a laptop with maps."

Kane bit his lip. "Cell service is irregular out there. Sometimes you get it, sometimes not. If you have trouble with the signal, climb up on top of a hill or a mountain. Anyplace high and you're more likely to get one. Please tell me you have a GPS."

"We could not avoid. I mean afford. We have a compass and map. The man in the shop showed us how to use them." Squinting at the deputy's face, Takara lowered her voice. "Are we not permitted to go?"

Kane put his hat and sunglasses back on. "No, this is America. You can do as you like even if it kills you." With that, the deputy walked away.

Takara watched him for a moment, noting the way the weight of his gun changed his gait. Then she turned to her friends and switched back to Japanese. “Are you ready?”

Shoda spread the United States Geological Survey map they’d bought that morning across the trunk of the Nissan. When Takara pinned the map with her hands, she felt the heat from the sun-baked metal lid.

Shoda pushed a broad finger across the map. “It’s less than three kilometers back to the top of Horse Mountain. We could start there and try to guess which way he might have gone.”

“How about lunch?” Jiro asked.

“What?”

“We should go back to town for lunch. I want tacos.”

Takara stared. “Jiro, we’re here to find a lost boy, not play tourist. What’s wrong with you?”

The spiky-haired fighter shrugged. “Nothing. I’m hungry.” He turned and marched west along the trail toward Horse Mountain.

Takara folded the map and stuck it in her pack. Shoda stepped close to her. “You ever notice how Jiro changes his mind a lot? He gets too excited about some things, and too negative about others.”

Takara shrugged. “Jiro is extreme about everything. Even his emotions.”

“I think Kyle is right. Jiro is manic depressive.”

“Before you said he was bipolar.”

“It’s the same thing,” Shoda said.

“Oh.” Tak watched Jiro troop up the trail. “I don’t know. Jiro’s not crazy.”

“I didn’t say he was. But we should keep an eye on him.” Shoda picked up his walking stick and swung onto the trail.

* * *

Tyler blew the lint off the juniper berries from his pocket, ate them, and drank the Spirits bottle dry.

He stashed the notebook behind a rock inside the cave, grabbed his spear, and hiked down to the stream. The rain continued, but the lightning had moved on.

As he pushed through the line of spruce trees, two mule deer stood up. The deer shook themselves, flicked their big ears, and trotted away.

Tyler watched them move, a pair of long, light brown blurs masked by the trees. They lifted their skinny legs and tossed their heads, and then they were gone.

His mouth watered.

He crouched in the bushes above the stream for a time, and when he was certain it was safe he slipped down for a long drink. After he'd refilled the bottle and ditched his shoes, he went into the current for lunch.

The first three tries brought nothing, and he wondered if the rain had sent all the fish to the bottom. But then he corralled a chunky fish by the bank and stabbed it with the spear. The strike only wounded the fish and it darted between his feet and zipped downstream. It took the boy another half an hour to catch two fish the size of his shoes.

Tyler gathered twigs and one small pinecone into the front of his shirt. He carried the two fish by their tails, and slipped back to his cave.

Inside, he rebuilt the branches hiding the entrance, and then piled the twigs he'd collected. He took off his belt, and slapped the edge of the flint knife against the buckle.

Sparks flew, winked, and disappeared.

He changed the angle, and tried again. The flint created plenty of sparks, but nothing caught. Tyler looked around, and then collected some smaller sticks from inside the cave, dry twigs the size of spaghetti noodles. He swung the knife.

A half dozen sparks bounced. One, just one, landed. A pencil thin stream of smoke rose up in the cool air of the cave.

Tyler smiled and fed the flame. A twig. A thicker twig.

A flicker, and then a hint of smoke rising and it was out. The fire died. Tyler frowned and reached for his belt.

He struck the flint and steel rapidly, raining sparks down onto the twigs. One caught and he leaned down and blew on the flame. It crept across to a second twig, and then a third.

The boy forced himself to feed the fire a bite at a time. When the flames were the size of cereal bowl, he pushed the pinecone in. It caught and burned fast. The heat touched his face and he reached for more fuel.

The flint knife cut heads, and tails and fins off with ease, but when he tried to scrape the skin away he mangled the fish. Tyler spread the middle sections of the fish across a green tree limb and held it above the fire, but the pieces fell through. He settled for arranging the loose bits on a bed of leaves and pushing them into the coals on one side of the fire.

When he couldn't wait any longer, he speared a fish chunk with a twig and popped it in his mouth. The outside was hot and smoky tasting, and the inside only warm, but it wasn't bloody.

Tyler ate his first cooked meal in the wilderness while the rain petered out and raced east.

Warm and full, he sat against the wall and examined his spear. He didn't need to keep the fire going, but he did. It was company of a sort.

Like the boy, the fire was always hungry. It fed. It breathed. It moved when the wind blew down off the mountain. It wasn't television, but Tyler found himself watching the flames.

The tip of his spear was as sharp as he could make the wood, but blunt to his touch. He shaved the end with the flint knife and cleared away the fish blood, but it was only a little sharper.

Tyler thought of Takeus throwing his magic spear at the zombies by the lighthouse. That spear had a bright metal tip. The boy reversed his spear and went to work with the knife.

He carved a socket into the blunt end, cutting away the wood a little at a time. He reversed the knife and pushed the handle into the socket. It wobbled, so he wrapped the end with long strands of tough, green grass and tied them in square knots.

The boy stood and brushed wood shavings from his pants. He hefted the spear with both hands, crouched and jabbed. He pictured a bear lumbering toward him. Tyler sidestepped and thrust.

The knife stayed in the socket.

Tyler crouched and threw dirt over the fire. Just before he smothered it completely, he thought of the skeleton. He wrapped a stout stick in dead grass and made a torch. He plunged it into the coals and waited it for it to light.

The torch burned much faster than the ones in *Lair of the Hydra*, so Tyler made two more. A forked branch with a pinecone and a clump of grass wedged between the limbs worked well enough for him to carry it deeper inside the cave to explore.

He reached the skeleton where he'd found the knife and stopped.

Is this person in Heaven? Or on a spaceship? Or is this it? Are they just dead, and I took their knife?

The boy took a long step over the skull and continued, torch high in his left hand, his spear in his right.

The floor rose under his feet as the cave tunneled up into the mountain. Despite the torch, the stone corridor was cold. A branch to his left narrowed and he squatted down to look, careful to keep the brand away from his face.

The short branch opened into a small cave with a high ceiling. Tyler pushed his spear ahead of him and ducked down. As soon as he was in the cave he stood and put his back to the wall.

It seemed just the sort of place a Gila monster would hide. Tyler imagined a massive, wet-skinned Gila monster curled up on a bed of bones, eyes shut, its tongue flicking out of its mouth to taste the air. Like a dragon in a story.

Tyler waved the torch.

Something glittered.

He edged forward.

More bones. A skull, bigger than his head. An adult. A rusted metal bucket that might have been a helmet. A long, red-black metal rod so rusted it looked as flimsy as cardboard.

Although his hands shook, Tyler stepped forward. The bones didn't look in the right order anymore, and he figured animals had played with them. And there was nothing he could salvage. He was afraid to touch the rusted items because they looked poisonous.

Tyler squeezed out of the passage and back to the main corridor. He looked to his right, but his torch was burning down, and his heart was pounding, so he went back to the entrance and sat.

He thought about the hollow-eyed skulls. Here, with the trees and the dwindling rain within arm's reach, the skeletons seemed weak and maybe sad. Tyler wondered how they came to the cave and what they did there, and how they died.

Did their families know what happened to them? Did their friends come to look for them? It looks like they each died alone, maybe sick and hungry or hurt.

Will I die in this cave? Die a lost, forgotten boy, like these unremembered dead?

In the half light of the cloudy afternoon sky, Tyler opened the notebook computer and logged into *Lair of the Hydra.*

* * *

Lair of the Hydra

The portal pulsed blue and Tyler stepped out onto the beach beneath the lighthouse. He darted in among the statues and stood still while he searched the hills and the sky for monsters.

It took him a moment to realize something was wrong. The sea oats on the dunes inland blew towards him. And yet the waves behind him were high, crashing hard onto the rocky shore.

The lighthouse was lit up, even though it was daytime, and the door stood ajar. Further along the coast toward the city, the water was as still as a pond.

Takeus was right, things are falling apart.

Tyler drew his sword and went inside the lighthouse and up the steps to the top of the tower. Takeus wasn't there, so Tyler decided to wait a while and hope the computer's battery didn't die.

He watched the waves. The patterns seemed wrong. Two waves, then four, and then nothing, utterly flat blue water. Something far out near the horizon broke the surface of the water, and Tyler caught a glimpse of scales, but the creature dove and Tyler wondered what he'd seen.

While he waited, Tyler went through his item inventory. He knew he was low on healing potions, and if monsters attacked before Takeus arrived, it might go badly.

Other than his sword and broken spear, he still had two healing potions, a bottle of Greek fire, flint and steel, a map of the caverns beneath Athens, a brass key, a scroll, three small rubies, and two torches.

Tyler knew time was slipping by and the notebook might fail. He couldn't wait much longer for Takeus, so Tyler tried to devise a way to leave the short warrior a message.

First he went down to the beach and wrote "Diablo Mountain" in the sand with his sword. He watched a fresh batch of waves assault the shore, and wrote the message a second time farther inland. Tyler nodded and walked back to the lighthouse. When he turned to shut the door, he saw that his messages had disappeared.

Tyler took a torch and tried to write on the outside wall of the lighthouse, but the torch didn't even mark the stone. He tried a dagger, but the dagger snapped in half.

Tyler went inside, shut the door and barred it, and stood under the light of a torch. He went back through his inventory and opened the scroll. The scroll was a single sentence--one of many clues characters had to collect in order to find the entrance to a maze on the island of Crete. Tyler had never been to Crete to attempt the quest.

He highlighted the text on the scroll and hit the backspace key. The text flickered and disappeared. He stared at the blinking cursor for a moment, then carefully pecked out "New Mexico Geodetic Survey.Diablo Mountain.8"

The cursor stopped. Tyler hit the keys but it wouldn't move further. "Not enough room."

A howl sounded from the beach below. Tyler looked over his shoulder and ran up the steps to the top room of the lighthouse. He typed again.

"NewMexicoGeodeticSurvey--"

The stone lighthouse shook. Tyler heard the oak door crack.

He typed faster. "--DiabloMountain8731." This time the message fit the scroll.

Grunts and heavy footsteps sounded from the stairs.

Tyler dropped the scroll near the door to the walkway and reached into his pack for his blue portal orb.

* * *

Chapter 34
New Mexico, USA
Day 7

Silas watched a lizard on a rock.

The lizard did not hurry. The reptile conserved its energy. But when it had to move, it moved quickly. A sudden strike, and a beetle twitched in its mouth.

Silas admired the reptile.

He finished his last can of beans-and-franks and drank stream water from a refilled bottle. He'd treated the water with purification tablets, and the liquid had an astringent quality.

Silas wondered what the bacteria in his stomach would do when they encountered the treated water. Would an epic war rage inside his intestinal tract? Thousands, if not millions, of organisms arrayed in battle. One side seeking the total destruction of the other. No truces, no diplomacy, no last minute mercies.

"The boy is dead," he murmured.

Somewhere between the horse hooves and the mountains, he'd lost the boy's tracks in the heavy rain. He'd circled, worked the area by spirals and pie-shaped quadrants, and stared at the map until his head hurt, but he'd lost the boy.

Stupid and out of his head with thirst, Tyler had probably stumbled over a rocky patch of ground and fallen into a ravine. Silas told himself that somewhere the boy lay senseless, dehydrated like an old apricot, dying in the heat.

Silas ground his teeth.

Reason said the result was the same whether it came from him or the careless indifference of nature. But it irked him.

It would be reassuring to see the corpse. Satisfying. He pictured the boy grown thin and weak from exposure to the burning sun and lack of food and water. A lifeless husk, like the bodies littering the ground at Jonestown. Litter. Something to be swept up.

Silas tossed the empty steel can away and opened a handy wipe. He inhaled the scent of lemon and alcohol as he cleaned his hands. It was time for discipline, no matter how bitter.

The compact man hiked east. Dark clouds formed a storm front behind him, but Silas didn't hurry. He decided to march to

Highway 15, and then hitchhike. Someone would stop, and Silas would persuade them to take him south to Silver City. And then he would get into his Jeep and leave the state.

As he walked alongside Turkey Creek, Silas reached a clear spot between the sand-scoured oaks and the pinon pines. A trail. But the trail ran north and south, and his goal was east.

Silas crossed the trail.

He looked down.

Shoeprints. Normal for a trail. A small shoeprint. A child's sneaker.

Silas froze.

The sand of the trail was loose, but the print was sharp, fresh. Not crumbled. He squatted next to it. The shoe left a spider web pattern. A spider web pattern with a capital 'S' at the big toe. Silas blinked.

A bigger shoeprint lay next to the mark. A hiking boot or a trail-running shoe--something with knobby, aggressive treads. It was about his own shoe size when Silas put his foot beside it.

He found a third set, also boots, several sizes larger than his. All three tracks traveled together, heading north.

The compact man unfolded his map. His eyes drifted over the square sections west of the highway until they settled on Trail 160, which ran north and south.

Silas stood and stretched his back. His right hand touched the pocket where the revolver hid. He considered the evidence and concluded that a man and a woman were hiking, found the boy wandering, and gave him water. "Then what?"

He went back to the map. As the clouds rolled in it was hard to read the small letters on the heavy paper. Trail 160 led north to the cliff dwellings and the Visitors Center. Silas assumed the Center would have a telephone, and maybe a ranger on duty. It would make sense for the couple to take the boy there.

Silas put away the map. He tightened the straps on his pack and jogged north along the trail.

* * *

Chapter 35
New Mexico, USA
Day 7

From the 6500 hundred-foot vantage point of Horse Mountain, Takara and Shoda shaded their eyes and looked north.

Shoda squatted in the sand to read the map. "Straight north of here is Sapillo Creek. He may have gone there for water."

Takara nodded. "What does Sapillo mean?"

"I have no idea. My English is okay, but my Spanish is awful."

Tak looked over her shoulder. Jiro stood near the cliff edge, holding a pebble at arm's length. "Jiro! Stop that. There are people down there."

Jiro turned. "No, the cops all went back up the trail. Just dead people now."

Shoda shook his head and passed Tak the map. "Maybe we should push him and get it over with."

Tak punched her stocky friend on the arm. "Do you see any tracks?"

"No, but the wind and the rain may have erased them. We will just have to guess where he might have gone. I think going to a stream for water makes sense."

"Me, too. We'll try Sapillo Creek first," Tak said. She waved to Jiro. "Come on, we're going."

The three marched through the afternoon heat. The sky to their left grew dark with clouds, but the temperature didn't seem to fall. Tak sipped warm water from a bottle and pushed on.

She was used to long walks through the city, but the wilderness was different. The air was hot but clean, and there weren't crowds to jostle her, or cars to honk at her. She didn't have to stop at every intersection and wait to cross, or duck to keep umbrellas from poking her in the eyes.

They reached an area thick with brown scrub grass and bushes. Shoda used his walking stick to scramble down a ravine, and Tak followed. Jiro trailed them, flinging rocks at bushes and singing pop songs.

Minutes later they struck a trail that ran east and west. Shoda stopped and leaned on his stick.

"You should drink some water," Tak said. She pushed her hair out of her eyes to look at the map. "If this is Trail 247, then that ditch was Sapillo Creek."

"It was completely dry," Shoda said between gulps from a canteen. "If it was like that when Tyler found it, he would have kept moving." He pointed at a faint, blue line on the map that ran parallel to a dotted black line. "The Gila River and Trail 724 go north together. We could follow them. If we don't find Tyler in a few more hours, we can hike east to the road and follow it back down to Wild Horse Mesa."

Takara nodded. "That makes sense. Shoda, you're pretty good at this."

Shoda smiled and looked away. Jiro chased a lizard with his machete. The reptile disappeared into a hole and Jiro kicked the dirt.

They followed the trail north along the Gila River. The march was easier than bushwhacking across the country and it was cooler near the flowing water.

When the trail bent back toward the east, Takara led them north past Brushy Mountain. As they ploughed through the junipers and under the semi-shade of the oaks and pinon pines, Tak expected to find coiled rattlesnakes and crouching pumas. Instead they saw toads, and lizards, a few squirrels, and the hind end of one scrawny rabbit.

Jiro sheathed his machete and stomped through the sand, red faced and sweating. "If it rains every afternoon, how will we ever find this kid's tracks?"

The trio stopped.

Shoda nodded. "He has a point, Tak. This park is huge. They shouldn't even call it a park. It's like its own country."

Tak sat with her back to a stumpy pinon tree and finished a bottle of water. "I don't know. I'm looking for places he described when he talked to me in the game, but he didn't know where he was." She watched the clouds, now the color of dense smoke, pile up above them. "Maybe we'd better turn toward the road soon."

"Try *Lair of the Hydra* once more," Shoda said.

"We don't meet at the lighthouse until nightfall."

Jiro rolled his eyes. "Just try it. Maybe the kid is perched in a tree a kilometer from here or something. Try it and then let's go back."

"Okay." Tak had to pull out her sleeping bag and snacks to get to the laptop. She balanced the computer on her knees and powered it up, but it was barely getting a wireless signal. Still, the connection held and she logged into the game.

* * *

Lair of the Hydra

Takeus of Thebes stepped out of the blue light of the portal onto the beach near Syracuse. A dozen dark figures surrounded him. The short hoplite snatched his sword from the scabbard but the creatures didn't move.

Tak realized he stood among the dead. Magic had turned men and monsters both to stone. He sheathed the sword and jogged toward the lighthouse.

The lighthouse stood straight and tall, but it cast no shadow. Takeus hesitated. The rough stone blocks barricading the door were gone. And the iron-banded door swung open at the touch of his spear.

Takeus stared at the door. It was brown, but flat brown. The wood had no texture. No shading. The iron bands were clean, not rusted by the salt air and the sea spray.

Something heavy thumped the ground behind him and Takeus felt it through the soles of his sandals. He spun, and saw a second statue fall. As the frozen creatures fell, the ground swallowed them like quicksand. Takeus watched, mouth agape, as the water on the beach receded. The entire blue-green line drifted backward away from the shore.

The lighthouse swayed. Flickered.

Takeus charged up the steps. The flat slabs of stone shifted beneath his feet. He ran near the wall where the steps were widest. Dust fell from above, clouding his vision. Tak put his hand on the wall as a guide and pushed up the last dozen steps.

"Tyler? Tyler!"

The platform shifted as Tak went through the door and she stumbled to one knee. Tak crawled onto the walkway and grabbed the lip of the wall for balance.

Tyler was not there.

Tak yanked the portal stone from her pouch.

The sea was gone and only a flat, tan layer of sand stretched to the horizon. The wall around the platform crumbled and stones dropped away.

A small yellow scroll rolled past her toward the edge.

Tak dove. She caught the scroll in one hand and spread herself flat to keep from going over.

As the lighthouse shook, she pushed the scroll open. It read, "NewMexicoGeodeticSurveyDiabloMountain8731."

The tower tumbled.

Tak activated her portal.

* * *

Chapter 36
New Mexico, USA
Day 7

"Look, it's a turtle!"

Emma Rowbury looked up from reading her map. Her husband sat next to her on the rock, eating a Snickers Marathon bar that had melted in the morning heat. Emma looked at the ring of chocolate around his mouth and smiled.

"Don't bother the turtle, Flower," Emma called to their eight-year-old daughter.

Twenty yards away from her spot on Trail 160, Flower leaned over a gully. "But Mom, it's hurt."

Emma lowered the map and nudged Andrew. "You want to get this one?"

Andrew shut his eyes. "Hey, I had to clean the dog poop off her shoes. Besides, this is one comfortable rock."

Emma draped a map over his face to block the sun, and hiked over to see what her daughter was doing. She hitched up her shorts as she walked. Already a petite woman, she figured she'd sweated off at least five pounds while hiking. "Flower, we need to get moving. The radio said there'll be a storm later today and we have to get back to the campground. We're going to drive into Silver City for dinner."

Flower tilted her head as if she was listening, but she continued to look down into the gully. Emma knelt next to her, one hand on Flower's belt. The gully was only eight or ten feet deep, but the walls were steep.

"See? It's a turtle. He's hurt." Flower pointed.

Emma stared at the jumble of stones below. "Honey, I don't see--" A stone moved. "Oh." A small, dark turtle, no more than five inches long, lay on its back. When it rocked side to side, she saw yellow marks, like splashes of paint, on its shell. "That's an ornate box turtle."

"What's ornate?"

"It means fancy. Hey Andrew, come here," Emma said.

Andrew groaned and then trooped over and bent down. "Ah man, that little guy is in trouble. He must have been tooling along the edge and fell off." Andrew pushed up his glasses and put one leg over the edge. "I'll get him."

Emma touched his arm. "Let me. I know your feet are hurting."

Flower sat up. "What's wrong with your feet?"

Andrew winced. "Blisters, baby. Really bad blisters."

Emma was glad Andrew still had his boots on. Flower couldn't stand the sight of blood and Andrew's blisters had split. She looked for a foothold and swung her leg over the edge. Her strong fingers dug into cracks in the rock and she worked her way down carefully, moving one limb at a time.

When her left boot touched the soft sand of the gully, Emma turned. She reached down to grab the edge of the turtle's shell and flip him over.

She heard a dry rattle.

Something slapped her left wrist.

Emma yanked her hand back.

A blur struck her left calf.

Emma stomped down with her right boot.

The snake whipped its head back under the rock, then struck a third time.

Emma jumped over the turtle.

She looked down. Blood was on her wrist. Not a lot, but it was bright red in the sunlight. There were two wounds on her leg. Emma struggled to catch her breath. She realized Flower was screaming.

Andrew hit the ground in front of her. The snake darted to his left. He stomped its head with his heavy boot.

Emma leaned back against the wall and watched her husband drive his foot down on the snake's head and all she could think was how much it had to hurt his blisters.

Emma squeezed her wrist with her opposite hand. "What kind?" Her teeth chattered. "What kind of snake?" She tried to look around her husband.

Andrew pinned the reptile's head with a fist-sized rock. He used one boot to extend the body. The snake was close to five feet long, and the diamond pattern along its back was clear. Andrew cleared his throat and turned around. "Em, it's a rattlesnake. A Western Diamondback."

"Those are poisonous," Flower called from above.

"Very." Andrew stood on his toes and reached up to touch Flower's shoulder. The girl looked over the rim, her face covered in tears, nose running over her lips and chin. "Flower, run to daddy's pack and get the snakebite kit. It's yellow."

The girl nodded, and disappeared.

Emma leaned against the rock wall. The bite wounds didn't hurt as much as she thought, but she shook from the adrenaline rush. "Can you boost me up?"

Andrew cupped his hands and lifted her one hundred and five pounds easily. Emma rolled over the top of the gully and sat up. When she stretched her left leg, she saw that her calf was swelling. Andrew scrambled up beside her just as Flower ran back with the kit and a canteen.

Emma took the kit. Flower squatted next to her, her long hair hanging in her red eyes. "I'm going to get the cell phone," Andrew called over his shoulder as he ran to their packs.

The snakebite kit was a yellow rubber cylinder in two pieces. Emma twisted it apart and spilled out the contents--a metal blade sealed in aluminum foil, a glass vial of iodine antiseptic, a piece of nylon string, and a page of instructions.

She spread the contents in her lap, but the string was stuck in the top of the rubber cylinder. Emma passed the rubber cap to Flower. "Baby, use your little fingers to get that string out, okay?"

Flower trembled, but she went to work on the cap.

Andrew dropped down next to her, his phone in hand. "I can't get a signal. This damn thing is--"

"Andrew, I need your help with this."

"Okay." He nodded several times. "We can do this. We have the kit. What do we do first?"

Following the instructions, they broke the ampoule of iodine and spread it around the wounds on her legs. There wasn't enough iodine left to clean the bite on her wrist.

"I got it," Flower yelled. She pulled the green string out of the cap.

Andrew looped it around Emma's arm. "How high does it say to tie it?"

"An inch and a half above the bite. Not too tight." Emma took off her belt and tied it around her leg. She read the directions aloud. "Okay, now it says to make a one-eighth-inch to one-quarter-inch deep incision over the fang marks. Not on fingers, toes or a blood vessel."

Andrew peeled the foil off the tiny blade. His hands shook. "Your calf is muscle, but there's blood vessels in your wrist. I'll make it shallow. You ready?"

Emma nodded and looked away. When Andrew cut, she hissed. She felt a tear run down her cheek. Flower turned pale and stepped back. "Flower, sit down." Emma passed her the water bottle. "Sit under that tree and drink."

Andrew threw the dripping blade into the gully. "What's next?"

Emma read from the paper. "Apply suction with the rubber cups."

Cradling her leg in his lap, Andrew worked on the wounds on her calf. The rubber cup stuck and pulled out her skin, but with the blood, Emma wasn't sure how much of the venom came out. "Okay, let's try my arm."

After he finished her arm, Emma put the cups in her pocket. "We may have to do this again. The instructions say most of the venom should be drawn out over an hour time period."

Andrew looked over her shoulder and bit his lip. "I may have to carry Flower. Can you walk?"

"I guess it depends on how far." Emma smiled, her lips tight across her teeth. "We'll have to stop and loosen the tourniquets every ten minutes. My leg is already starting to swell."

Wind blew her hair off her neck. It was almost cool. Emma looked up. Black clouds gathered in the west and crept toward them. "We better get moving."

Andrew helped her up. "We'll follow this trail north to the Visitors Center at the cliff dwellings. We can use the phone there."

* * *

Chapter 37
New Mexico, USA
Day 7

Deputy Kane sat in his car. The rain came down so hard the front windshield was a light gray cascade with a view of nothing, like plunging your face into a waterfall.

The total lack of visibility made the cruiser seem small. Kane wiped moisture off the driver's side of the window with his hand. He knew an ambulance was parked ten feet from his front bumper, but he couldn't see it.

When his cell phone went off, he flinched, then shook his head. "Spooking myself." He picked the phone up off the passenger seat. "Kane."

"Hey." His wife's voice came in low and the connection crackled.

Kane sat forward in his seat. "Kayla, is everything okay?"

He listened, but she didn't say anything. Kane pictured her sitting in their kitchen, one hand over the phone. The other wiping away tears. "Did the doctor call?"

"Yes. He said...he looked at the test results and he says I can't have babies." She coughed hard.

Kane rubbed his free hand across his eyes and down his nose. "Damn. Baby, I'm sorry. It's okay. We'll be okay, we just need to keep trying."

"But we've been trying so long," she said.

"I know. I know we've tried." He stopped talking because he didn't know what to say.

"The physician's assistant said we should look into adopting, and she gave me a brochure...but I can't read it right now. I want our own baby."

Kane's phone rattled. Another caller was trying to reach him. He squinted at the screen. "Damn it. Kayla, the Border Patrol's on the other line. We've got a murder case out here and I--"

"Go, answer it." She sniffled once, then her voice strengthened. "I'll see you tonight. Come home safe." She hung up.

Kane took a deep breath and unclenched his fist so he wouldn't smash it through the windshield. He put the phone back to his ear. "Deputy Kane. Grant County Sheriff's Department."

"Kane? It's DeWitt. Damn, I can barely hear you."

"Storm is bad up here. Where are those ATVs?" Kane asked.

"The side of the road. The trailer had a flat tire. I tried to put the donut spare from my cruiser on it, but it doesn't fit. I'm waiting for a guy to bring a new tire."

Kane shrugged. "Don't stand out in the lightning trying to change it. The rain is so heavy the trail may have washed out by now. You know how fast those arroyos flood."

"Yeah, we pull dead hikers out of so-called dry streambeds every year. I have my laptop in the truck and I'm giving the databases a quick look while I wait," DeWitt said.

Kane sat forward in his seat. "Find anything?"

DeWitt sighed. "I'm not sure. I found a male and female Burroughs who applied for a loan in Albuquerque two years ago. A Discover Card account cancelled eighteen months ago. A library card in Sacramento, California. Stuff like that. It might be two of the people at the bottom of the cliff. But there's no record of them having a son. Or a daughter, for that matter."

"No birth certificate for a Tyler Burroughs?"

"Not that I could find. No school records either."

"Miss Murakami said Tyler told her he was home schooled. But still, there should be something." Kane chewed the edge of his mustache. His wife had reminded that morning that it was past time to trim it. "I don't get this. Like you said, Mr. and Mrs. Burroughs may be among the dead in those rocks, but the girl couldn't identify any of them as Tyler. So how could he know about the crime unless he was there and ran away?"

"I've been thinking about that," DeWitt said. "The other possibility? He did it."

"What?"

"This guy sent those people off the cliff, and now he's posing as a child to lure in his next victims. Did those Japanese kids go back to their hotel?"

Kane slapped the steering wheel with his free hand. "No. Damn it. They went to look for the boy."

"Oh, hell."

"Yeah. We carried up three of the cliff bodies on stretchers, but the ambulance is full now, so we're waiting on the rest of you to show up. I'm going to look for the Japanese."

"What's the point? You'll never spot them in this weather. They're probably hunkered down under a rock somewhere."

"Yeah, but I have to try. They may walk right into this psycho's trap." Kane shut the phone and reached for his hat.

* * *

"What did you find? Was he there?" Jiro asked.

Tak looked up from her laptop computer and blinked. "*Lair of the Hydra* is...collapsing. It's like watching a world melt."

Shoda came out of the scrub with a roll of toilet paper in one hand and a bottle of hand sanitizer in the other. "What happened?"

"The world melted. Probably because it's so damn hot here," Jiro said.

Tak shut the computer. A fat, warm drop of water hit the back of her hand. It almost stung. "I found a scroll with the name of a mountain and a number. Tyler must have left it for me. Shoda, check the map for Diablo Mountain."

The stocky young man squatted under a pinon pine and spread the map. He squinted and stabbed the map with a thick finger. "It's here. West of us. Seven, maybe eight, kilometers. What was the number?"

"8731."

"Oh, that's the elevation. Diablo is the highest mountain around here, judging by the other peaks listed," Shoda said.

A drop hit the map and rolled past his hand. Shoda quickly folded the paper and put it in a plastic bag. A cobalt blue rope of lightning arced between two swollen clouds. Half a second later, it whipped down onto an oak on the hillside.

Shoda jumped. "Damn. We need to get away from these trees."

Tak crammed her gear back into her pack, slung it over one shoulder and led them out of the thicket at a run. Her pack slapped against her spine as she powered up over a ridge. Individual drops of rain melded into a continuous vertical flood.

She blinked her eyes, but the water poured down her face and under the collar of her shirt. Lightning struck again, close enough to shake the ground. The thunder became continuous.

The three stumbled down into a creek bed and under the shelter of a fallen tree trunk. Tak took the compass from her pocket and held it out until the needle stopped spinning. The water of the stream rose to touch the edge of her boots.

"We can't make Diablo Mountain in this," Shoda shouted over the storm. "The lightning will cook us."

Tak nodded. "Let's go north and east. The Cliff Dwellings National Monument is just a few kilometers. They have a Visitors Center. We can ask for shelter there."

Jiro poked his head between them. The rain had flattened his spiky hair and he looked ten years younger. "Use your cell phone and call that deputy. Tell him about the scroll. And tell him to pick us up from the Visitors Center."

Takara dug out her phone and leaned to keep the rain off of it. The tiny icon in the top left indicated no signal. The battery was charged, but without a signal from a cellular tower, the phone was useless. "No signal. We'll have to keep moving. There will be a phone at the Visitors Center."

Shoda nodded. "Okay, let's go."

As the stream rose over the toes of their boots, the three splashed across and up the far side.

They hiked at a fast walk for half an hour, and the storm lagged behind them as they moved east. The rain pelted their heads and made their backpacks twice as heavy, but the lightning subsided.

Shoda pulled alongside Tak and spoke over the rain. "We should either hit Highway 15 or the west fork of the Gila River. I'm sure there will be signs for the Visitors Center."

"You think they'll have hot tea?" Jiro called.

Tak shrugged and kept moving. Carrying her lunch and an umbrella on the long walk to the metro station was not the same as marching across the Gila with a 15-kilogram pack. The rocky, broken ground made her watch every step, and her rain-soaked boots rubbed her ankles raw.

The panting trio slowed to ascend a hill and the storm caught up. Thunder shook Tak's heart in her chest and the rain poured down so hard she had to put a hand over her mouth to breath.

Although it was only late afternoon, they ran through an eerie twilight. Jiro pulled ahead as they went up a steep incline. He stopped and pointed and yelled, but Takara couldn't hear him.

She pushed herself up the hill and paused next to Jiro, gasping for air.

"It's a trail," Jiro said. "We must be close."

The trail led them up, but it went north and east and it was easier than cutting cross country, so they followed it.

Tak had her head down against the torrent, watching the ground ahead of her, when she ran into Jiro's back. He stumbled and turned. "Look."

Ahead rose a tall cliff with lumpy, rounded walls as if the rock had melted like the terrain in *Lair of the Hydra*. Takara blinked rain away. Above the tree line she spotted a void, a black gap in the cliff. Then a second gap, and a third.

"Caverns," Jiro yelled into her ear.

As Shoda caught up with them, a barbed bolt of white-hot lightning struck an oak twenty paces away. A gout of flame erupted from the tree.

Shoda grabbed Takara's arm. "Run!"

The three dashed forward. In the gloom it was hard to be certain, but as they ran, Takara looked up and noticed regular lines within the huge caverns.

While lightning stitched the ground around them, they dashed under the lip of the rocks and into the nearest cavern. Wind blew the rain in, so they pushed forward into the gloom. Jiro ran to a series of stone steps. "It's the cliff dwellings. We can wait out the storm here."

Takara flicked on a flashlight and followed Jiro up the steps. Her wet hair clung to her neck and she shivered. They passed a numbered marker and the floor leveled out.

The first structure was nothing more than a few waist high walls with no roof. She wondered if it had been a pen for animals. The uneven ceiling of the cave soared high above them. They scrambled up a modern wooden staircase and found a room with complete walls, but it, too, did not have a roof.

Takara stepped inside and the wind died instantly. The air was cold, but she felt safe from the lightning. Jiro sprawled against one wall and opened a bottle of water. Shoda squatted by the entrance to watch the lightning play over the canyon. “I guess the Indians could see their enemies coming from up here, but it’s kind of creepy.”

Tak sat next to him. “It’s better than being out in that storm.”

* * *

Chapter 38
New Mexico, USA
Day 7

Takara sat next to Shoda in the cave, and checked her phone for a signal. When the phone didn't pick up any bars, she set it aside and tore the top off of a foil packet of runner's gel. In the dim cavern, she couldn't read the label. She sniffed the carbohydrate syrup; it smelled like strawberry lip gloss. The gel was so sweet she almost gagged, but half of a bottle of water pushed it down, and Tak reasoned she needed the energy.

Shoda ate from a can of tuna with a plastic spork, while Jiro lay with his head on his pack, snoring.

The storm grew worse. Lightning peppered the canyon floor 60 meters below them. When the wind gusted, the rain blew sideways into the cave and over the wall of the ancient house.

Shoda shook himself when a sheet of rain came in the open roof. "Maybe we should move further inside."

"I hate to wake Jiro. He's snoring like--" Tak paused. "Did you hear something?"

The blocky young man shrugged. "The thunder is so loud I can't hear anything." But he stopped and listened. His eyes narrowed, and Shoda reached for his hickory walking stick.

Tak picked up her flashlight, but it was too short to be much use. She touched Jiro's face with a cold hand. He twitched and opened his eyes. She put her finger across his mouth and leaned down. "There's something here. In one of the chambers."

Jiro sat up and slid his machete out of its sheath.

A massive figure plunged into the room, swathed in a green plastic poncho.

Tak leaped back. Jiro rolled to his feet. Shoda took his stick in both hands.

"Help!"

The man fell to his knees. A woman spilled out of his arms onto the cold floor. A child ducked into the entrance and froze.

Tak grabbed Shoda's arm. "Wait! What's wrong?" she asked in English.

The man pushed the hood of his poncho back. Rainwater poured off of him. He crawled to the woman. “A snake bit my wife. Flower?”

The man turned. A small figure in a pink poncho ran to him. The woman on the floor moaned.

Takara flicked her flashlight on and knelt by the woman. The American’s left arm was swollen to her shoulder socket. A thin string cut into her skin.

The man fumbled with the knot on the string, but his wet hands shook. “We kept it on too long. To stop the poison from going to her heart.”

“Let me try.” Tak plucked at the knot, then tried her teeth, but the nylon was strong. The man loosened a leather belt from the woman’s left leg.

“It bit her three times. Twice on the leg. We were hiking, she tried to save a turtle and--”

“It’s okay,” Tak said.

“Do you have a phone?” the man asked.

“Yes, but I can’t get a signal. It might be the cave walls.”

The man pushed himself up to his feet. “I couldn’t get a signal on the trail, but maybe now. I’ll go outside and try.” He turned to the child. “Flower, stay with your mom.”

The man tucked his phone under the hood of his poncho and ran out. Thunder boomed on the cliff top above and the little girl whimpered.

Tak waved her flashlight around. “We should move deeper into the caves. Shoda, help me lift her. Jiro, go check on the man. Tell him what we’re doing.”

Shoda slipped his hands under the woman’s ankles, but hesitated. “Maybe we shouldn’t move her. She looks bad,” he said in Japanese.

“It will be worse if she lays here with the rain blowing on her.” Takara lifted the woman beneath the shoulders. The American was small, more the size of a Japanese woman, and light. The girl followed, a miniature pack on her back.

“It’s my fault,” the girl said.

“I’m sure it isn’t,” Tak replied.

“I told her to help the turtle and the snake bit her.”

The thunder was loud and Tak was unsure of her English. She shook her head. They carried the woman across an open courtyard and into a stone house whose walls rose all the way to connect to the ceiling of the cave. The back wall of the house wasn't cut stone, but rather the raw bedrock of the mountain.

They eased the woman down and put her head on a pack. She stirred, but didn't open her eyes. Tak dug in her gear for a fresh bottle of water to give the woman.

Shoda aimed the flashlight at the woman's injured leg. It was swollen to twice its normal size and the skin looked so tight Tak thought it might split. The area around the bite wounds was bruised dark, but it was hard to see what color.

The girl crouched next to her mother and put a small hand on her forehead.

"Hey, Tak, Shoda," Jiro yelled. His voice bounced around the walls of the cavern.

Tak went to the low doorway. "In here."

Jiro and the man ducked in, both dripping. "I can't get a signal," the man said. He leaned over his wife. "Emma, can you hear me?"

The woman didn't respond. The little girl began to cry.

The man sat back. His face was slack with exhaustion. He trembled.

"She walked most of the way herself. I was carrying Flower when Emma fell. She said her leg was burning. And the swelling...got bad. Emma has a high tolerance for pain. You should have seen her when she had Flower." He shook his head. "I'm going to the Visitors Center for help. It's a mile down the mountain."

He got to one knee, swayed and would have fallen if Shoda had not caught him.

"Mister?" Tak took his other arm.

"Rowbury. Andrew Rowbury." The man sagged and Shoda propped him against the rock wall by his wife.

"Mister Rowbury, we'll go for help." Takara mangled the surname, but the man nodded. "You stay here with your wife. We will leave our packs with you so we can run fast." She turned and spoke Japanese. "Jiro, Shoda, bring flashlights and the map. Leave behind anything that will slow us down."

Tak tucked her flashlight in her pocket and knelt by Andrew. “While you were hiking, did you see anyone?”

“See anyone? We saw people at the campground two days ago, but they were packing to leave. Why?” Andrew asked.

“We’re searching for a boy named Tyler. He is lost. I think he may be on Diablo Mountain, but the storm forced us here,” Tak said.

“Diablo is five, maybe five and a half, miles west of here. In this storm...” Andrew leaned his head back against the wall. “No, I’m sorry, but we didn’t see a lost boy.”

Takara nodded. “We’ll run to the Visitors Center and bring help.”

Andrew reached up and squeezed her hand. “Thank you. Please hurry.”

* * *

Chapter 39
New Mexico, USA
Day 7

Lightning played across the treetops.

Even when the rain began to melt the spider web shoeprints, Silas stayed with the trail. Trail 160 guided him through the thunderstorm and all the way north to where Highway 15 ended at the Gila Cliff Dwellings National Monument. The compact man stepped onto the road, looked from under the dripping brim of his hat, and turned right.

The parking lot in front of the Visitors Center was empty except for a white pickup truck with an insignia on the driver's door. The Center was a low, stone built structure with a flat roof and a flagpole out front. A stout figure stood beneath the pole, hauling down a sopping flag.

Silas touched his coat pocket, and then splashed across the parking lot. "Hello!"

The person, in a slicker and a wide brimmed hat, spun, half draped in the flag. "Sir, what are you doing out in this weather?"

Silas stood bent against the wind. Water pooled above the toes of his boots. Lightning arced from cloud to cloud above him. "I got caught on the trail. Can I go inside?" He pointed at the Visitors Center.

The woman tried to fold the wet flag, then gave up and draped it over her shoulder so it wouldn't touch the ground. She secured the rope to the pole and waved. "Come on."

Silas followed the ranger inside.

"Summertime we stay open until five, instead of four thirty, but it's four fifty already," she said. "The bookstore is closed, too."

"That's fine. I just want to get out of the lightning. Had a close call on the trail. I swear my hair stood up under my hat."

The ranger chuckled. "Yeah, these afternoon storms catch people off guard." She worked to fold the flag. "I can't believe I forgot and left this out. Never happens."

"Here, I'll help." Silas took one end of the flag and tugged it taut while she folded.

"Thanks. I'll take it home with me to dry, but you can't just wad up Old Glory, you know?"

"I feel the same way. It's appalling how some people treat our flag these days," Silas said. She walked toward him as she folded the cloth, so that the flag ended in Silas's hands.

He passed the thick triangle to her. "On behalf of a grateful nation..."

"Oh, don't even kid. My husband is in the National Guard. Last year he did a tour in Iraq and I had nightmares about hearing those words." She took the flag and turned toward the door. "Can I give you a ride to your vehicle?"

Silas drew the pistol from his pocket. He pointed the short-snouted gun at the back of her head. "No, thanks."

He pulled the trigger.

In the enclosed space, the noise was tremendous.

She hit the floor with the flag cradled in her arms. Water ran off her slicker.

Silas took a long step back and checked himself over. He was wet, but it was all rain, not blood. Silas inhaled. In the dim light, he couldn't see the smoke, but he tasted gunpowder in the back of his throat.

He tucked the revolver in his pocket. The barrel was warm for a moment.

Silas put his boot on the dead thing's head and pushed it over. Its face was whole, so the bullet must have lodged inside the skull. He touched his forefinger and thumb together.

Five bullets minus one equals four left.

He examined the Visitors Center. There was a tall glass case with three pots on the bottom shelf and some shards of pottery on the top. He read an exhibit about the Apaches. It had a drawing of an Apache warrior and a wooden bow and three arrows on display.

Three pots. Three arrows. Things come in threes. Three threes makes nine. Six of nine complete, three to go. A male hiker, a female hiker, and a stupid boy.

A helpful brochure had a map of the monument grounds. The picture indicated the road led north past a campground and ended at the trail up to the cliff dwellings. He wondered why Tyler and his rescuers weren't here since they'd been ahead of him on the trail.

Silas stared at the bow and arrows while blood leaked out of the ranger's head onto the floor. He figured the storm might have forced them to take shelter at the campground, where they could have a tent or a vehicle.

Where else could they go?

He examined a picture of the cliff dwellings. They looked old, but sturdy, protected by thick rock walls. Silas nodded.

The compact man put his pack by the door and worked his way through the entire building. He found a landline phone and disconnected it from the wall. He carried the heavy plastic unit to the trashcan, but stopped with his arm in midair. Although he couldn't bring himself to reach into a filthy garbage bin, he could imagine someone else doing it to retrieve the phone.

Silas carried the phone to the body. He wrapped an empty plastic sandwich bag around his hand and pushed his fingers into its pockets. He pawed out a set of keys, a cell phone, and a tube of Chapstick.

He took the two phones out to the restroom and dropped them in the toilet. Bubbles came out of the landline phone.

Silas went back and looked at the body. It was too near the door, and someone might see it if they looked inside.

He covered one hand with the plastic bag, and the other with a spare T-shirt from his pack. Silas took the corpse by the wrists and pulled it to the back wall and let it thump to the ground. More blood leaked out of its head while Silas tore open a foil packet containing an alcohol-soaked cloth. As he scrubbed his hands, Silas stared at a picture of an Apache. He took the keys, flipped off the lights, and locked the door.

The ranger's truck took three tries to crank, but it finally caught, and Silas eased down the road to the campgrounds. The rain was so heavy that even with the windshield wipers at full speed, he could barely see.

One vehicle sat in the parking lot. A blue Toyota Matrix with Arizona license plates. Silas could see that it was empty, but he knew the boy might be hiding on the floorboard, so he leaned on the windows and checked.

The Toyota was empty.

There were no tents pitched. No recreational vehicles. No campers. Just darkness smothering twilight and the cold drops of rain running down the back of his collar.

He drove the truck half a mile west to the end of the road, and parked. Rain drummed on the roof. Silas shut his eyes for a moment, and then shook his head and opened the door.

The noise tripled. Thunder, lightning, wind, rain. He locked the truck, put the keys in his pocket, and entered the trail leading up to the cliff dwellings.

The trail angled south and west. At points it was narrow and the drop off to his left grew steep. Silas stopped to take a breath.

Ahead on the trail, something flashed yellow in the growing dark. Silas squinted. A second flash.

He looked behind him, but the trail was narrow there. Silas raced forward, his pack slapping against his shoulders. Fifty paces on he found a thick patch of scrub trees.

He crouched at the edge of the trail and lowered himself by hand, boots digging for a grip in the wet earth. Silas slithered into the thicket and lay still.

Voices sounded. The thud of boots struck the ground. He saw the yellow light and sank deeper into the gloom. A figure ran down the trail, then a second, and a third.

The leader held a flashlight. All three were too tall to be children. Adults. Running down a trail in a lightning storm. Silas watched them go by.

Three pots. Three arrows. Three people. Pots, arrows, people. But not two hikers and a boy.

Silas shivered as rain ran down his face. He crawled up over the edge onto the trail. Even with the rain, he spotted voids in the cliff where the caves were.

According to the exhibit in the Visitors Center there were forty rooms in the pueblo. At thirty seconds per room, Silas calculated he could search the caves in twenty minutes.

Four bullets left. Three people. One extra bullet.

Silas ran up the trail.

* * *

Chapter 40
New Mexico, USA
Day 7

The first cave in the cliff dwellings was simply a shallow shelf ten yards deep into the mountain. Silas went through it in twenty-two seconds, flashlight in his left hand and pistol in his right.

He slowed in the second cavern. The Mogollon Indians had built eight rooms there in a mushroom-shaped cluster under the lip of the cliff. His LED flashlight was powerful and Silas was careful not to shine it in his own eyes, but then a rope of lightning arced down and wrecked his night vision.

Silas wondered if his violet eyes contained more visual purple than ordinary humans did.

The eight rooms were cold and empty. Empty for seven or eight hundred years.

Silas moved to the next cluster, keeping close to the wall and working left to right. He did not want to leave any unexplored rooms, but when he saw the high shelf of rock behind the houses, he debated whether to explore it.

Why would they sit in the dark, he reasoned. Silas knew hikers would have a lantern or some kind of light that he could look for.

After searching nine more rooms, he went back out into the rain and around the rock wall to the next set of dwellings. He crept up a modern set of wooden steps and found a courtyard running between two rows of houses.

Silas checked the three buildings on his left, then moved along the inner wall. He kept his flashlight pointed down, angled so he could see where to put his feet.

Ahead, a rectangular patch of yellow light shone on the cave floor.

The compact man clicked off his flashlight. He skulked through the shadows and listened at the low doorway.

"Hang on, baby. Help will be here soon," a man said.

Silas ducked through the doorway.

A woman lay with her head on a pack, her boots toward the entrance. A man sat next to her, holding her hand. A child, swathed in a poncho, crouched opposite the man, holding a canteen. Two stubby candles flickered on the floor near the woman's head.

Silas inhaled the sweet scent of beeswax. "Hello, Tyler."

The man looked up. "What? Who are you? My wife needs help. She's been bitten by..."

Silas didn't listen.

The small figure in the poncho turned. She pushed long hair out of her face and stared.

She.

Silas blinked. "You're not a boy. Where is the boy?"

The man bent one knee to get up and Silas fired.

The 130-grain bullet hit the man in the belly. The man took one step and collapsed.

The shot was very loud in the small stone room. The smell of powder supplanted the scent of beeswax.

Silas darted to his right and cornered the girl. "You're not Tyler. You're not Tyler!" He shook the gun in her face.

The girl dove across the prone woman. When the child fell on her, the woman's eyes fluttered and she raised her right arm to wrap it around the girl.

The man groaned and rolled over.

"Give me your shoes," Silas yelled at the girl. "Take them off and give me your shoes."

The girl tugged at the laces, but her fingers shook so much she couldn't release the knots. She tore them off and kicked them to Silas.

Silas scooped one of the red and blue sneakers off the stone floor and examined it in the candlelight. "Spider web with an 'S.' The track is the same. The exact same!"

He laughed. Then hiccupped once. The sound echoed off the walls. Silas bent over. His lungs clenched tight and fluttered against his ribs. His vision narrowed, darker and darker at the edges until all he could see was the shoe in his hand.

The compact man staggered back. "Three pots, three arrows, three people. Things come in threes. Three more people. Twelve. Three too many. Too many. Where is the boy?"

He pointed the gun at the man, who lay pale and panting. Silas shifted the barrel to aim at the child's back where she lay across her mother. “The bullet will go through. Two for one. Five minus three is two.”

The wounded man raised himself on one elbow. “We didn’t see any boy,” he groaned. “There were people here earlier. Three people searching for a boy. Don’t hurt my baby. She’s just a little girl.”

“Three people searching for a boy? What did they say?” Silas took aim at the child’s spine.

“Diablo Mountain,” the man gasped. “They think he’s on Diablo Mountain.” He crawled over his wife and child, shielding them.

Silas held his aim. *Diablo Mountain. It’s on the map. I saw it on the map.*

He slid out of the circle of candlelight. *If they go to Diablo there will be Tyler plus three. The ranger was one. This man was two. Three bullets left. I can’t shoot these wretches, I have to save the bullets.*

He kicked the girl’s shoe across the dirt floor. It knocked one of the candles over, but the wick continued to burn.

Silas went out into the rain.

* * *

Chapter 41
New Mexico, USA
Day 7

Takara leaned back as gravity yanked her down the trail. Her right boot slipped, and she fell into Jiro.

They tumbled into the mud in a heap.

Shoda hauled Jiro up, dropped his stick and knelt beside her. "Are you hurt?" he asked in English.

Jiro slapped Shoda's arm. "It's just us here. Speak Japanese."

Takara sat on the trail, water soaking through the seat of her pants. She stretched both legs, flexed her quadriceps and looked up. "I'm okay."

She took Shoda's hand and got up. Shoda continued to hold her hand until she shook him loose. "I'm fine. Let's go."

"I know you like me, but you don't have to throw yourself at me," Jiro said as he passed her on the narrow trail.

Tak shook her head. Her wet hair clung to her face. "Dream on."

The three dashed over the mud-slick rocks and soon found themselves on the level ground of an asphalt road. An empty white truck sat parked at the trailhead. Jiro tugged on the door handle. "Should I break the window?"

"Do you know how to hotwire a car?" Shoda asked.

"No."

"Then what's the point?" Shoda followed Takara east along the road. "Come on."

Tak slowed as they passed the camping area, but she didn't see any tents and only one car. They followed the road as it curved around to a parking lot in front of the Visitors Center. Tak couldn't decide if the rain was letting up, or if she was simply getting accustomed to it.

They jogged through the parking lot, past the flagpole and to the door. The Center was dark. There were no cars in the lot. No people. No pay phones.

They huddled together by the door. Tak pressed her flashlight to the glass and looked in. Her breath fogged the glass and she pulled her head back. Shoda pounded on the door so hard it shook.

Jiro stepped forward. "We have to get to a phone. Shield your eyes."

Before Tak could object, Jiro drove the hilt of his machete into the glass. She heard it crack, but she couldn't see it in the dark. Tak raised her flashlight.

Jiro hit the same spot again and the glass broke. Shards fell inward. Jiro snaked one arm in and twisted the lock. He pulled his arm out and opened the door.

The beam of Tak's flashlight played over a loose tube of lip balm and a thick, colorful triangle. She bent and picked it up. "It's an American flag. A wet flag."

Shoda touched the cloth. "Why was it on the floor?"

"Something's wrong." Jiro slipped past her. "I smell blood."

"Are you sure?" Shoda asked.

"We have car accident victims brought in every night at the hospital. Trust me, there's blood in here."

Tak bit her lip. *Don't let it be Tyler.* "Maybe an animal broke in."

Jiro looked over his shoulder at her and pointed. "I see something back there."

They found the park ranger by the far wall. Tak put two fingers to the woman's neck. Her skin was cold. "No pulse."

"Let me borrow your flashlight," Shoda said. "I'll go find a phone."

Shoda trundled off into the dark. Jiro turned the woman's head. "Wound on the skull. Might be a bullet hole. Or maybe they hit her with something sharp like a pickaxe or a drill or a--"

"Jiro." Tak folded the woman's hands over her uniform shirt. "This is murder. Someone killed her."

Jiro dug under the woman's poncho.

"What are you doing?"

"Seeing if she has a gun. We might need one." Jiro rocked back on his heels. "No. Damn, I thought she'd have one."

The flashlight beam swung over them and Shoda slumped against the wall. "I can't find a phone. No desk phones, no cell phones. Nothing. I even found a phone jack in the wall, but no phone. I don't get it."

"I do," Jiro said. "Someone killed her and took the phones. There's a murderer loose." When he looked down at the dead woman, a glass chip fell out of his hair.

Takara stood. "We have to go back to the cliff dwellings. Those people are alone," she said.

Shoda shrugged. "Maybe we should go south along the road, back to Silver City. Tell the police."

"It's 50 kilometers, and there won't be any people on the road in this weather to pick us up. We have to warn Mr. Rowbury about the killer."

"What about Tyler?" Jiro asked. "That American is a big guy. He can protect his wife and daughter."

"From a gun?"

"I don't know," Jiro said. "We came here to find Tyler..."

"And we will. But we should help these people. Tyler was hiding the last time I talked to him. He's safe for now," she said.

"Okay." Shoda looked around. "Do either of you have any food? Climbing back up there is going to be tough."

They went out to the vending machines, but none of them had any coins. Jiro raised his machete. "Stand back."

Tak caught his wrist. "We can't just break in. That's stealing."

"You owe me a giant Mexican dinner when we get back," Jiro said.

The three took turns drinking from a water fountain, and then ran back out into the rain.

As they jogged along the road past the campground, Tak was certain there was less lightning in the sky, but the rain continued to pour.

The hike up the trail ground them down to a fast walk. The mud seemed to suck their boots in and hold them. The incline gave Takara shin splints and she trailed her right hand along the rock wall. Shoda drew alongside her and stopped. "Tak, we're almost there. Switch off your flashlight."

She couldn't see his expression in the dark. "Do you think the killer might be up there?"

"It's possible."

Jiro passed them, his machete out and ready. "I hope he is. I'll kill him for making us hike back up here."

The three pushed up the last hundred paces and stumbled into the sudden stillness of the cavern. The wind died and without the rain beating on their heads, they could hear again.

Takara started into the courtyard, but Shoda touched her arm. He motioned Jiro ahead, then he went next. Tak frowned and followed.

They crept into the courtyard. Doorways opened like deep, toothless mouths all around them. Tak shivered. Then she spotted the warm yellow glow of a candle, and smelled melting wax.

Jiro peeked around the doorway, and ducked inside. Shoda and Tak went in after him.

The girl, Flower, screamed.

Andrew Rowbury's head came up off the ground, but when he tried to sit up, he fell back. He lay on the cold floor, hands pressed to his belly while blood leaked between his fingers.

Takara darted to the family. "Don't be afraid. It's us. We're back from the Visitors Center."

Flower curled into a tight ball with one hand on her mother's head.

Jiro stood over them. "What the hell happened?" he asked in Japanese.

Shoda translated. "What happened?"

"A man came," Andrew gasped. "He walked in and shot me. I don't even know him. He shot me." Andrew held his stomach with both hands.

Takara retrieved her pack and found a dry T-shirt. She wadded it and pressed it to Andrew's wound. He groaned. Warm blood soaked through the shirt onto Tak's fingers.

"Did you get help?" the big American whispered.

Takara looked away. The woman lay very still. In the candlelight, Tak couldn't tell if her chest was rising and falling.

Shoda picked up a candle and brought it close.

Andrew gripped Tak's arm. His fingers were sticky. "Did you get help?"

"No." She shook her head. "There are no phones. And the ranger is dead. We came to warn you."

The American lay his head back. "Oh God." He released Tak's arm and reached to touch his wife. "She hasn't woken up. I put the tourniquet back on her leg after you left, then he came. I can't get it off."

"We'll cut it off her." She wrapped Andrew's hands around the T-shirt. "Hold this here."

Andrew opened his eyes. "He asked about the boy."

"What?"

Shoda and Jiro stepped closer.

"He said the name 'Tyler' and asked where he is." Andrew closed his eyes and swallowed. "He pointed the gun at Flower and Emma. I'm sorry. I told him about Diablo Mountain."

Takara sat back on the floor, one hand still on Andrew's wound. "Tyler warned me," she said to Shoda and Jiro in Japanese. "He said Silas was hunting him. We have to go after him. To the mountain. One of us should stay with them." She nodded at the family.

Shoda looked from Tak to the family and back. "Tak, maybe you should stay. Jiro and I can--"

"Tyler doesn't know you," Takara said. "He'll hide if he sees you. I have to go. But someone needs to stay and care for these people, so--"

"Shoda can watch them," Jiro said as he stepped into the circle of candlelight.

"Silas has a gun," Shoda said. "I still think Jiro and I should go."

Tak touched Jiro's arm. She felt his bicep tense beneath the sleeve. "You said you took a first aid class at the hospital."

Jiro shrugged. "Everyone has to. That doesn't mean--"

"Yes, it does. Shoda and I have no training at all. You're the only one qualified to help these people."

Jiro opened his mouth. Closed it. "Damn it. Here, take this." He took his machete from his belt and handed it to Shoda. "Good luck."

Tak looked at Shoda, who nodded. She bent over Andrew. "Mister Andrew, what does this man look like?"

Andrew blinked. "He was short. Wiry."

"He has creepy eyes," Flower whispered from her spot in the shadows.

Jiro took an audible breath and loosened the belt around the woman's leg. His hands shook. He looked up. "I'll do what I can for them."

Tak nodded. "Okay." She lifted her pack. Shoda waited by the door. "Take care. We'll be back as soon as we find Tyler."

The two went into the night.

* * *

Chapter 42
New Mexico, USA
Day 7

As he hiked to Diablo Mountain, Silas stopped and looked over his shoulder. He glanced up the canyon, one hand rubbing the back of his neck.

A faint, washed out yellow glow flashed for a second. He blinked rainwater from his eyes. Opened them and it was gone.

Flashlight. Flashlight tag. Silas squared his shoulders under the weight of the wet pack. *Tag. I am it.*

He scrambled up the canyon slope on his left for a better view. Silas sat on a rock with his hands in his pockets, shivering when the wind gusted along the canyon floor. His purple eyes strained wide, gathering all possible light.

He saw a flash, yellow, not blue-white like lightning. Silas nodded and touched the cold steel pistol. *Who are they?*

He thought about the three people who passed him on the trail to the cliff dwellings. Their light was yellow, like this one. Silas wondered if they were relatives of Tyler's, or park rangers, or FBI agents.

Silas yawned so wide his jaw popped. He sat with his head in his hands and rubbed his temples. Rain stung his neck.

How can they follow me in this storm?

They aren't following me.

They know where I'm going.

He looked over the top of his fingers and saw the light again. It was closer.

Silas scrubbed his face with a cold handful of rain. He stood and hitched up his pack.

* * *

Shoda slowed the pace as they went downhill, careful not to step in holes or walk off cliffs. Tak kept her flashlight beam aimed a few steps ahead to check their footing, and wondered how long the batteries would last.

When they reached the floor of the canyon, the flat was easier on their legs, but the brush was thicker. They walked on the slope for a while, but Tak's ankles ached so she led Shoda back to the base of the canyon.

"Maybe we should rest," Shoda said. His breathing was so ragged Tak could hear it over the rain.

Tak swung the flashlight to keep the beam ahead of them. "It can't be far now. We'll rest when we reach the foot of the mountain."

Her flashlight beam dipped. She stopped to look, hands on her knees. Despite having drank most of her water and eaten all of her snacks, the pack seemed heavier with each kilometer. "There's a gully ahead. Watch your step."

Shoda came up beside her and peered down into the dark. "It's steep."

Tak seized the limb of a stunted tree and slid over the edge. Her boots scrambled in the mud, then caught. She followed a thick line of roots by touch, her flashlight in her mouth and mostly useless since she faced the wall of the gully.

"You okay?" Shoda called from above.

"Yeah, it's just slick. I can see the bottom. It's not that bad." She slid the last three meters, and landed with a splash. Cold water swirled around her calves, but it dulled the pain in her shins.

"There's a stream, but I think we can cross it," she said. Tak kept the beam of the flashlight pointed at the wall so Shoda could see to climb down. A minute later he thumped down next to her.

Raindrops bounced on the surface of the water, splashing Tak's pants up to her thighs. She started to wade in, but Shoda caught her arm. "Wait."

He held his walking stick by the top and poked it into the dark water. The tip hit bottom. "Okay. It's not too deep, but let me go first to check for drop offs."

Five steps into the stream and the current became a persistent tug at her waist. She reached forward and held the strap of Shoda's pack.

As they scooted across, shuffling their feet on the bottom, the far wall rose up before them. The west side of the gully was as tall as the east, but the incline was less steep.

"Almost there," Shoda said.

"Tag. You're it," a voice shouted from above.

"What?" Tak looked up. A figure loomed on the wall above them. She tilted her flashlight and saw the man shield his eyes with one hand.

The other hand held a gun.

"Flashlight tag. I haven't played since I was a boy," the man yelled over the rain.

Shoda stopped and Tak stood next to him, still holding onto his pack. "It's him. Silas," she whispered.

The man put his other hand on his wrist to steady the gun. "There were three of you. Where's the other one?"

Tak opened her mouth, but no words came. Her teeth chattered. Beneath the water her knees shook.

The man tilted his head as if listening. "No matter. Two bullets. Five minus four equals one. One left for the boy. One is perfect."

The wind dropped. A hum ran through the mud beneath Takara's boots. She heard a noise. Dull at first, then louder. A rumbling roar from the north.

Tak turned.

She saw a blur a hundred meters further up the gully. The water rose around her.

The man stepped back from the edge and laughed. "Guess I'll save my bullets."

A ten-foot-high wall of black water swept down the arroyo. It carried small trees, rotting logs and rocks in it frothy grip. The sound was immense. A mind-numbing roar.

Shoda shoved Takara back toward the east wall. He screamed, "Climb!"

Tak staggered in the rising water.

Shoda snatched Jiro's machete from the sheath and bolted up the west slope toward the gunman.

The man fired.

Shoda fell backward.

Tak climbed, grabbing handfuls of roots and wet earth.

The wall of water hit her.

It snatched her from the slope. Tak tumbled in the maelstrom. Something struck her shoulder. She bounced off a rock. Tak forced her eyes open and clawed at the water. Caught a gulp of air. Went under. Collided with something. Pushed her chin up. Caught a breath and a nanosecond glimpse of the flood before it sucked her under again.

Tak could not distinguish between the black water and the black sky. She kicked, but the pressure in her ears increased, and she realized she was diving instead of rising.

* * *

Chapter 43
New Mexico, USA
Day 7

At twilight Tyler sat behind the brush pile at the entrance to the cave and watched the rain come down. He stretched his hands to the small fire beside him and spread his fingers.

The fire crackled. Tyler smiled and nudged a pinecone into the flames with the toe of his sneaker. He took a juniper berry from his pocket and tucked it into his lip and savored it.

There was plenty of water in the Spirits bottle and Tyler was still full from the fish he'd eaten for lunch. A pile of wood lay drying on the floor behind him.

Tyler reached for the notebook computer, flipped it open and held down the power button. The hard drive whirled. The screen came up, then flickered. The small light above the keyboard was normally green, but earlier when he'd left the scroll at the lighthouse, the light turned orange. It blinked red now.

He pushed a dirty finger across the touchpad, but the screen went blue. And then black. The drive stopped. The computer was silent.

The boy stared at it for a moment and then closed it and set it aside.

After a moment, Tyler pushed it further away. He drew his knees to his chest and watched the rain fade to a drizzle. He thought of the small skull he'd found, and the big one, too.

He imagined himself an old man, coughing as he lay next to a fire in the same spot, in the same cave. It seemed possible. The picture was as clear in his mind as the image of the little skull further back in the cave.

Tyler touched the cool flint blade at the tip of his spear.

He thought about his mother's voice. The smell of his father's aftershave. The little girl in the trailer next door. The dog, Rufus, and how his ears felt between Tyler's fingers. Soft. Softer than anything in the world except his mother's cheek.

Tyler went to the woodpile. He took a few of the driest slivers and put them in the inside pocket of his jacket. He picked up his spear and went out into the night. The last drops of the storm hit his shoulders.

* * *

Silas contemplated probability.

While he climbed the mountain, he thought about the rain-slick grip of the gun in his hand and how it jerked when he pulled the trigger. The dark shadow of the man falling backward into the even darker water. A second figure across the gully, climbing, and then swept away by the dirty gray wall.

Who were they? Silas pushed aside a low-hanging limb as he walked along the deer trail.

And why did they come to rescue a useless boy?

And there was the wall of water. Silas had wandered the southwest long enough to know that every year hikers died in arroyos. The afternoon storms sent too much water for the dry streambeds to manage, and the water poured down in a wave that uprooted trees and tumbled huge stones. And drowned hikers.

But the timing of it fascinated him. It was almost miraculous.

Although it was nothing compared to what he'd done on the cliff. Sending 24 people over a cliff with the power of his voice was a stunning feat. The flood may well have been luck, and Silas accepted that.

Still, the timing was perfect. Despite his weary legs, he marched up the mountain, sure of his strength. And as he marched, the rain thinned to a drizzle.

It was difficult to determine when he reached the top. There were two wide shelves separated by a tumble of boulders, and ringed by stubborn evergreen trees.

Silas smelled the smoke of the fire before he saw it. He slowed his pace and crept through the spruce trees until he saw the dancing orange glow.

The fire was only the circumference of a car wheel, but in the night the flicker carried a long way. Wrist thick logs cracked and smoked and collapsed on top of each other and into the glowing bed of coals.

There wasn't anything cooking over the fire. Tyler wasn't sitting with a squirrel on a stick held over the flames.

It's not a cooking fire. It's a signal fire.

Silas watched the flames for a moment, and realized when he turned his head away that he'd ruined his night vision. He blinked and sank to one knee.

After he counted to 99 by threes, Silas rose and began a loop around the clearing. He knew Tyler must be hiding nearby waiting for help. That's what signals were for. And someone had come.

I am here.

But after a complete circle of the fire, Silas stopped. *The boy isn't here. He must have gone to gather more wood.*

Silas waited.

* * *

Chapter 44
New Mexico, USA
Day 7

Takara twisted and fought the cold wall of water. Her shoulders burned and she sank. She thought of the tale of the village girl swimming circles in the ocean, searching for a lantern light.

Then the leading edge of the wave tossed her aside, out of the center of the current. Tak slammed into an uprooted tree and clawed for a hold.

Her head went under, but her right boot touched bottom. Takara staggered out of the water, and collapsed on the rocky shore, her legs still dangling in the river.

Tak spit out a mouthful of muddy water, and pushed up to her knees.

She rose and stumbled up the bank, not sure whether she was east or west of where she'd started. Her pack was gone. Her knee hurt. She pushed her fingers under the tear in her pants and felt warm blood. Her flashlight was gone.

Tak stopped.

Shoda.

She remembered Shoda running with the machete, halfway up the slope. The roar of the water. The flash from the gun.

She sat down among the rocks. Tak opened her mouth to call to him, but hesitated.

Is Silas near?

She shivered. Tak got up and searched among the rocks. *If Shoda is lying unconscious, I might walk right past him.*

Her teeth chattered so hard her jaw ached.

She tottered to a thick growth of scrub grass and fell to her hands and knees and crawled inside. Tak curled up and looked at the sky. She saw a star.

It took her a moment to realize the rain had stopped. Clouds stampeded east, driven by a steady wind.

Tak tried to focus on the star, but her vision blurred. She felt a sore spot on her check and ran her fingers through her wet hair to check for wounds. Her fingers found leaves tangled in her hair, but no blood.

She blinked. Closed her right eye. Her vision cleared. Opened her right and closed her left. Blurry.

Lost one of my contact lens.

She felt in her cargo pockets. When her fingers found her glasses case, Tak bit her lip. Tears ran down her cheek. She shut her eyes. The other pocket held a fat rectangle the size of a cell phone. She pulled it out and held it close to her face.

Tak tore the plastic wrap open with her teeth, and unfolded the foil space blanket. She wrapped it around her, pulled one corner up over her head, and lay shivering.

I must find Akira. No. Not Akira. Tyler.

The storm moved on. The wind died. Stars shoved twinkling points of light through the gloom. The night became still.

Takara pressed the face of her watch to illuminate it, but the watch did not glow blue. She felt a deep crack in the watch face and sat up.

Her shivering stopped.

Tak sat in the shadow of a mountain, wrapped in the space blanket.

I don't have Shoda. I lost the map, the compass, my water. Silas has a gun. I don't even have a knife.

She bent her head for a moment and breathed. In through her nose, deep into her stomach, then up and out through her teeth. Once, twice, three times. Just like she did before sparring at Midnight Judo.

Tak searched the sky. After a few minutes she found a faint smudge of a star. The pole star. She knew the pole star was north, and Diablo Mountain was west.

She folded the space blanket, but couldn't make it as small as it had been packaged and finally crammed it into her cargo pocket.

Tak opened her eye, removed her remaining contact lens, and tossed it away in the grass. She opened her case, blew water off the lenses and put her glasses on.

She stood.

West of her, high on the mountain, a fire glowed orange.

Tak nodded and began to climb.

* * *

Half way up Diablo Mountain, Takara paused and dug in her pocket for her eye drops. Her eyes burned from the filthy storm water. The tiny white bottle wasn't there. She clenched her fists.

Her stomach rumbled, deep down, and she wondered about the muddy water she'd swallowed in the gully. Yet somehow her mouth was dry.

Once she was under the trees, the meager light of the stars disappeared. She climbed steadily, but when she raised her head, the pinpoint of flame at the top seemed no closer.

She put her boot down on a stone that rolled away beneath her foot and she fell. Takara reached back and felt along the ground for the rock. It was heavy and smooth in her hand.

Will I die on this mountain? Will they find my skull?

Shoda is dead. Shot and drowned. That man, Andrew, in the cliff dwelling is probably dead. And his wife with the snakebite. And the people at the cliff.

So much death. It must stop. I have to save Tyler.

She pushed through a thicket, and pencil-thin limbs raked her glasses, but not her eyes. Tak ducked lower, crawling through the dirt like an animal.

The ground and everything on it, the leaves, the cones, the rocks, were wet. The rain left everything limp and slick, but quiet. Tak's heavy boots made little sound as she drove herself up the side of the mountain.

Her tongue was thick, but Tak didn't hear a stream or even step into a deep mud puddle. The earth soaked up the water, and what it didn't drink ran downhill to the canyons.

Takara's lungs ached, and knots formed in her calves.

The gap between the trees increased and she felt the ground level out beneath her. Tak leaned on a tree, panting, and pushed her filthy hair out of her eyes.

She stood on a shelf, with only the sky and the cold stars above her. On a slight decline below her lay a jumble of rocks, and then a flat space. And a fire.

Tak waited, and watched.

The sudden stillness brought the night chill back around her shoulders. She shivered once, and crossed her arms. The day's heat was a faint memory.

She wondered if she'd somehow passed Silas in the dark and arrived at the top first. Takara moved forward on her hands and knees, making as little noise as she could. She crept into the boulders.

A rustle, so brief she wasn't sure she'd heard it, made her freeze.

Then a small figure, bent low under a pile of brush, darted to the fire. The shadow knelt to feed handfuls of fresh sticks to the hungry flames.

Movement on her right.

A shape melted out of the tree line. A head. Then an arm. The arm came up. It held something shiny.

"Tyler, run!" Takara surged out of the bushes. "Run, Tyler!"

The boy looked up.

The man in the shadows turned.

Takara charged the man. Long fast strides coming so quick she almost sprawled.

The gun spat flame.

Something punched her in the shoulder. Takara spun, suddenly facing the fire. She saw the boy's back as he sped into the trees. She fell and lay still.

The gunman ran past her without a word.

She felt the heat of the fire through the soles of her boots.

Her right hand slipped up to probe her left shoulder. Her shirt was still damp from the rain. Tak's finger touched the wound and she winced.

She sat up and the world spun around her for a moment, then her eyes focused and the flames danced on the lenses of her glasses.

Tak clenched her left fist and moved her arm. Fire roped down her limb from shoulder to elbow to wrist. She bit her lip to keep from screaming.

She heard the thump of boots in the trees, careless of their noise.

"Get moving, Tak," she whispered. "Move."

She rose. The downhill steps jolted her, and blood ran under her shirt to the waistband of her cargo pants.

Someone hit a line of bushes fifty paces down the mountain. The scrubs shook. Tak ran straight down, empty handed and wide-eyed.

The stars became bright. Colors departed, but the shapes of trees and rocks grew sharp, like figures cut from paper. The thump of boots and the scatter of stones were harsh to her ears. She dashed beneath a spruce and the scent was so strong and sweet in her nose that she gagged.

She saw the gunman vault a fallen log and stumble when he landed. He took two steps, fell, and scampered forward on his knuckles like an ape.

Takara drew closer.

She spotted a small head bob as it turned and cut down a switchback. The boy skidded down the rough trail. Without thinking, Takara grabbed a tree limb to slow her slide and her arm burned white hot.

She sank to her knees, hands over her mouth. She choked for a moment.

Tak looked up.

The boy was gone. The gunman, Silas, was gone.

Takara growled.

Then she saw the void. The spot where the side of the mountain was blacker than the sky.

A cave.

She staggered forward. Warm blood dripped from her fingertips.

Takara stopped at the entrance. She pushed one hand inside and cold air caressed her like breath from a tomb. Tak shook. The entrance was wide as a car door, but she hesitated.

Tak thought of the immense weight of the mountain above, crushing down on the cave--the dirty, narrow pit into the earth. Her heart shuddered hard against her sternum.

It's like the earthquake. Trapped beneath the rubble. All that weight. Can't breathe.

She gulped a lungful of air and forced one boot forward.

The ground beneath was gritty with wind-blown sand. Tak trailed her right hand along the wall and pushed herself one step at time into the hungry black mouth.

Keep moving. Don't stop. Tyler needs you.

Her vision was useless, but her eyes strained anyway. She sniffed the air and caught wood smoke and sweat, and strangely, the smell of fish.

A click.

Tak turned.

A cone of white light exploded in front of her, driving her back.

Silas stepped out of the shadows, a flashlight in one hand, and a gun in the other.

Tak shielded her eyes.

"Who are you?" Silas asked. He raised the gun.

"No!" Tyler burst from the darkness.

Silas spun.

Tyler drove a flint-tipped spear into Silas's gut.

Silas howled. The gun barked. The bullet struck the stone ceiling.

Silas dropped the gun and the light and grabbed the spear with both hands. He yanked the spear out, knocking Tyler backward.

The boy hit the floor.

Silas reversed the bloody spear.

Takara leapt forward and snaked her right arm around Silas's neck. She squeezed. Groaning, she raised her left arm to push his head forward and complete the jiu-jitsu chokehold.

Silas dropped the spear. He drove them both backward into the cave wall. He tried to tuck his chin in and bite her forearm, but she had the hold locked in tight. He clawed at her fingers.

Tak held on.

She squeezed until white spots burst in front of her eyes. Silas's hands fell away. He drooped. Tak held the choke until her arms went numb and shook. Finally, her grip failed and she dropped him.

Takara took a ragged breath. Tyler stepped forward into the white ring of the flashlight. "Let's go," Tak whispered.

The wiry boy nodded.

When they got outside the cave, Tak bent forward, her hands on her knees while the world spun around her. She shut her eyes.

The boy touched her shoulder. "I...I'm Tyler. Of Silver City. That was my spear."

Takara wiped tears from her cheeks. “I know you, Tyler. I’m Takeus of Thebes.”

“You’re a girl?”

* * *

Chapter 45
New Mexico, USA
Day 7 and Day 8

Silas rolled over onto his back. He couldn't see the ceiling high above him. He stretched out his hand for the glowing flashlight, but could not reach it.

He flexed his knees, dug in his heels and pushed. A second time, a third. He writhed across the cold cavern floor, leaking hot blood.

He heard a sound like a wood saw, closed his mouth and it stopped. Realized the sound was his own ragged breathing.

Inches at a time, he slithered into the weak yellow glow of the fallen flashlight.

Silas reached out again. Instead of the metal cylinder, his hand found a smooth orb. He drew the object to him and held it up to the light.

It was a skull. Empty sockets. Slits for a nose. A top row of teeth, but no jawbone.

Silas stared at it.

His arm collapsed. The skull hit the floor and rolled away.

The flashlight flickered, and went out.

* * *

Inside the cliff dwellings, Jiro took a deep breath. He looked at the child crouched by her mother and asked, "Do you have any more candles?"

When the girl looked blank, he realized he'd spoken in Japanese. Jiro switched to his halting English. "More candle?"

The girl looked at her pack, but wouldn't leave her mother's side. Jiro opened the miniature pack and dug through. He found a short, fat candle and lit it from the one next to the man. The candle nearest the woman guttered, the light casting shadows across the wall like puppets in a play.

Jiro shuddered.

"Have knife?"

The girl shook her head. “Only scissors. I’m not old enough for a knife.” She pulled her bag closer and sorted with her free hand. Her right hand remained on her mother’s forehead. “Here.”

She passed him a pair of blunt-nosed scissors.

The lean man held the scissors up to the light. The tool was cold to the touch, so he knew it was metal, but the blades didn’t feel sharp. Jiro turned them sideways and pushed under the nylon cord around the woman’s arm.

He twisted the scissors and worked them like saw. The cord parted. “Good.” Jiro nodded to the girl. He had to cinch the belt around her leg in order to open the buckle, but he had it off in a moment.

The woman’s leg twitched violently and she moaned. The girl began to cry again.

“Okay,” Jiro said. “Okay. Blood flow to leg. Stings. Like foot asleep. Okay?”

“Okay,” the girl whispered.

He duck walked around the woman until he was opposite the girl, and then put his ear above her face. Although the woman’s eyes were shut, Jiro felt her breath on his cheek. He held up a candle and watched her chest rise and fall.

“Sleeping bag? Blanket?” he asked in English.

“We threw them away. Dad said they were too heavy because he had to carry Mommy.”

“Okay.” Jiro yanked every piece of dry clothing out of their backpacks, and draped them across the woman. The girl stretched out one hand to help arrange the loose clothes.

Hot wax spilled onto Jiro’s fingers when he carried the candle over to check on Mr. Rowbury. “Awake?”

The man nodded. “Yeah. I’m still here. How’s my wife?”

“Breathing. She is strong,” Jiro said. As he examined the bullet wound in the man’s stomach, he listened to his ragged breathing.

“How feel?” Jiro asked.

The man looked at him for a moment, and then blinked. “I’m cold. Feels like my heart is beating too fast.”

Jiro felt the pulse at the man’s wrist, and then at his neck. “When less blood, less, ah, pressure in system. Heart must pump faster. Hard to explain English.”

The man shut his eyes. "Makes sense." He hissed out a breath. "Hurts like a son of a bitch."

Jiro wasn't certain what the man said, but his expression was obvious. He held a bottle of water to the man's mouth. "Drink."

Some of the water ran down his cheeks, but the man drank most of the bottle. When he couldn't hold his head up any longer, he sank back and sighed. "Chest hurts."

"Heart works very hard," Jiro said.

Jiro moved the candles to give better light, and dug his last bottle of water out of his pack. He opened it and poured a tiny measure into the cap, and put it to the woman's lips. The water went down, but the woman didn't respond.

He handed the bottle to the little girl. "Give her more?"

Thunder boomed along the canyon outside, but the lightning no longer flashed as often. Jiro lifted the man's cellular phone from the floor and ducked through the low door.

Jiro ran across the courtyard and scanned the cave entrance, but after just leaving the candle-lit room, he couldn't see anything more than shapes in the darkness. He squatted in the lee of the wall, and flipped the phone open.

The screen was so bright he squinted. The phone searched for a signal, but found none. Jiro noted the time on his watch and was amazed to see an hour had passed since Tak and Shoda left.

A fresh band of rain swept along the cliff face and down the canyon, driving him back into the shelter of the caves. Jiro switched the phone off and jogged back to the room.

Inside, the man was on his knees, grunting as he tried to push up to his feet.

"What? No." Jiro jumped to catch the man as he fell backward. "What are you doing?"

"I can't find my phone. I need to call work," the man gasped. "I'm taking sick leave."

Jiro lowered the man and held him down as gently as possible. "You can't move. Wound will bleed more." He took the blood soaked T-shirt from the floor and pressed it against the man's stomach.

When he checked the man's pulse, it was rapid. His arm was clammy. Jiro wiped his hand on his shirt and felt the man's forehead.

As he leaned across a smell hit him and he knew the man had voided his bowels.

Jiro grabbed his backpack and placed it under the man's boots to elevate his legs. He wrapped the man's hands across the bloody T-shirt and covered him with his poncho. The man's breathing faded to a weak panting, and Jiro moved two of the three candles closer. In the small room, the candles heated the cool night air.

The young man swallowed and sat down between the husband and wife. The girl was asleep, curled around her mother's head. Jiro watched his patients' breathing, and took turns checking their pulse--the woman's right wrist, and the man's left wrist.

He picked up the water bottle he'd given the girl, but it was empty and the cap was lost in the dark shadows.

* * *

The last of the three candles burned out and died, but Jiro realized he could still see. He jerked his head up.

Light, feeble and without a hint of heat, shone across the courtyard and through the low doorway. He checked his patients.

The man was cold, but still breathing. And the bleeding had stopped. The woman's pulse was faint, and her breaths were irregular. Jiro found the little girl awake and watching him.

"What name?" he asked. He thought Tak had said it, but he couldn't remember. His head ached.

"My name is Flower," the girl whispered.

"Flower, can you go to the wall and watch? Watch for help."

The girl shook her head.

"Okay, I'll go." Jiro stood. His back was tight from bending over, and his tongue clung to the roof of his mouth.

He crossed to the door and ducked down, spine popping.

"Wait!"

Jiro looked back. Flower had her hand above her mother's nose and mouth. "Help."

He ran to the woman. When he couldn't get a pulse, he tilted her head back and checked her airway. Her breathing had stopped.

Jiro leaned down, but he couldn't feel her breathe or see her chest move. He pushed the loose clothes aside, put the heel of his palm on her breastbone, locked his elbows, and pushed.

He shoved her chest down. Her ribs flexed under his hands. Jiro counted aloud until he'd pushed 30 times, and then pinched her nose and put two long breaths into her lungs.

Her chest moved.

He began another set of chest compressions. After 30, he put two more breaths into mouth.

Flower sat with her knees drawn to her chest, tears trickling down her face and off her chin.

The woman gasped a long, rattling inward breath, sat halfway up, and sank back. Her chest continued to rise and fall as she breathed.

Jiro sat back. Sweat ran down his cheeks. The little girl continued to cry, one hand over her eyes, the other on her mother's forehead. Sunlight filtered into the cliff dwellings.

"Is there anyone here?" a voice yelled in English.

"Here," Jiro called.

Two men ran into the room. They wore different uniforms, and one wore a hat. The one in the hat hesitated, his hand on his pistol. The other yanked a fat, black radio from his belt, and barked into it.

The woman on the floor opened her eyes.

* * *

Chapter 46
New Mexico, USA
Day 8

"You're tall," Tyler said as Takara led him down Diablo Mountain.

Takara nodded. When they were clear of the trees, she tilted her head back to look for the North Star. The sky spun and she staggered.

Tyler caught her arm. "He shot you. Maybe we should rest." He looked over his shoulder.

She leaned on the boy and continued down the slope. "He won't be coming after us. I just want to get off this mountain."

"Okay." Tyler put one of her arms over his shoulder, like he'd seen football players do when helping a teammate off the field. "I left the Spirits bottle in the cave. And the computer, but it's dead."

"We'll find you a new computer. What's a Spirits bottle?"

"It's a brown bottle that holds a lot of water. But don't worry, I know where the stream is."

They worked their way down the mountain, Takara guiding them east. They drank from a stream and Tyler picked juniper berries while Tak sat against a tree.

The sky ebbed from black to blue. A shimmer of fire lit the east.

Tyler squinted at the rising sun. "Where are we going?"

"To the road. If we go east, we'll--"

"You know where the road is?" He skipped and almost yanked Takara over.

"Yes. Slow down, please."

They hiked for another half hour until a helicopter flew over them. Tak waved her good arm, and Tyler hopped up and down and shouted.

The helicopter made a wide turn and came back. They shielded their eyes when it landed, spraying sand in a wide arc.

A big man in a uniform got out and jogged over to them, one hand holding down his hat. He didn't have sunglasses on and his eyes were bloodshot.

Tyler held Takara's hand.

"Miss Murakami, is this Tyler?" Agent DeWitt asked.

Takara nodded. And fell over.

* * *

Deep in the Gila National Forest, Deputy Kane sat by a flooded arroyo and watched the rain water go by. The level of the river fell almost fast enough for him to see it. It was only a few feet deep now, but still frothy.

A canteen sat beside him on the rock. He'd dropped two purification tablets into it, and shaken the container with the cap loose, so the water ran down the sides and cleaned the lip.

He waited for the tablets to finish their work. Sticks with green leaves on them floated past in the center of the stream. The air was clean, and the scent of rain persisted until the rising sun burned it away.

Kane watched a bird soar, so high above he could not identify it. He watched the water, and sat in the canyon and tried not to think about the people at the bottom of the cliff.

The deputy realized he might think about those people for the rest of his life. He looked east along the canyon. His eyes lit on a patch of white in the sand above the water.

A strip of bark from a tree perhaps, or... Kane stood up. "Or a shirt."

He walked downstream. His canteen remained on the rock.

He saw an arm move.

Kane broke into a run.

A thick Japanese man with a bloody head lay on the sand just above the water's edge.

When Kane rolled him over, the man groaned.

* * *

Takara woke and found a needle taped to her wrist. Her eyes followed the needle to a tube leading to a clear plastic IV bag hanging on a pole. The bag was half full.

The sheet across her feet was too tight, bending her toes. She kicked her long legs and pulled the sheet loose.

"You're awake."

Jiro slumped in a chair, eating a bag of Twizzlers and drinking a Sunkist. Dark half moons hung below his eyes.

"Give me one of those." She reached.

Jiro pulled the bag to his chest. "Maybe we should check with your doctor. They pulled a bullet out of you, you know."

Tak glared at him.

"Okay, okay." He passed her the bag.

"Where are my glasses?"

"On the nightstand. I'll get them." He pushed up out of the chair. "Here."

Takara put on her glasses and everything in the room jumped at her at once. She sank back on her pillow. "What happened to the people, the Americans?"

Jiro looked her in the eye. "They're alive. They put them in a room together down the hall. Around dawn, two cops came and found us." He bit his lip. "It was a tough night."

"I lost Shoda," Tak blurted. "We were crossing a stream, and Silas--"

"I know. He told me."

"What?"

"Yeah, Shoda told me all about the flood and how he lost my new machete and--"

"He's alive? Go get him."

"Do you always wake up this demanding? Hang on." Jiro went out the door.

A moment later she heard two voices speaking Japanese, and then laughing. Takara sat up and smoothed her hair back over her ears.

Jiro maneuvered a wheelchair into the room. Shoda sat wrapped in a blanket like an old man. The left side of his head was shaved to the scalp, and a bandage was taped above his ear. "Good morning," Shoda called.

"I always said he was hardheaded, but I had no idea," Jiro said.

Shoda stepped out of the chair and leaned over her bed.

Takara smiled. "You look ridiculous."

Shoda touched her hand. "I met Tyler this morning. He's a nice boy."

"Yeah." Takara's eyes filled. "Charging up the side of that gully was stupid."

Shoda shrugged.

She squeezed his hand. “Thanks.”

The door swung open and Deputy Kane and Tyler came in. Kane rested one hand on Tyler’s shoulder. “See, I told you she’s all right. Already sitting up eating candy.”

Tyler looked up at the two Japanese men. One was lean and spike haired, with sharp eyes. The other was muscular, and half of his hair was cut away.

The boy squared his shoulders and walked right between them. He stood at the side of Tak’s bed and gripped the metal railing. “Can I please have a Twizzler?”

When Tyler marched past the other men, Kane smiled.

Takara looped a long arm around Tyler’s neck. “Hey, you.”

* * *

Chapter 47
New Mexico, USA
Day 9

Tak wrapped her wet hair in a towel, and reached for the toothpaste. A hot spike shot up her arm when she extended it, and Tak snatched back her hand.

I should have put the sling on.

Someone knocked on the door and then opened it.

"Are you dressed?" Shoda marched into the hospital room. "Or not."

Tak poked her head out of the bathroom. "Aren't you supposed to be in a wheelchair?"

Shoda pointed. "Aren't you supposed to be in a sling?"

"I won't tell if you don't." Tak brushed her teeth twice. "I swear I can still taste that river water."

"Yeah, my stomach's been weird. Hey, they just released me." Shoda raised a thick arm. He slid one finger under the pink plastic hospital bracelet around his wrist and pulled. And pulled. "Damn, what is this made of?"

While Shoda gnawed at the bracelet like a trapped coyote, Tak limped out and sat on her bed. "Did you find out anything about Tyler's relatives?"

Shoda stopped chewing. "I found an aunt in the white pages who lives in California, but--"

"That's great," Tak said. She slipped her feet into a pair of flip-flops. "I'll get them to release me, and we can go tell Tyler. Kane told me he's with Child Services."

Shoda held up a meaty hand. "Tak, wait. I called. The listing was out of date. Tyler's aunt died last month." He sat in a chair next to the bed and itched the shaved side of his head around the bandage.

Tak's shoulders slumped. She leaned back against the pillows. "Did she have children? Cousins of Tyler's?"

"No. And her husband died years ago."

"Damn. I don't want him in some orphanage."

"Yeah." Shoda gave the hospital bracelet a half-hearted tug.

They limped down the hall to the desk. Shoda carried the bag of Takara's clothes they'd brought her from the hotel. Jiro sat in the lobby, drinking a can of Sunkist. He popped up. "Are we out of here?"

Tak held up her good arm. "I have to sign some things first. They may even want us to pay them."

The paperwork took nearly an hour. While they struggled through a stack of forms, a short man in a white coat stopped by the desk. He spoke to a woman in hospital scrubs, who pointed at Jiro.

The man came around the desk and extended a hand to Jiro. "I have two patients who are alive because of your efforts. Thank you." He pumped Jiro's hand.

The spike-haired young man nodded and spoke in slow English. "I am glad they live."

The doctor picked a file up off the desk and walked to the door. "You ever consider a career in medicine?"

Jiro shrugged.

The nurse insisted Takara ride in a wheelchair out to the entrance. Jiro pulled the rental car around and hopped out to get her door. Shoda put her bag in the trunk.

Jiro thumped down in the driver's seat and put on a huge pair of gold plastic Elvis sunglasses. "I'll take you invalids back to the hotel for a nap, and then I'm thinking we go out for a Mexican dinner. I saw this place on TV that looks very authentic. The waiters wear sombreros."

"Can we eat something that isn't spicy?" Shoda moaned from the back seat. He held his stomach with both hands.

Tak flipped the visor down to block the afternoon sun. "Let's go by the Sheriff's office. I told Deputy Kane we'd check in."

"I don't know how to get there," Jiro said.

"Take a left up there." Tak fished a map out of the glove box and squinted at the tiny print. While she navigated Shoda went to sleep, mouth open and his head against the window.

"He has a concussion. He's been napping a lot," Jiro said softly.

Tak glanced back at the snoring man. "I'm glad he's sleeping in your room."

"Thanks." Jiro turned into the parking lot. Three Sheriffs cruisers sat baking in the sun. "Shoda, wake up you lazy ape."

The three shuffled inside. The sudden passage from heat to air-conditioned cool made Tak sneeze. Kane sat at his desk, stirring a steaming mug of coffee.

The rangy deputy stood. "Good to see you all back on your feet." He pulled two extra chairs over.

Tak smelled the coffee and her mouth watered. "Deputy Kane, Shoda and Jiro searched the Internet for relatives of Tyler, but found no one."

"I found an aunt in California, but she's deceased," Shoda said.

"Did you learn anything about his family?" Tak asked.

Kane chewed his lower lip. "I put one of our young guys on it. He's a techno wizard. He found grandparents in Texas, but they're long dead. So no luck with his father's side of the family. And he didn't find any living relatives on the mother's side, either."

Tak removed her glasses and rubbed the bridge of her nose. "What can we do? What will happen to Tyler?"

"As of now, he's a ward of the state of New Mexico," Kane said. "Child Services will place him in temporary foster care until they find something more permanent."

"Tyler has been through a lot," Takara said. "He needs a good home."

The deputy leaned forward with his elbows on his desk. "There might be another option. My wife and I have tried to start a family, but...the doctors told us it's not going to happen. We've talked about adopting."

The deputy shifted in his seat. "It's a long process and there's a lot of paperwork involved. I can ask the Sheriff to write a recommendation. Talk to our pastor, and Kayla's doctor, and get some folks to vouch for us. I thought maybe you could ask Tyler and see what he thinks. I don't make a lot of money. He won't have a fancy life, but I can teach him things. And Kayla's a schoolteacher. He won't lack for learning."

Takara smiled. "Will you take Tyler horse riding?"

Kane nodded. "I will."

"Our flight is tomorrow. I'd like to see Tyler before we leave."

"Sure." Kane picked up the landline on his desk. "I'll call Child Services and set it up."

* * *

Day 10

Jiro yawned as he parked the rental car. "I'm almost looking forward to the flight, just so I can sleep without listening to you snore."

Shoda chuckled. "Tak, can we say goodbye to Tyler, too?"

Tak opened her door and eased out. "Sure. Come inside." She draped her backpack over her shoulder and limped across the parking lot.

The three entered the Child Services building and checked in at the desk. A woman led them down a hallway and out a back door into the morning heat.

Four children played badminton on a sandy court, flailing at the plastic birdie. Tyler sat alone on a swing, eating a Popsicle. When he saw them, he smiled and stood up. "Hey, Takara. Shoda, Jiro."

Tak hugged the boy. Shoda shook his hand. Jiro slugged him in the arm.

The woman's cell phone rang and she walked back to the shade of the building, talking while she paced.

Tak nodded at the badminton players. "You're not playing?"

Tyler shook his head. "Maybe later. I feel tired a lot. The lady told me I have to eat more." He finished the Popsicle and licked the wooden handle clean.

"That's the same thing the doctor told me," Takara said. "They kept waking me up to eat."

She walked to the swing set and sank onto one of the faded plastic seats. She put her backpack between her feet and unzipped it. "I brought you something."

The thin boy perked up. "A present?"

"Yes." Takara pulled her laptop computer out and passed it to Tyler. "I know you lost your notebook model, so here is a replacement. This way we can keep in touch."

Tyler held the computer to his chest. "You're going back to Japan already?"

Tak nodded. "I have to. I've used all of my leave time from work. And all of my money." She watched Shoda and Jiro join the badminton players. The birdie hit Jiro in the head and the children laughed. "Jiro has to go home and see how his mother is doing. And Shoda is starting a new job at a bank."

She touched his arm. "With this computer we can video chat and talk every day. I'll send you some games, too."

"Okay." Tyler nodded. "I'd like to talk. I guess we can't play *Lair of the Hydra* anymore?"

"No. That world is gone. But we'll find a new place to play." Takara pushed off and swung just fast enough to feel a slight breeze on her face. "Tyler, what do you think of Deputy Kane?"

Tyler shrugged. "He's nice to me. He bought me a Capri Sun. And he told me we'd go fishing some time." He kicked a rock with the toe of his battered Spiderman shoe. "I told him I already know how to catch fish."

They swung in silent synchronicity, back and forth in the morning heat, the hot air stirring their hair. The sun rose in the sky.

Takara checked the time on her cell phone. "Tyler, I have to go. I set you up an email account. Deputy Kane or one of the people here can show you how to use it. I'll write you as soon as I get home, okay?"

She hugged the boy. After a moment, Tyler hugged her back.

Takara put her sunglasses on to cover the hot tears seeping down her cheeks. She collected Shoda and Jiro and crossed the playground to the building. When the lady opened the door, Tak looked back over her shoulder.

Tyler squatted on the sidewalk, patiently rubbing the wooden Popsicle stick on the rough concrete. Filing the stick to a point.

* * *

Epilogue
Tokyo, Japan
6 Months Later

Tameko's head swiveled. Tak felt the cat move in her lap and opened her eyes. The sliding door opened and Aunt Shiori stepped out onto the tiny patio.

Takara sat up and rubbed her eyes. When she lifted the cup of tea on the table next to her it was cold. She took a sip anyway.

Shiori tucked her hands under her arms. "I'm ready for spring."

"How was lunch?" Tak asked.

"Good. But the restaurant was crowded and we had to sit by the kitchen. It was warm, though."

"Is Sergeant Shimada over his chest cold?"

"He's fine now. That man is made of granite." Shiori blushed.

Tameko dropped off Tak's lap and shoved his head into Shiori's ankle. She reached down to rub the cat. "You look like you didn't get much sleep."

Takara smiled. "I talked to Tyler a long time last night. The adoption process is complete. Deputy Kane and his wife, Kayla, are Tyler's new parents."

"That's great news!" Shiori sat in the other chair. Tameko rolled on his back and showed his snow-white belly. "Is Tyler excited?" Shiori asked as she rubbed Tameko's stomach.

Takara nodded. "And relieved. He and Deputy Kane became close these past months. Tyler worried the adoption might not happen." She pulled her knees up in her chair and sipped her tea. "I bet winter isn't this cold in New Mexico."

"Probably not," Shiori said. "Do you have work tonight?"

"No. I'm going out."

"Your Midnight Judo club?"

"No. Jiro has his night class. And...Shoda and I are going to a movie."

The End

About the Author

Stories matter to me. I write because I hope my novels will make someone's life a little better.

If you have strong feelings about this book, good or bad, please consider leaving a review at Amazon.

Sign up here to learn about my new books, special deals and bonus content: http://markboss.net

Please search your preferred bookseller for my other novels:
HIRED GUNS
THE CULTIST
DEAD GIRL
DEAD GIRL 2: FADER BOY
ONE BULLET
SUPERHEROES ALIENS ROBOTS ZOMBIES (SARZverse Book 1)
ROBOT REVOLUTION (SARZverse Book 2)
ALIEN INVASION (SARZverse Book 3)

Visit my author site: http://markboss.net
My blog: http://www.chimpwithpencil.com

Made in the USA
Columbia, SC
24 September 2024

42254167R00155